# T'on Ma

## By Magnolia Belle

Note for Librarians: A cataloguing record for this book is available from Library and Archives
Canada at www.collectionscanada.ca/amicus/index-e.html
ISBN 1-4120-9729-0

*Printed in Victoria, BC, Canada. Printed on paper with minimum 30% recycled fibre.*
*Trafford's print shop runs on "green energy" from solar, wind and other environmentally-friendly power sources.*

# TRAFFORD
### PUBLISHING™
*Offices in Canada, USA, Ireland and UK*

**Book sales for North America and international:**
Trafford Publishing, 6E–2333 Government St.,
Victoria, BC  V8T 4P4  CANADA
phone 250 383 6864 (toll-free 1 888 232 4444)
fax 250 383 6804; email to orders@trafford.com
**Book sales in Europe:**
Trafford Publishing (UK) Limited, 9 Park End Street, 2nd Floor
Oxford, UK  OX1 1HH  UNITED KINGDOM
phone +44 (0)1865 722 113 (local rate 0845 230 9601)
facsimile +44 (0)1865 722 868; info.uk@trafford.com
**Order online at:**
trafford.com/06-1485

10  9  8  7  6  5  4  3  2  1

This book is dedicated to my Native American ancestors.
I don't know your names or your faces,
But I feel your heartbeat
And hear your voices in my dreams.

## The team:

**Editor:** Connie Webb
prairiewhispers@gmail.com

**Web Design:** Kirk Osburne  Web Graphics Source
webgraphicssource@gmail.com
http://www.webgraphicssource.com

**Illustrator:** Ken Faulks
http://kenfaulksillustration.com
kfaulks@islandnet.com

www.blackwolfbooks.com

# Table of Contents

# Chapter 1 — T'on Ma

Seventeen-year-old Lana sat beside the slow-running river and pulled off her shoes and socks, her toes wiggling in delight at their newfound freedom. Late August afternoons in Texas were the hottest part of the day, of the year — too hot to do chores or to stay inside the sod house where there was no air. This was a perfect time to swim and maybe to wash her hair.

Lana stood, removed her dress and underthings, and carefully laid them across a bush. She gingerly picked her way across rocks and around grass burrs, and then walked into the river until the water came to just under her navel. As she undid her braid, she let her long, brown hair fall loose down her back and shoulders. She leaned forward and gently fell into the water, its coolness a delight against her hot, sweaty skin. This was heaven!

The young woman swam and floated for a few moments but, wanting her soap, she stopped and took a few steps in the waist-deep water toward the riverbank. A noise behind her made her whirl around.

Several yards away, a Kiowa brave sat on a magnificent black horse, staring intently at the nude woman. Lana froze, not sure what to do. She hadn't brought a gun with her. The house was so close, she hadn't thought she needed to.

"*Don't show him you're afraid,*" she thought to herself. "*Stare him down and he'll leave.*" Calmly, she faced her uninvited visitor while she tried to slow her breathing.

He was young, maybe a few years older than Lana — wild, fierce, haughty. No paint adorned his face, so she decided that he must simply be hunting or traveling.

The brave continued staring at her with fearless, piercing brown eyes. Then his eyes flicked away, searching for the men he knew must be near. When his gaze returned to her blue eyes, she read her death in his face. But something stopped him; his expression softened. She didn't know that her beauty caused a debate in his mind — kill her or take her captive? Before Lana knew her fate, a man's voice called from behind the rise on the other side of the river, causing the brave's head to jerk at the sound.

"Lana? Girl, where are you?" Joshua Cooper yelled.

"I'm right here, Pa," Lana answered, not turning away from the Kiowa. "At the river."

"Well, hurry up! Your ma needs you in the kitchen."

"Pa? I'm in trouble."

As the words left her mouth, the brave reined his horse away and trotted across the prairie. Lana sank to her knees while she tried to quit shaking.

"What kind of trouble?" Her father's voice sounded much closer as he neared the small rise. Lana hurried out of the river and grabbed her dress, holding it against her.

"Kiowa. But he's gone now."

Her scowling father walked past her and forded the river where he made a close inspection of the area.

"Just one of 'em?" he asked as she scrambled into her clothes.

"Yes, Pa. Just one."

Making his way back, Joshua shook his head at her. "Come on to the house. I reckon he's gone."

\* \* \*

Two Hawks made his way to the summer camp of his village as he thought of what he had just seen. Homesteaders had come to the plains and had driven his people out, killing game, grabbing the land as if they owned it, making Kiowa life difficult. Tension and hostility broke out continually. The whites' Great Father kept making and breaking promises. Two Hawks didn't know what to believe. Apparently, the whites had more than one Great Father. It must be confusing for them, he decided. No wonder they were so strange.

And the woman in the river? He shook his head. Rumors of people with blue eyes had reached his village, but he didn't believe them. No one had blue eyes unless they were from the spirit world. Yet, hadn't he just stared into crystal blue eyes? And hadn't they stared back unafraid? What if she *was* a spirit woman? Maybe it was a good thing that he hadn't killed her. Nodding his head once, he decided he would call her *T'on Ma* (Water Woman).

\* \* \*

Joshua Cooper had survived the Mexican-American War of 1846-1848, but it left him exhausted in body and in mind. There had been too much hatred, too much death, too much turmoil, and he was done. Moving with his wife and family of three sons and one daughter, he made his way to north Texas. A farmer by trade, he thought perhaps he could raise cattle as well.

They reached their land in June of 1850. It set just south of where the Salt Fork and the Double Mountain Fork of the Brazos River met. Kiowa Peak rose in the distance.

With the help of his three sons, Nathan, nineteen, Paul, sixteen, and Jake, thirteen, Joshua soon had a sod house constructed. Being scarce, timber was used mainly for a door and for framing the windows. Perhaps one day there would be enough to cover the dirt floor. The Coopers had no money for glass windows, so sheets of waxy paper stretched across the window openings to let in a dim, muted light. Wooden shutters had been made to keep out rain and arrows. Netting hung across the ceiling to keep mice from falling through the sod roof onto unsuspecting sleepers below.

The rectangular house had three rooms. One bedroom, on the left, was for Joshua and his wife, May. Their three sons slept in the bedroom on the right.

The last and largest room set between the two bedrooms. It featured a fireplace on the left, and a long wooden table and several chairs in the middle. A kitchen counter ran along the front wall, underneath a window. The only family luxury, an oak hutch, had come straight from England with May's grandmother many decades before. The blue and white pattern of the Delft dishes that set on the hutch lent the only splash of color to the otherwise dark room. Lana had a cot against the far right corner where she would pull across a blanket hung from the ceiling for privacy.

With the house built, the next projects were building a barn, smoke house, and root cellar. Through careful planning, Joshua had enough provisions to keep his family going through the winter until next spring.

While the men were building, Lana and her mother were expected to collect as many buffalo chips as they could find. These would be used as fuel. The women would also forage for roots, berries, and herbs and would cut and dry as much prairie grass as they could to keep the horses fed through the winter. Every spare minute of each day was spent providing for their survival so far away from civilization, from stores, from medicine.

* * *

Once back at his village, Two Hawks tethered his horse outside his mother's tipi and went to find his father. "I've seen a white woman today," he announced as he sat beside his father, who was busy making arrows.

"What?" Many Deer looked up at his son. "Where?"

"About two spans[1] from here. She wasn't alone, either. I heard a man's voice calling to her."

Many Deer scowled. When would these people go away and leave them in peace?

"Should we go back tomorrow and kill them?" Two Hawks asked.

"Perhaps. Let me talk to some of the Dog Soldiers[2] first." Many Deer picked up an arrow shaft and inspected it for straightness. "Do you know how many there are?"

"No. I didn't see. They were behind a hill." His father only nodded. That wasn't much information to plan a raid on, though Kiowa were renown throughout the area for their fearless attacks.

"The woman was different," Two Hawks said after a moment. "Her eyes were blue like the sky."

*"Blue?"* Many Deer looked carefully at his son. "Are you sure?"

"Yes. Even from a distance, I could see that they were blue."

Many Deer scowled. This could be a sign, an omen. Like his son, like everyone in the village, they had all heard the story of people with blue eyes. But to have actually seen one...

"Perhaps we shouldn't kill them without learning more. I'll ask the others and see," his father decided. Many Deer continued with his arrow making, waiting until the fires were lit, supper cooked, and everyone's stomachs full before bringing this discussion to the Dog Soldiers.

Later that evening, after much debate and counsel, the Dog Soldiers finally decided that three of them should go on a trading mission. While there, they could look around and see how many settlers there were, how many guns they had, and if there were any horses worth stealing. Two Hawks would be one of the

---

[1] Span – a hand width that equaled about one hour measuring from the horizon to the sun.

[2] Dog Soldiers - a society of warriors who protected the village

trading party, to show them the way. Broken Man, as the eldest, would lead them, and Crying Fox would go along as added protection and an extra pair of eyes.

* * *

Two days after the river incident, Lana gathered eggs from the hens that had survived their journey to this new place. The fourth egg had been carefully placed in the bottom of the basket when she heard horses. Looking up, she saw three Kiowa riding slowly toward the house.

"PA! — PA! Come quick!"

Joshua and his sons stepped from behind the sod wall of the partially-finished barn, each bearing a rifle. Nathan stood behind his father. Paul kept his hand on Jake's shoulder.

Joshua cautiously approached the three Kiowa, his rifle barrel pointed toward the ground. They didn't look like they were there for trouble.

"Get in the house, girl!" Joshua ordered.

Lana scurried across the yard and ducked into the house with her mother. Peering through the crack in the door, she looked at the braves and recognized the one from the river. Two older men accompanied him. All three had their braids wrapped in fur, their ears adorned with Mexican silver. The man in the middle raised his hand toward Joshua in a sign of peace. Joshua returned the gesture and invited the braves to step down.

The men dismounted, Two Hawks throwing his right leg over his horse's neck and jumping lightly to his feet. They took a few steps toward Joshua and then sat on the ground. The oldest brave produced a pipe and tobacco.

"Paul," Joshua said to his middle son, "get coffee enough to go around. Put lots of sugar in theirs. Nathan, you help him."

The two sons obediently went into the house and returned a few minutes later carrying the hot, sweetened beverage in tin cups. Nathan had a folded blanket under one arm. Joshua reached for it and spread it in front of the Kiowa. Then, taking the coffee from his sons, he sat a cup down in front of each brave. The four homesteaders joined the Kiowa on the ground, sitting on the opposite side of the blanket.

After the amenities were observed, Two Hawks rose and walked to his horse, where he untied a large bundle. He threw it into the middle of the blanket and then repeated the same process twice more.

Nathan spread the bundles out for a quick inspection.

"They've got rabbit and coyote pelts in here, Pa. It's all prime, too." The Cooper family needed those pelts to make clothing against the bitter, subzero winter weather common on the high plains.

"I guess they want to trade." Joshua said, and then turned to shout over his shoulder. "Ma, bring the trading sugar and molasses out."

In a few minutes, the door opened and May and Lana stepped through, carrying their trade goods. May set a small sack of hard sugar on the blanket in front of Broken Man. Lana placed two jugs of molasses beside it and stepped back. As she did so, she glanced nervously at Two Hawks, who had watched her since she came out of the house. Opening one of the jugs, he poked his finger in and then pulled it out, covered in rich, sticky sweetness. As he stuck his finger in his mouth, he looked at Broken Man and grinned, nodding.

Crying Fox said something to Two Hawks, then rose and mounted his horse. Two Hawks picked up the two jugs and handed them to Crying Fox. The Coopers stood up as Broken Man also mounted his horse. Two Hawks returned to the blanket and stepped over to Lana. Holding her chin in his right hand, he stared deeply into her eyes. Yes, they *were* really blue.

Lana quit breathing, afraid to move or to blink. She desperately tried to remove the fear from her eyes. But, if she could hear her heart pounding this loudly, she was sure he could, too.

"*T'on Ma*," he said, pointing to her chest. "*T'on Ma*."

"Let her go!" Joshua ordered, his rifle pointing straight at the young Kiowa. Two Hawks looked disdainfully over his shoulder at Joshua, dropped his hand from Lana's face, and grunted. Swooping down, he picked up the sugar sack and then effortlessly jumped back on his horse, his long braid swinging behind him.

The three braves turned their horses and rode away without any concern for the rifles at their backs. The trade had been a good one. There would be feasting tonight.

## Chapter 2 — Blackberries

The trading party rode back to the village, triumphantly announcing their arrival with shouts and song. Small children ran around them like so many clucking hens pecking grain. Two Hawks slid off his horse and held the sugar sack above his head.

"Sweet!" he proclaimed. Crying Fox stood beside him and lifted the two molasses jugs as well, looking proudly at the people. This was a rare treat, indeed, for his village. Two Hawks gave his mother the sugar in an honorary gesture, just as Crying Fox gave the molasses to his wife. The two women were in charge of these luxuries until the feast that night. Their men had made them proud, had given them esteem in the eyes of the village.

The three braves then met with the elders to give their report.

"It's only one small family," Broken Man said. "One man and three sons, his wife and daughter."

"But the men all had rifles," Crying Fox added.

"What of horses?" someone asked.

"I only saw two of them. Even our poorest are better than those."

"Hmmm." The men looked at each other and at the ground as they considered this information. How much trouble would one family with two poor horses be? Or, for that matter, how much trouble would they be to get rid of?

"What of the blue eyes?"

"I saw them," Broken Man said. "It's just like Two Hawks told us. The girl has blue eyes."

"Hmmm."

This was the tricky part. What did those blue eyes mean, exactly? Was she a spirit woman? Was she a medicine woman? Would harming her bring a curse to their village? These questions needed time in order to be answered properly.

"I touched her," Two Hawks said. "She *felt* real. Also, I've given her a name. I told her what it is, but I don't think she understood."

"What name?"

"Water Woman."

* * *

"Pa, that was the Kiowa from the river," Lana said once they were all inside.

"The one that grabbed you just now?" May asked.

"Yes'm." Lana walked over to the fireplace and poked at the fire. "Pa, why was he staring at me like that?"

"I have no idea, child," Joshua shook his head.

"I don't think he would have hurt me. He just wanted to stare," she added.

"You need to stay close to the house from now on," Nathan ordered in his position as her oldest brother. "Unless you're with one of us." Nathan was as tall as his father, but more muscular. He wore his dark brown hair to his shoulders; his light brown eyes and handsome face much like his mother's.

"Paaaa," Lana whined.

"No. He's right. You stay close. And from now on, you take a gun with you. You hear me?"

"Yes, sir."

16

That night, after supper and chores, Lana wearily climbed into bed. It had been another exhausting day. But this time, her mind wouldn't get quiet and let her sleep. She thought of Two Hawks standing so close, staring so hard at her. What was he looking at, anyway? Hadn't he ever seen a girl before? And then she blushed, covering her face with her blanket. He had seen much more of her at the river than she ever intended.

* * *

That evening, in preparation for the feast, Two Hawks put on his best leggings and the moccasins with the intricate beadwork that his mother and sisters had labored over. Their beading skill was unsurpassed in the village. Skunk tails pompously trailed behind each of his heels. His freshly braided hair had red vermilion down the center part. Two Hawks felt as handsome as he looked.

When he joined the others at the feast, he deliberately sat close to a young woman he liked. Corn Flower was shy. In the past, whenever he tried to catch her eye, she would only look down, never at him. Once he threw a plum stone at her, trying to get her attention, but she acted as if nothing happened, as if nothing stung her cheek. Other young men were also interested in her, but she treated them all the same way.

That night, however, in the flickering light of the fire, Two Hawks caught her looking sideways under her long lashes at him. He sat up straighter and ignored her. He had brought the sugar; let her work for *his* attention this time. There were other young women smiling at him across the fire. He deliberately winked at one of them, aware that Corn Flower could see. Her scowling face made him secretly grin.

Strips of buffalo hung from sticks over the fire, where the fat melted and dropped, sizzling and hissing, into the flames. The enticing aroma sharpened everyone's hunger. People chatted and gossiped among themselves, all the while keeping one eye on the meal. All who had contributed pelts for the trade that day would get to taste the sugar and molasses first. The others could squabble over any that remained.

After the meal, the people grew quiet when Broken Man rose and stood close to the center. He recounted the day's events in great detail. They all shook their heads at the description of so many guns. Laughter filled the camp when he imitated a hen with its ungainly walk and funny sound. A hush fell over them as he told of the woman with blue eyes. So the rumors were true then.

When he told of Two Hawks touching T'on Ma's face, several of them looked wonderingly at Two Hawks. Had some of her power gone into him now? Or perhaps he would fall ill. They would have to wait and see. But he had done a very brave thing. On that, they all agreed.

* * *

Several days later, Lana and her mother picked rosehips not too far on the other side of the river. Rosehips were good for medicine and tea. Properly dried, they would last all winter. Each woman had her basket as well as a rifle. They spent almost an hour picking their way through the bushes when May stood up, holding her head.

"I've got the fiercest headache," she told Lana. "Too much sun, I reckon."

"Maybe you better get back to the house."

"Probably should."

"Give me your basket," Lana offered, "and I'll finish filling both of them. It won't take too much longer and then I'll come back."

"All right. Keep your gun handy, though."

"Yes'm."

Lana watched her mother walk away and then turned to continue her work. She labored steadily for twenty minutes, occasionally stopping to wipe her forehead with her apron. One basket was completely full and the other almost. As she straightened up to stretch her back, she saw huge blackberry vines a few yards away. Picking up both baskets and her gun, she clumsily made her way over to it for closer inspection. Though late in the season, lush, juicy berries covered the vines.

"Oh, what a pie these will make," she murmured as she popped one into her mouth, closing her eyes in ecstasy at the burst of rich, sweet flavor. When she opened them, she reached for more berries and caught a movement out of the corner of her eye. Turning her head, she saw Two Hawks as he stood on the other side of the vines and intently watched her.

She had seen him three times now. This couldn't be a coincidence, and she determined to find out if he was friend or foe.

"Hello," she said softly. When he didn't move, she picked three berries and held them out in her open palm toward him.

"Here. Try these. They're good."

Two Hawks watched as Lana took a few steps closer to him. When he still didn't move, she picked up one of the berries and held it to his lips. Staring at her, he tried to decide what to do. If he refused the food, she might bewitch him and turn him into a rock or a bird. Thinking it for the best, he opened his mouth and let her push the berry in, all the while never taking his eyes off her.

For the first time, he saw her smile at him, watched her eyes light up. Picking up a second berry, she ate it herself. "Mmmmm," she continued smiling. "Good." When she offered him the last one, he took it from her hand and, to her surprise, held it to her mouth. In the custom of his people, it didn't do to accept a gift and not give something in return. Cautious, she let him feed it to her, and then stepped back toward her baskets.

Two Hawks followed and waited for her to face him. When she did, he touched her shoulder. *"You are Water Woman,"* he informed her, "*because I saw you first in the river. And I am Two Hawks.*"

She shook her head, not understanding. He touched her shoulder again and, to her ears, said, "T'on Ma. T'on Ma." Then he touched his chest and told her his name, "Yi Ceŋtas[3]."

"T'on Ma," Lana repeated, pointing to herself. When he nodded, she repeated his name, "Yi Ceŋtas," and touched his chest. He nodded again.

"Oh. All right. Nice to meet you, Yi Ceŋtas." Tilting her head, she asked, "What does T'on Ma mean?" Once he understood her question, he pantomimed the words for water and woman.

"Water Woman?" Lana's puzzled expression faded as she realized why he named her that. The first time he'd seen her, she had stood in the river.

"And your name? What does it mean?" she asked in pantomime again.

He held up two fingers. "Yi."

"Two?" she copied his gesture.

He nodded and then searched the sky. An eagle flew low on the horizon. Pointing to that bird, he shook his head 'no'. Waiting for a moment, he pointed again, higher in the sky, to a hawk and nodded. "Ceŋtas."

"Oh, your name is Two Hawks." Lana smiled, proud of this breakthrough in communication. At least now she knew her name as well as his. "I'm Lana. Lana," she repeated.

"La-*nah*," he echoed. When she nodded her approval, a light of satisfaction filled his eyes.

She turned to pick more berries, scratching her hands on the thorns as she did so. Two Hawks saw the light traces of blood on her skin and realized that she wasn't a spirit woman. He nodded. At least that was one mystery solved.

Two Hawks relaxed now that he knew she wouldn't whisk him away to a cloud or turn him into rain or anything. Spending time

---

[3] Yi Ceŋtas – Yee (two) Shenta (hawks)

together gave him more information to take back to the elders. Besides, he enjoyed looking at the pretty woman. He lay down on his side, stretched out his long legs, and leaned on one elbow as he watched her. It never occurred to him to help. Picking berries was woman's work.

* * *

After a short while, Lana decided she had enough berries for a pie. Besides, it was getting late and her family would worry about her if she didn't hurry home. She tried to get the two large baskets and the rifle gathered up for the long walk back, but it proved to be cumbersome. To her surprise, Two Hawks picked up one of the baskets and began walking in the direction of her house. She fell into step beside him.

When they waded through the river, he set the basket on the ground, held up his hand, and turned to go back.

Lana touched his elbow, stopping him. "Yi Ceŋtas, thank you." She smiled and nodded.

He studied her face for a moment and then slowly returned her smile. With that, he walked away.

* * *

"Well, she's not a spirit woman," Two Hawks told his father that evening. "Her hands were bleeding from thorns."

Many Deer nodded. The elders hadn't yet come to a decision on what to do with them. This bit of information would help.

"Wait. How do you know her hands were bleeding?" Many Deer asked.

"I was with her when she picked berries."

Many Deer shot a look of concern at his rash son. "And her father, her brothers?"

"I didn't see them."

"You need to be more careful than that," he scolded. "They could have been close. She could have screamed and you would be dead now."

"I don't think she'll scream. As a matter of fact, she smiled at me today."

"What?" His father's face scrunched up in a frown. "Why was she smiling?"

Two Hawks knew that if he told his father they fed each other blackberries, it would only cause more confusion, more consternation. "I'm not sure," he finally said. "Perhaps because I helped carry her baskets."

Many Deer rose to his feet, agitated. "Have you lost your *mind?* Leave her alone. She'll get you killed!" He bent over to leave the tipi, muttering to his wife as he left. He needed air — air and time to think about his crazy son!

## Chapter 3 — The Hunt

Lana made her way to the house, lumbering slowly with her burden of baskets. That night at dinner, she happily showed her family the blackberries.

"And there's more. A lot more," she informed them. "If you can spare Jake tomorrow, Pa, maybe we can go pick them."

Jake's eyes lit up. He hated working on the barn. Picking berries sounded like a wonderful reprieve.

"I don't know," Joshua frowned. "Do you think we can get along without him for one day, Nathan?" He winked at his eldest to let him know he was teasing Jake.

"Well, Pa." Nathan scratched his head like he was thinking on it real hard.

"Oh, pleeaassseee," Jake begged, making his face look as pathetic as possible.

"I reckon we could," Nathan finally said.

"Well, then, I guess you're going berry picking with your ma and sister tomorrow."

Jake wanted to jump up and down in his excitement, but felt he was too old for such behavior now. Instead, he sat in his chair, beaming.

That night, there were two in the Cooper family who had trouble falling asleep — Jake, over the excitement of the next day's adventure, and Lana, over that day's.

Once she had relaxed around Two Hawks, she had studied him, and her thoughts went back to that. He moved gracefully, like a panther, with his muscles rippling through his bare chest and arms. He had surprised her when he let her feed him the berry. Whatever had possessed her to do that? Maybe it was a gesture of friendship. Perhaps it was a gesture of trust. Whatever it was, it had worked.

And when he fed her, it surprised her even more. Not just his gesture, but the way she felt when he did. There had been a gentleness in his hand that she hadn't expected. Thinking back on his smile, how his whole face softened, how he became handsome to her when they said goodbye at the river, she felt herself blushing again. This wasn't right. She shouldn't allow herself to think this way. Her pa would skin her alive if he knew! Turning over — again — she tried desperately to calm her thoughts so she could sleep.

\* \* \*

August sped by with a velocity that only came from being too busy. There was too much to do if the Cooper family were to survive the winter. With the barn finished, the horses now had shelter. But that was only one part of the larger picture. The Cooper family rolled out of their beds each day before the sun came up, ate a cold breakfast and hurried to their respective tasks. They met again for a big lunch and then quit work through the hottest part of the afternoon. There would be a few hours of work before sundown, at which time they ate a light supper that had been cooked during the cooler, early morning hours. Many times it was nothing more than heavy cornbread with molasses drizzled on the top. Falling exhausted into bed, they slept until time to get up and start all over again.

\* \* \*

24

The Kiowa band worked just as hard. During the summer, they hunted buffalo and dried meat, tanned hides for tipis and winter clothes. Scouring the land, the women looked for anything edible that could be saved for the long, barren months ahead.

Shortly after Two Hawks met Lana at the blackberry vines, the men of his village planned a buffalo hunt and sent scouts out to locate the herd. When the scouts returned, telling of their find, the village moved to the location. The next morning, the scouts led the hunters out.

After making a final survey from a hill, one of the scouts returned, crawling backward down the slope, until it was safe to stand up. He walked over to the hunters and nodded. There were hundreds of buffalo beyond the ridge. It would be a good day.

Horses and men alike were painted with symbols of the animal they hunted, and with symbols of strength and power. Spears and lances, bow and arrows were honed and ready. Only the best horse, the best hunter, would come away unscathed from this dangerous game.

Two Hawks' horse pranced nervously underneath him, sensing the tension in the men. Many Deer sat not too far away on his own mount. Nineteen of the twenty in the party had been on hunts before. There was only one novitiate, Corn Flower's younger brother, Laughing Turtle. Sitting on his pinto, he did his best not to show his nervousness. It would be too shameful, especially in front of some of the best hunters in the entire Kiowa nation.

Broken Man lifted his feathered lance high in the air, as all eyes watched in anticipation. The lance dropped, signaling the hunters to begin their slow ride down the ridge. They rode calmly, approaching as close as they could without spooking their prey. Some had actually made their way into the midst of the large animals when one of the bull buffalo lifted his massive head and snorted his warning. The charge began as a melee of thousands of pounding hooves raised dust almost too thick to see through.

Horse and buffalo began the dangerous death dance at breakneck speed.

Riding beside one of the massive beasts, a hunter looked for the spot just above or beside the animal's heart to plunge the long lance deep and stop the buffalo's charge. It took a steady, fearless horse, a steady, fearless rider to do this. Many a warrior had been trampled to death, or gored, leaving them maimed for life. This type of hunting was not for the faint of heart. But the lives of their band depended on their success that day. What was the life of one hunter weighed against the hunger of an entire village?

Laughing Turtle chose a small cow for his first kill. He rode beside it, looking for the best spot for his lance. The animal's movement made it difficult for him to aim. Finally, lifting his arm as high as he could, he plunged the lance into the running buffalo, but it didn't penetrate deeply enough. When the animal turned in mid-step and charged toward him, his horse reared. Laughing Turtle fell backward to the ground, in imminent danger of being trampled. He sprang to his feet, grabbed the buffalo's mane, and jumped on its back while he pulled out his knife. Stabbing the animal's neck repeatedly, he only made it angrier.

Two Hawks saw Laughing Turtle's dilemma and made his way to the young man. Pulling an arrow out of his quiver, he aimed carefully and sent it deep into the buffalo's left eye and brain. The animal dropped underneath Laughing Turtle, who tumbled head-over-heels at the momentum. He jumped quickly to his feet and ran back to the cow to make sure it was dead. Then he lifted his arm above his head and 'ki-yied' above the tumult to Two Hawks. With a wave of his hand, Two Hawks turned his horse around to make his third kill of the day.

After what seemed like hours of intense activity, the herd disappeared over the horizon, and the hunt was over. Warriors stood beside their prey while a call went out to the women who were anxiously waiting not too far away. The women cut through the tough hides, going straight for the livers, which were passed to the hunters' eager hands and eaten raw on the spot. Then the hard, bloody work of butchering began. That night, there would be a feast and a dance to honor the buffalo.

\* \* \*

Two Hawks proudly joined the festivities, but not as proudly as Laughing Turtle or his parents. Making his first kill, even with Two Hawks' help, was a big achievement. Hadn't he faced the danger, ridden into the herd, and used his lance? The women in his family sang his praises as Laughing Turtle sat there, beaming.

Corn Flower had heard the entire story of the rescue by Two Hawks from her brother. When she could, she made her way over and knelt beside him.

"Thank you for helping my brother," she said quietly, as she looked down at the ground.

"He didn't need much help," Two Hawks said generously. "He was very brave today."

Corn Flower looked directly into Two Hawks' eyes and smiled her gratitude. She knew without his help, her mother, her sisters, and she would be singing a dirge rather than a victory song that night. Reaching out, she touched the back of his hand and then stood up. With a full heart, he watched her cross the ground toward her friends. Perhaps tonight he would ask her to walk with him by the cottonwood trees. Perhaps tonight he would tell her how he felt about her. Perhaps tonight...

But, as his mind filled with these wishful, love-filled thoughts, another young brave, Iron Crow, walked over to Corn Flower and held his hand out. She took it as she rose to her feet, and the two walked out of the circle of firelight. Scowling, Two Hawks also stood and stomped back to his mother's tipi. He hadn't seen that coming.

\* \* \*

The Kiowa elders decided to live in peace with the Coopers as long as the Coopers lived in peace with them. They based part of their decision on the possibility that Lana was a medicine woman.

Broken Man, Crying Fox and Two Hawks went to trade with the Coopers again a few weeks later. This time, they took fresh venison to barter for coffee, beads and two axe handles. Joshua hadn't had time to do much hunting, so the fresh meat was gladly welcomed. Also, he wanted to try out his new smokehouse, and this gave him the perfect opportunity.

Throughout the trade, Two Hawks and Lana exchanged several glances, though neither spoke to the other. As the Kiowa rode away, Two Hawks glanced over his shoulder. When Lana saw him looking, she held her hand up in a gesture of goodbye. Two Hawks raised his in return, nodding once to her, and then turned back.

"What are you doing, Two Hawks?" Crying Fox asked after they had been riding for a few minutes.

"What do you mean?" Two Hawks looked puzzled.

"Waving to Water Woman."

"Nothing. Just waving."

"Are you sure it's nothing?"

"Of course I'm sure," he protested.

"So, if someone like, say, Corn Flower were here, you'd still wave to Water Woman?"

Two Hawks scowled at that.

"That's what I thought," Crying Fox laughed, his point made.

## Chapter 4 — Fire!

Late September found the weather finally cooling down. No hint of fall tinged the air — not yet — but it was coming. Lana could feel it in her bones as she walked alone, carrying a basket and her rifle, far away from the house, through rain-starved prairie grass and brush. That day, she hunted for chicory, sage, wild onions, and anything else edible that her family could use. Cherubic, contented clouds filled the azure sky. The weather suited her mood. She hummed to herself when, from behind, a stag ran past her, unafraid of her presence.

*"That's odd,"* she thought as she watched the white tail disappear into the brush. A few minutes later, two coyotes loped past her. Curiosity made her stop and turn around. Her eyes filled with horror at what she saw. One huge, roiling cloud of bitter, furious smoke filled the entire sky. The blackness raced closer at an alarming rate. She continued to stare, motionless, while she struggled to understand. Then, on the horizon, wicked yellow, orange and red flames shot skyward.

"Prairie fire!" she exclaimed as she twisted around in indecision. What should she do? The fire lay between her and home. Could she outrun it? But run where? The river!

She hoped she could make it to the river in time. Dropping the basket, but still clutching the gun, she hiked up her skirt and ran as fast as she could through the brush and tall grass. The brambles tore at her dress, scratched her legs, but she ran on. Soon, she could hear the crackling flames behind her. A light wind fanned them higher, faster. Her side began to ache, but she could feel the heat on her back now, so she kept running. At last — at long last — she saw the twisting river a short distance away. She was almost there when she tripped — on what, she wasn't sure — but she fell hard, hitting her head on a rock, and passed out.

* * *

Two Hawks was hunting alone when he saw the fire. He knew to go to the river and hurried his horse toward it. Walking his horse chest-deep into the water, he sat there to wait out the fire while he tried to calm the nervous animal. To his amazement, he saw Lana running toward the water, and he wondered why she was so far away from her house. When he saw her fall and not get back up, he jumped into the water and, holding the reins, hurried to her. Grabbing her by her shoulders, he pulled her down the small embankment into the river. He could see blood on her left temple. Letting her body float, he took her and his horse to the deep part of the river and held Lana steady while he waited for her to regain consciousness. After a moment, she moaned.

"*Be careful,*" he told her. "*You're hurt.*"

Confused and dazed, Lana thrashed against the water and against whoever held her. Her efforts only made her choke from breathing water as her head plunged beneath the surface. While she struggled to stand on the riverbed, she steadied herself by holding Two Hawks' arm with one hand while she held her head with the other.

Looking back from where she had just fled, she could see the prairie engulfed in flames and smoke. Animals of all types crossed the river, running for their lives. Finally realizing what had happened, she looked up at Two Hawks with wide, fearful eyes.

"Yi Ceŋtas?"

"T'on Ma." He gestured that she needed to lower herself into the river until only her head showed. The fierce heat from the fire made the air hard to breathe. Pieces of grass floated on the wind, some soot-blackened and some still burning, sticking in their hair. It looked like hell had come to earth.

Glancing over her shoulder, Lana saw that the fire, picked up by the wind, had jumped the river and had been carried across the narrowest part, where it continued on its path of destruction. Finally, after what felt like an eternity, the flames died down around them; there simply was no more grass to burn. Only a charred, twisted nightmare remained.

When it was safe, they both stood up. Lana shook uncontrollably from the shock and injury. She turned toward Two Hawks and saw the same look in his eyes that she knew was in her own.

"Oh, Yi Ceŋtas!" she cried as she threw her arms around his neck. "You saved me! We're alive!"

The astonished, young Kiowa stood still for a second and then, feeling her trembling against his chest, put his arms around her, glad to have someone to hold at that moment, as well. When she raised her head up to look at him, he carefully touched her wounded temple. It didn't look too bad, he decided.

As he held her, he looked into her eyes, her beautiful, blue, bewitching eyes. His expression changed as he slowly dropped his arms from her and took one step back. He wasn't supposed to feel like this. He wanted Corn Flower. Didn't he?

"I ought to get home," Lana said after a moment, and then began slogging her way through the river, weighed down by her wet skirt and petticoat. She walked over to the river's edge where she had tripped, and searched for the rifle. Most of it remained, though the stock was charred and still too hot to pick up.

Two Hawks realized that she was determined to go home at once and followed her to the riverbank. Touching her shoulder, he pointed in the direction of her house and shook his head 'no'. "*The earth is still too hot to walk on.*"

She frowned, not understanding. He took her hand and put it, palm down, on the ground for a second. She quickly jerked it back. "Ouch. That's hot!" she complained.

Making the motion with his index and middle finger for walking, he shook his head 'no' again and, this time, he saw understanding in her eyes.

"Oh, I see. We need to wait." Her shoulders slumped in frustration. "Ma and Pa are going to be worried sick about me."

Two Hawks gathered up his horse's reins, got on, and then motioned for her to do the same. Her heavy, wet clothes made it difficult, but, with his help, she managed. They began working their way slowly down the meandering river, letting the horse find its footing as it went.

Lana slid her hands around the brave's waist, holding tightly to him. She had never ridden bareback before and had trouble keeping her balance. Every time the horse stumbled on a submerged rock, she grasped Two Hawks even tighter. He began to enjoy himself. Fifteen minutes passed when he felt her lay her head on the back of his shoulder and heard her sigh. Maybe she was enjoying herself, too. He wondered.

It was dark when the two young people arrived at her home. On one side of the river, the earth was scorched. On the other, the homestead remained untouched by flames. Lana knew that her family had had a narrow escape.

Stopping at the riverbank, not willing to go close to her house, Two Hawks slid off the horse and helped her down. She took his hand and started to lead him up the slope when he stopped her, shaking his head. Her family wasn't the only one worried that night. He needed to get home, too, but he didn't know how to tell her that. All she knew was that he wouldn't come in to be properly thanked.

"All right, Yi Ceŋtas," she sighed. "I can't make you come in." She looked over her shoulder in the direction of the house and then turned back to him. "I wish we could understand each other. I want you to know how much I owe you. Thank you for saving me back there."

As he stood in the dim light, he watched her while she talked. He liked her voice, even though he had no idea what she was telling him.

"At least let me do this," she continued talking. To his surprise, she reached up and kissed him quickly on his cheek.

"That was a kiss," she explained. "Kiss," she said again, pointing to her lips and then to him.

"Kiss?" he repeated and then shook his head 'no'. If Lana had been a Kiowa maiden, he wouldn't have done this so soon after meeting her. But she wasn't, and he was intrigued. Taking her in his arms, he leaned down and kissed her long and sweet, taking his time, enjoying himself.

Lana had never been kissed before and wasn't quite sure what to do. After a moment, she relaxed and put her hands on his arms. Unconsciously, she slid her hands across his chest and around his neck as she molded her body to his.

Two Hawks felt the change in her, and what had started out as a lark to the young man now became something different, something hungry. Holding her tighter, he kissed her again, but now with real emotion. Finally, he let her go and stepped back, looking thoughtfully at her.

"Kiss," he said softly as he touched the curls that lay against her cheek. Looking up at him, she took his hand and kissed his palm, overwhelmed by what she felt. He leaned down and kissed her once more, then grinned and jumped back on his horse, hurrying home.

Lana stood there for a few moments, watching him ride away while she composed herself. Then, sighing once, she turned toward the house.

"Ma, I'm here," Lana announced as she opened the door.

"Lord be praised!" May exclaimed as she jumped up from her chair.

"Girl, we thought you were dead! Your brothers and I went looking for you until it got too dark." Her father walked over and hugged her. Even her youngest brother, Jake, hugged her. Lana sat at the table and recounted the day.

When she got to the part about being rescued by Two Hawks, her father stopped her. "Who's Yi Ceŋtas?"

"He's the one that grabbed my face the first time they came to trade. He calls me T'on Ma, which means Water Woman. And his name in English means Two Hawks."

"You didn't leave him outside, did you?" Joshua looked toward the door.

"No, Pa. He wouldn't stay." Her mother inspected her head and began to dab it with iodine. "And, Pa, I'm sorry about the rifle. I tried to save it. I really did!"

"That's all right, Lana," he reassured her, though losing the gun was costly.

"I can show you where it is and maybe you can get another stock for it later," she offered.

"Maybe we'll do that," he agreed. "But for now, I'm just grateful you're alive."

## Chapter 5 — Water Buckets

Two Hawks made it back to his village a few hours after dark. Turning his horse loose with the herd, he trotted toward his mother's tipi, knowing his family would be worried about him. His mother was sitting outside by the supper fire when he approached.

"I'm here."

"Where have you been?" His mother, Gray Dove, looked up from her cooking, relief clear in her eyes.

"I was caught in the prairie fire."

"We saw the smoke. Are you all right?" she asked as she handed him a bowl of venison stew.

"Yes. I'm fine. The fire didn't reach here, I see."

"No."

Hearing his son's voice, Many Deer stepped outside and sat beside him. He watched Two Hawks eat for a minute and then commented, "The fire was some time ago, son."

Two Hawks nodded as he swallowed. "I had to rescue Water Woman from the fire. I saw her running, but she fell and was knocked out, so I dragged her to the river." He took another bite of food before he continued. "Since she was hurt, I took her home. Then I came back."

"Did you speak to her people?"

"No. I didn't go into their house. I didn't see anyone."

"So there's no trouble with them?" Many Deer wanted to be clear on this point.

"No. No trouble at all. Water Woman seemed very grateful for my help."

Corn Flower walked by their fire for the fifth time that evening, worried about Two Hawks, wanting to know if he was home yet. Seeing him, she smiled. He nodded once briefly at her, and then resumed eating.

His lack of interest bothered her. Usually, he would have done or said something to tease her. But not this time. She might as well have been one of the camp dogs for all of the attention he paid her. Turning on her heel, she tossed her head and flounced away. Two Hawks barely noticed, but his mother watched the whole thing with great interest.

"She likes you, you know," Gray Dove teased her son.

"She likes Iron Crow," he retorted as he handed his empty bowl back to her.

"That's not what her mother tells me." Expecting to get an eager response to that, Gray Dove was surprised when Two Hawks simply shrugged his shoulders and announced that he was turning in for the night.

When he had gone, she turned to her husband, looking worried. "That's not right," she said. "He's been pining for Corn Flower for a long time. Why would he suddenly lose interest?"

Many Deer shook his head. He wished he had no idea, but a suggestion of a reason nagged the back of his mind. It was so preposterous, though, that he dismissed it before it ever became a full thought.

\* \* \*

As he lay on his buffalo robes, Two Hawks looked up through the smokehole, where the moon had gotten snagged on top of the lodge poles. He put his hands behind his head and let his thoughts drift back to the fire, back to the river. Closing his eyes, he could feel T'on Ma's hands around his waist, holding on for dear life as she rode behind him.

He smiled at that, but the smile faded as he recalled her — what had she called it? Oh, yes, her kiss. And then his kiss. And then *their* kiss. He rolled on his side, trying to shake the memory of her body pressed against his, of how she felt in his arms. But it didn't work. Sleep eluded him until the dark, early morning hours.

\* \* \*

The next day, a small group of young men went hunting, Two Hawks and Laughing Turtle among them. The hours went by with some success. They killed several rabbits and one stag. On their way back home, Laughing Turtle rode beside Two Hawks so they could talk.

"My sister is mad at you," Laughing Turtle grinned, his eyes twinkling.

"Why?" Two Hawks asked.

"Because you didn't talk to her last night."

"If I had, she wouldn't have said anything, anyway. She never does."

"I know. But this time, you didn't even try. And now she's mad." He laughed.

"Why is that so funny?" Two Hawks asked.

"Because she is so sure you'd do anything to get her attention, it's funny to see her wrong. She thinks she knows everything." Laughing Turtle sounded like a typical younger brother.

"Well, I guess she *doesn't* know everything, then," Two Hawks said quietly.

Something in his tone made Laughing Turtle look over at him. "You still like her, don't you?"

Two Hawks shrugged his shoulders in a noncommittal fashion, refusing to discuss it any further. They rode the rest of the way home in silence.

That evening, after a delicious rabbit supper, Two Hawks sat beside his mother's tipi to enjoy the night air when Corn Flower and Iron Crow walked by. When she saw Two Hawks, Corn Flower deliberately took Iron Crow by the hand and looked adoringly up at him, ignoring Two Hawks as they passed. Two Hawks shook his head at the irony. Now that he wasn't sure that he wanted her, she was doing all she could to make sure he did.

* * *

Three days later, the sun leisurely rose in the east, sending streaks of pink and orange through purple and midnight blues in the western sky. With a bucket in each hand to get the day's water, Lana walked down the slope toward the river. She saw Two Hawks on his horse and, when he saw her, he slid down and walked over to her.

"*Good morning, T'on Ma*," he smiled.

"Yi Ceŋtas!" Lana looked over her shoulder, but no one could see them from the house. "What are you doing here?"

He took the buckets from her and set them on the ground. Then he pulled her close. "Kiss."

"Uh — uh," Lana didn't know what to do.

"Kiss?" he asked sweetly.

She paused for a moment, looking into his handsome brown eyes, and then nodded. "Kiss."

Holding her tight, he kissed her just like he had imagined at least a thousand times since the last time he saw her. Her soft hands touching him just so. The sweetness of her lips tasting just like that. Her breasts pressing against him.

"*LANA*! Get in the house this instant!" Joshua's voice boomed angrily down at the young couple.

Lana whipped around, jumping out of Two Hawks' arms. "Oh, Pa!"

"Git!" Joshua strode furiously down the slope, pointing back at the house. *"Now!"*

Lana gathered up her skirts and ran back to the house as fast as she could, water buckets forgotten.

Joshua stood in front of Two Hawks. "You need to get home, boy!" he ordered, gesturing to Two Hawks' horse. Two Hawks didn't need to know English to understand 'mad father'. He raised his hand up once, palm out, nodded, and then jumped on his horse, splashing through the river on his way home.

Lana burst into the house, engulfed in tears, and flung herself into her astonished mother's arms.

"What happened?" May asked with great concern.

Before Lana could quit crying enough to speak, Joshua stormed inside. He jerked Lana around by her shoulders to face him. "I ought to whip you till you bleed!"

May looked in alarm at her husband. "What happened?" she asked again.

"I caught your daughter kissing that Kiowa boy down by the river."

*"What?"* May whirled around to look at Lana. "Have you lost *all* good sense?"

"But, but Ma, it was just a kiss," Lana cried.

"That's not the point!" her father growled. "He's Kiowa. He'd just as soon rape you and leave you for dead!"

*"That's not true!"* Lana wailed. "He's kind and gentle. He saved me from the fire, didn't he?"

Her lack of understanding of the Kiowa's ruthless reputation scared the life out of Joshua. They took captives and sold them into slavery in Mexico. Their legendary hatred for white settlers resulted in burnt homesteads, stolen horses, mutilated dead. He didn't know how to get her to see the danger. Grabbing her face in his left hand, he leaned in close.

"If I *ever* catch you with him again, I will *beat* you. And I'll *kill* him!"

Lana had never seen her father look that harsh, that hate-filled. It frightened her. For the first time in her life, she was afraid of her own father.

"All right, Pa," she said quietly. He slowly released his grip on her face, red marks remaining where his fingers had been.

"Go get the water," he told Nathan, who, along with his two brothers, had watched the drama with great concern. If their father had to kill a Kiowa, they would have a fight-to-the-death on their hands with the rest of the tribe. Lana better do what she was told, or she endangered all of their lives.

# Chapter 6 — Guests For Dinner

"That girl is going to be the death of me," Joshua complained to his wife when they had a moment alone in the barn. "I aged ten years this morning."

"Sweetheart, I know." May stepped into his embrace. "Me, too. But, like she said, it was just a kiss."

"Oh, honey. No." Joshua shook his head. "There's a kiss like this." He leaned down and gave his wife a quick, sweet kiss. "And then there's a kiss like the one I saw this morning." He leaned in again and kissed her with passion and heat and longing, his hands moving across her back, pressing her closer to him. May momentarily forgot what the object lesson was.

When he finally let her go, she looked up into his eyes and nodded. "I understand."

"May, I don't know what to do." He ran his hands through his hair, his eyes filled with worry. "Bringing the boys out here was one thing. I'm not afraid for them in the same way as I am for her. She's my only girl, and when I think of all that could go wrong, I almost want to pack up and leave."

"We knew all this before we came out here," May reminded him. She reached for his hand, patting it once. "You need to understand something, Joshua. Lana is growing up. If we lived near a town, she'd be getting married soon to some fine young man that you couldn't stand."

He chuckled at that.

"But out here," May continued, "there is no one for her. Absolutely no one. Except for this Kiowa boy."

"He's not really a boy, May. You've seen him. He's a grown man."

"I know. But it doesn't change the fact that he's all that she has. And I really don't think he'd hurt her. He's had too much opportunity before this, if he was going to."

"I hope you're right. God in heaven, I hope you're right." Joshua sighed his prayer and then turned to his chores.

\* \* \*

Two Hawks rode slowly back into camp, trying to decide what he should do with the rest of his day. He didn't feel like hunting. Making arrows with his father held no interest. What he wanted lived back at the sod house. He tethered his horse outside his mother's tipi and went in to the empty lodge. His father entered a few minutes later and was surprised to see him sitting there, doing nothing.

"Are you ill?" Many Deer asked, looking closely at his son.

"No. I'm fine."

"Then why aren't you out hunting?"

"I don't feel like it," Two Hawks murmured.

"You'll feel like it this winter when there's nothing to eat," his father scolded.

"I know. I'll go in a moment." Two Hawks rested his elbows on his raised knees. Many Deer found the whetstone he had come in for and turned to leave. But something in his son's tone stopped him.

"What is it?" Many Deer sat across from him. "Something's on your mind."

Two Hawks sighed heavily, knowing that if he told what was really on his mind, it would only bring an argument. "Nothing."

"Son, whatever it is, tell me."

"You won't like it."

"Tell me anyway." Many Deer braced himself for whatever it might be.

"I went to the whites' house this morning."

"Why?" His father's face wrinkled in a question.

"Because I like Water Woman — a lot. And I wanted to see her again."

Many Deer closed his eyes, his jaws flexing. "Well, you were right. I *don't* like it. And what do you mean 'see her *again?*'"

"Ever since she fed me blackberries..."

"Wait. When did she feed you blackberries?"

"Oh. That's right. I never told you about that. When I carried her basket home for her, I've liked her ever since then." Two Hawks deliberately made himself look straight into his father's eyes — as a man, not a boy, would do. "When I took her home from the prairie fire, I kissed her. And she kissed me back. Then, this morning, when I was kissing her, her father caught us."

"You are a *fool!*" Many Deer exploded as he jumped up. "I don't know who should shoot you, her father or me!" He paced around the lodge for a full minute, so angry that he didn't trust himself to speak or even to look at Two Hawks.

"This is too dangerous," he finally spoke. "Someone will get hurt if you don't stop this insanity now!" He took a few more steps and then stopped to ask, "What did her father do?"

"He yelled at me."

"But he didn't try to shoot you?"

"No."

"You are *very* fortunate!" With that, Many Deer stormed out of the lodge, looking for Gray Dove. Maybe the boy's mother could talk some sense into him! After a few minutes, Two Hawks left as well, deciding that hunting would be better than staying in camp close to his father.

When he got home late that afternoon, his mother and sisters were busy preparing a small feast. "What's going on?" Two Hawks asked, looking at all the food.

"We're having guests tonight for dinner," his mother explained.

"Who?"

"Corn Flower and her family," his youngest sister, Shy Bird, informed him.

"Oh." He sounded completely disinterested, making his mother frown. It was the only thing she could think of to try and stop his madness.

"Corn Flower is very beautiful and very skilled," Gray Dove commented to no one in particular as she sliced turnips. "She is going to make someone a wonderful wife. Did you see the moccasins she beaded for her brother? They are magnificent!"

"I suppose you've talked to Father about this morning," Two Hawks surmised. "And this is all for my benefit." He gestured to the food.

"Not just for your benefit, son. If there is trouble with the white woman's family, our whole village will suffer. The bluecoats will come. You need to remember that."

Two Hawks gritted his teeth and went into the lodge. His mother was right. He *knew* she was right, but it didn't stop how he felt.

Corn Flower arrived with her family a short while later. The young woman wore her elk-tooth dress, which was supposed to have magical powers, making the young man of her desire unable to resist her charms. As the two families sat around the fire, making polite conversation before the meal, Corn Flower held something out to Two Hawks.

"I made this for you," she said quietly.

He accepted the knife sheath she handed him. Some of the most intricate design work he had ever seen covered it.

"You did this?" he asked. When she nodded, he praised, "This is very good. *Very* good. Thank you." He took his bone-handled knife out of its old sheath and carefully put it in his new one.

The two mothers exchanged hopeful glances and then passed out the food. After the meal, which included much teasing and story telling, Two Hawks got a silent signal from his father and, reluctantly shrugging his shoulders, stood up.

"Would you like to take a walk?" he asked Corn Flower.

"That would be nice."

They walked together into the night, neither speaking for a long time. "That was a good meal," Corn Flower said in the face of his prolonged silence.

"Yes. It was." They continued walking silently for a few more minutes.

"If you're not going to talk to me," she complained, "then why did you ask me to walk with you?"

"For our parents. They seem to think you and I should be married."

Corn Flower ducked her head down at that, embarrassed and hopeful at the same time. "What do you think?" she finally asked.

"I don't know. I think you prefer Iron Crow. I know I prefer someone else."

That bit of news stunned her. "Who? Little Tree? Wind in Hair? Who?"

"You don't know her."

"I don't *know* her?" Corn Flower was really puzzled now. "She's not from our village?"

"No. She's not even Kiowa."

*"What?"* Corn Flower stopped and turned to face him in the dim light. "Not Kiowa?"

"She's the one with the blue eyes," he finally admitted.

Corn Flower took one step back in astonishment, her mouth opened in disbelief. "Blue eyes!" She stood there looking at him, searching his face for any sign of insanity. "She's bewitched you, then," Corn Flower concluded.  That had to be it.  There was no other reason why Two Hawks suddenly didn't want her any more.

Two Hawks just laughed and shook his head.

## Chapter 7 — Don't Touch Me!

"Husband, I want to talk to you about something," May said quietly, once they had gone to bed. Joshua rolled over and put his arm around her shoulder while she snuggled against his chest.

"All right," he kissed the top of her head. "Talk."

"We need at least two buffalo hides for this winter, but three would be better. I need to make blankets out of them. Can we trade with the Kiowa?"

"I see." He lay there silently for a moment. "And what do you propose we trade for these hides?"

"I've got all of that blackberry jam I made up. I bet the Kiowa would like that."

"But that's *my* blackberry jam," he whined, teasing May.

"I'll hand you a jar when you ask for a blanket come January."

"Let me think on it. I'll let you know in the morning."

"All right, honey. Good night."

The next morning, at breakfast, Joshua looked at Nathan and asked, "Do you know how to get to the Kiowa camp?"

"Yeah. I've seen it while I was out hunting."

"All right. We need to do some trading — blackberry jam for buffalo hides. You'll have to show the way."

"When are we going?" Nathan asked.

"Right after breakfast."

"Can I come?" Jake asked eagerly. He was dying to see a Kiowa camp.

"No. You stay here with your ma and sister."

"Wait a minute, Joshua," May stopped him. "I'm not staying home alone with both you *and* Nathan gone."

"Then what do you propose, wife?" He sounded irritated.

"That we all go."

"No! Too much could happen."

"Too much could happen if we don't go, too," she reasoned. "At least this way, we'd all be together. Besides, it's not like they don't know us. We've traded before."

"What about her?" He nodded toward Lana. "That's the *last* place she needs to be."

May looked across the room and studied her daughter, considering the risks. "She'll be with us, Joshua," she finally said. "She won't leave my side once. I promise."

Joshua searched May's face. He had seen that stubborn expression many, many times and knew he wouldn't win this argument. "All right." His doubtful sigh expressed his reservations. "Get ready."

Jake jumped to his feet, so excited he could hardly stand it. Lana looked at both of her parents, unable to believe what she was hearing. First, they tell her never to see Two Hawks again, and now they're taking her to where he lived.

"I'll get the jam, Ma," Lana volunteered as she rose from the table.

They spent two hours walking to the Kiowa camp. Nathan took them straight to the bustling village, where they arrived by midmorning. Joshua, Nathan and Paul led the way into the middle of the camp. There, the Cooper family waited. Camp dogs barked and growled at the strangers and their strange smell while young children clung to their parents' legs and stared wide-eyed at the pale people.

Broken Man watched their arrival with great curiosity before he walked over to greet them. He bent over and said something to a young boy, who quickly ran off with an important duty to perform.

Leading them all to his wife's tipi, Broken Man motioned for Joshua, Nathan and Paul to enter, but barred Jake, May and Lana from the lodge. They were to wait outside by his fire. Broken Man's wife hurried back into camp when she heard the commotion, and walked warily past the two women and boy as she went into her lodge. Stepping outside a few moments later, she motioned for them to sit down around the fire.

They had no sooner gotten settled when Crying Fox sprinted across the yard, having been summoned to the impromptu trade. Ignoring the women and boy, he bent over and went in.

A moment after that, Two Hawks rode into camp and slid off his horse, also hurrying to Broken Man's lodge. Seeing Lana stopped him in his tracks. He stared first at her and then at her mother. *"What are they doing here?"* he wondered. As he walked to the lodge, he looked at Lana, but she wouldn't look up, afraid of incurring her mother's wrath. He, too, bent over and entered the tipi.

It would take some time observing the amenities before actual trading began. Lana clutched the basket of jam in her hands as she studied the camp to pass the time.

It was all May could do to keep Jake still. He desperately wanted to join in the game of stickball being played by several boys his age at the edge of the camp. When the rawhide ball came rolling toward them, a young Kiowa ran up to get it and motioned for Jake to join them.

"Can I, Ma? Please, can I?"

"It's 'may I.' And, yes. You may." May smiled as her youngest leapt to his feet and ran to the game.

It was then that Lana noticed a beautiful young woman staring at her with an odd expression on her face. Lana turned her head, pretending not to see her. But it didn't do any good. She could feel the woman's eyes boring holes in her. Finally, she said something her mother.

"That girl keeps staring at me and I don't know what to do. I don't want to start trouble."

"I've noticed that, Lana. Be still and ignore her. Maybe she's just curious."

"I hope so. But she looks mad."

\* \* \*

Corn Flower hurried to her mother's tipi when she heard about the white family in camp. Standing beside the lodge with her mother and sisters, she glared across the yard at Lana.

"*So, that's the one with blue eyes. Water Woman. Huh! She doesn't look* so *beautiful,*" Corn Flower thought to herself. But, in spite of all that she told herself, she couldn't quit staring. What did Two Hawks see in her, anyway? Deciding to get a closer look, she grabbed her younger sister by the arm and, together, they walked over to Broken Man's lodge.

Standing a few feet in front of Lana and May, Corn Flower silently continued to stare. After a moment, Lana had all she could take. She set the basket down and rose to her feet.

"Hello," she said without smiling. "I'm T'on Ma. Why are you staring at me? I don't like that!"

"Lana," her mother warned. "Be nice."

"Ma, she doesn't know what I'm saying." Lana kept looking at Corn Flower while she spoke.

"Maybe not. But she can hear your tone of voice, same as me."

Corn Flower heard the challenge, saw the expression on Lana's face. She deliberately leaned in close to look into those blue eyes. Only a few inches from Lana's face, she pointed to Lana's eyes. Lana pushed her hand away, frowning. Corn Flower straightened up, indignant, and pushed Lana's shoulder.

"*Don't touch me!*" she warned Lana.

50

"Don't you shove me!" Lana ordered, pushing her back, harder. Even though neither woman knew the words of the other, the meaning was crystal clear.

Corn Flower let out a startling trill and lunged for Lana's throat. Lana balled up her fist and socked Corn Flower in the face, just like Nathan had taught her. Corn Flower went flying backwards.

Men, white and Kiowa alike, spilled out of the lodge, alarmed at the commotion. Corn Flower jumped to her feet and rushed at Lana, who was only too happy to retaliate. Broken Man hurried to Corn Flower and held her by the arms. Two Hawks dove for Lana and grabbed her by the waist just as she leapt at her opponent.

Corn Flower screamed epithets at Lana, swearing she would scratch her eyes out even if it were with her last breath.

"Let me loose!" Lana struggled to get out of Two Hawks' grip.

*"Lana!"* Her father's stern voice stopped her. When she became quiet, Two Hawks cautiously stepped back, waiting to see if she was going to lunge at Corn Flower again. Corn Flower's mother came running at the first sign of trouble and now led her fuming daughter to her lodge.

"What is this all about?" Joshua demanded to know.

"I'm not for sure, Pa," Lana said, shrugging her shoulders. "She wouldn't quit staring and then she came over and pointed at my eyes. That's when we started fighting."

He shook his head and looked at his wife. "I *told* you that you should have stayed home."

"Can we talk about this later?" May asked.

With everyone's attention elsewhere, Two Hawks caught Lana's eye and winked at her. He'd learned enough from Corn Flower's yelling to understand what had happened.

Once everything quieted down, Broken Man gestured for the men to go back in and finish trading.

"Let me have the jam," Nathan said to Lana. When she handed the basket to him, he leaned in and whispered, "Try to be good for *five* more minutes. All right?"

She stuck her tongue at him and flounced down to sit by her mother.

Nathan wasn't far wrong on his timing. Within ten minutes, the men emerged from the lodge, all satisfied with the trade. Three prime buffalo hides were placed at Joshua's feet. The blackberry jam was carefully stashed away for the next great feast.

## Chapter 8 — Red Flint

When Joshua picked up the first fur-covered hide, he frowned. Even though it only weighed about twenty pounds, its bulk made it difficult for one person to carry. Two of them were needed to carry one hide on the two-hour walk back home. Joshua wasn't sure if his wife, daughter and youngest son could manage.

As Joshua considered their predicament, Two Hawks led a horse up to them. Picking up the first and then the second hide from the ground, he put them across the horse's back. He motioned for Joshua to do the same with the third. Once those were tied down, he started leading the horse southeast toward their homestead.

"I guess he's going with us," Nathan remarked. "He doesn't have to. I could bring the horse back later."

"You could," Joshua agreed. "But I think we've done enough damage here for one day. I don't want to make them angrier." He scowled at his daughter with these words. She meekly hung her head, knowing she would hear more about her behavior later.

In order to minimize her father's anger, she kept as far from Two Hawks as she could during the trek home. But Joshua couldn't stop them from watching each other with hungry eyes.

Once at home, May invited the young brave in for food. He had never been inside a house before and entered with some trepidation. The chairs looked odd and he watched how Jake sat in one. That looked uncomfortable. But then, everything looked uncomfortable in the house. Seeing the Delft china, Two Hawks walked to the hutch to examine the glassware closely. He had never seen anything like it before and thought the porcelain was quite beautiful, though he was afraid to touch it.

Nathan pointed to a chair for Two Hawks to sit on, which he did, reluctantly. May put a plate of cold venison and cornbread in front of him, with molasses in a bowl. Lana set a cup of hot coffee beside him and then sat across the table. Jake kept everyone's ears full while he recounted the stickball game, play for play. Joshua sat at the head of the table and drank coffee while Two Hawks ate his meal.

When Jake's chatter finally died down, Nathan turned to Lana. "What happened out there?"

"Like I told Pa, I don't know. She just pointed real close to my eyes. Like this." Lana demonstrated. "And, when I brushed her hand away, we started fighting."

Seeing Lana gesture to her eyes, Two Hawks knew that they were talking about the fight. He stood and walked around the table to her. He lifted her chin with his hand and pointed to her eyes, just like Corn Flower had done.

"*Blue*," he said. "*You have blue eyes.*"

The family didn't understand, so he pointed out the door to the sky and then back to her eyes. Looking around the room, he walked over to the hutch and carefully picked up one of the teacups. He carried it back to Lana, pointed to one of its blue flowers and then to her eyes.

"Oh. I see," May exclaimed. "They've never seen blue eyes before."

"Then why was she so mad?" Lana asked, confused. She looked up at Two Hawks and pointed to herself and then toward his camp. Then she played like she was fighting. "Why?"

He could see the question in her eyes and hoped he understood what she was asking. Cautiously looking at her father, not wanting to anger him again, he began to explain. Pointing to himself and then Lana he said, "Kiss." Then, he pointed toward his camp and made the face of someone getting angry, shaking his head 'no'.

Nathan laughed out loud.

"What's so funny?" Lana asked.

"That girl you were fighting with must have heard that Yi Centas likes you. She's jealous."

At this revelation, Lana went beet red and covered her face with her hands. She had no idea she had been fighting over a man.

"That should be enough to convince you, girl," Joshua said gruffly. "Leave him alone!"

She hung her head in a sign of docility. But, with Two Hawks still standing close to her, she secretly touched the back of her hand to his leg, leaving it there until he finally, reluctantly, moved.

Shortly after this, Nathan and Joshua escorted Two Hawks out the door, not giving him any time alone with Lana. He turned to look over his shoulder once, but she didn't see him. Gesturing goodbye to the two men, he jumped on his horse and went back home.

* * *

Two Hawks arrived to find his father waiting to talk with him.

"Why did you go with them?" Many Deer asked. "I *told* you to leave them alone."

"They couldn't carry those hides all the way back. So, I took my horse."

"*You* didn't have to go with them. It didn't have to be *your* horse."

Two Hawks listened to his father without saying anything. He didn't want to get into another disagreement.

"I suppose you haven't seen Corn Flower yet," his father continued.

"No. Why?"

"Water Woman gave her a black eye in their fight. The whole village is talking about that." He scowled at his son. "This is *not* good."

"A black eye? Really?" Two Hawks tried to remain expressionless, but he thought proudly to himself, "*That's my girl.*"

The next time Two Hawks saw Corn Flower, she gave him a look that would have dropped a charging buffalo. He saw it, but didn't care. It would be better if he chose Corn Flower, or any other Kiowa woman, for his wife. But he couldn't get Lana out of his mind or his heart.

* * *

Sundays were days of rest for the Coopers. After breakfast, Joshua read scripture from the family Bible and then said a prayer. After that, everyone was left to their own devices. Sundays provided Lana with the rare opportunity to indulge in her favorite pastime — reading. They only had four books and she had read each several times, but it didn't matter. She loved those books.

One Sunday afternoon, she announced that she wanted to read outside and would be back in time for supper. Picking up her worn copy of "The Complete Works of William Shakespeare," her ever-present rifle, and a blanket, she headed for her favorite place. Half a mile from the house stood a small copse of cottonwoods and cedars on a small rise overlooking the river. Even on the hottest days, a breeze blew from the river, making it one of the cooler places on the homestead. She considered this to be 'her spot'.

Lana spread her blanket close to the trunk of the largest tree and soon had her back propped against it, her book opened on her knees. She was soon magically transported to Denmark where she dashed up castle stairs with Prince Hamlet, looking for ghosts.

* * *

Two Hawks rode with four friends, presumably to hunt, but in the heat, all the game hid in shady places. Now, the men simply meandered across the plains, talking about the young women in camp and who liked whom.

"You like *her?*" Two Hawks shook his head. "She's crazy."

"So? I like them crazy," Black Stag defended his choice. "She's better than Red Sky."

"Hey! I like Red Sky," Tall Lodge argued.

"Why? She's so shy, she never says anything," Black Stag made a face.

"It's better than yours. Talk. Talk. Talk," Tall Lodge made the universal gesture with his hand for talking.

"Of course, we *all* know who Two Hawks wants. Corn Flower," Big Hand laughed and looked sideways at his friend. They all wondered at Two Hawks' silence on the matter.

"Look!" Howling Dog exclaimed, nodding his head over his shoulder. All the young men turned to see Lana across the river, totally engrossed in her book, unaware of her visitors.

On reflex, all but Two Hawks jumped off their horses, pulled their weapons, and searched the area for Lana's people.

"Get down!" Tall Lodge hissed up to Two Hawks. "She's got a gun."

Ignoring his worried friends, Two Hawks prodded his horse closer to the river. Hearing the horse splash through the water, Lana finally looked up. When she saw Two Hawks, she closed the book and stood up, taking a few steps toward him.

The Kiowa braves watched in consternation. What was Two Hawks *doing?* And why wasn't the white woman screaming and trying to shoot them?

When Two Hawks crossed the river, he dismounted and climbed the small rise. To their surprised amazement, she stepped into his outstretched arms and reached up for his kiss.

"Hmmm. I guess he *doesn't* want Corn Flower," Big Hand corrected himself.

With his arm around Lana's shoulders, Two Hawks waved to his friends to go on without him. Tall Lodge raised his hand once in acknowledgment. They mounted their horses and rode toward the village, full of curiosity at what they had just seen.

"Is that the one with blue eyes?" Black Stag asked.

"They say she's bewitched him," Tall Lodge frowned.

"I wish a pretty girl would bewitch *me* like that," Big Hand sighed jealously.

\* \* \*

"Hello, Yi Ceŋtas," Lana stood in his embrace and smiled into his handsome brown eyes. Then she glanced over her shoulder toward the house, but it was too far away. No one would see them.

"T'on Ma." He kissed her once more and then let her lead him to the blanket. Lana sat down and picked up the book. When he got settled beside her, he reached for the book and turned the pages, wondering what the strange marks meant.

Gesturing his question, he held the book out to her for explanation. Lana studied his face, trying to figure out how to explain reading and writing to someone who didn't speak English. Finally hitting upon an idea, she picked up a stick and brushed clean an area of dirt. She slowly wrote in big letters "T'on Ma" and pronounced the letters as she wrote them.

Next, she wrote his name, pronouncing the letters. When Lana looked into his eyes, she saw understanding there. He pointed to his name written in the dirt and then to his chest.

"Yes." Lana took his hand and traced the 'Y' and 'I'. "Yi," she held up two fingers. "Two." She repeated the process for 'hawks'.

Two Hawks took the stick from her hand and traced his signature in the dirt: a man's head with two bird figures overhead. "Yi Ceṇtas," he nodded. "Two Hawks," he spoke haltingly.

Their English/Kiowa lessons began that day under that stand of cottonwood trees. When they could, the young couple surreptitiously met on Sunday afternoons not only to continue the lessons, but mainly to be together. They kept each tryst short, an hour or less, but in those brief hours, they developed a deep friendship and their own lover's language. Each time, the young brave rode away a little deeper in love with his blue-eyed woman.

* * *

Two Hawks found his mother's father, Red Flint, sitting outside his lodge late one afternoon as he smoked a pipe and enjoyed the cooler weather.

"Grandfather," Two Hawks greeted him and sat beside the older man. Red Flint sent puffs of smoke from his mouth and watched them twist and curl, turning into wisps and then disappearing on the air.

"I've been expecting you," Red Flint finally spoke.

"You have?"

"Yes. Your mother spoke with me and I think you need someone to listen to you instead of telling you what to do." He puffed on his pipe once. "You are at the age where you should consider taking a wife." The gray-headed man turned to look at his grandson. "Your mother tells me there is trouble with that. You're confused."

Two Hawks frowned, looking down at the ground. When he looked back up, he spoke. "I'm not confused. My mother is unhappy with my choice. That's all."

"A choice with blue eyes and not one with brown?"

Two Hawks nodded.

Red Flint continued. "Even though you've grown up with Corn Flower? Even though she is Kiowa? Even though, up until this summer, she was all you could think of?"

"Yes, Grandfather. Even though."

Red Flint smoked his pipe while he considered this. When he had been Two Hawks' age, he would have simply stolen the woman and brought her back with him. But now, there were soldiers to consider — soldiers who would search for the stolen woman, terrorizing all Kiowa villages, not just the one that took her.

"Corn Flower's mother says Water Woman has bewitched you with her blue eyes."

Two Hawks nodded. "Yes. Corn Flower told me the same thing."

"And what do you think?"

"If she's bewitched me, Grandfather, it wasn't with her eyes. It was with her heart."

"Are you sure this isn't simply lust for her? I saw her in camp. Even as pale as she is, she's beautiful."

Two Hawks knew better than to give his grandfather a glib answer. Only honesty would do, would be accepted. He picked up a handful of dirt and watched it slowly fall through his fingers as he considered his answer.

"Maybe, if it had been two summers ago, when I was younger, that would be true. But now, I don't think so." He tossed the rest of the dirt down and wiped his hand clean. "When we are together, it's easy to be lost in her. And, when we are apart, I'm still lost in her. I need her. I can't explain it any better than that." Two Hawks looked somberly at Red Flint, hoping he understood what the clumsy words weren't saying.

Red Flint nodded his head a few times. "Then you have a difficult road ahead of you. She doesn't know your ways or the ways of your people. You don't know hers. Be prepared for all types of trouble. The two of you will be making your own road, one which none of us have been down before. We can't help you. Is she strong enough for that?"

"Grandfather, I haven't even told her how I feel about her. But she's strong. Of that, I'm sure."

"Do you know how she feels about you?"

"Yes. I see it in her eyes, in the way she touches me."

The old man's eyes grew distant as he recalled far away days. "Your grandmother loved me like that," he finally said. Now that his pipe had gone out, he rose to his feet. "Be patient with your parents. They won't understand, but they love you. I don't know what to tell you about her parents. Just be prepared for their anger."

Two Hawks only nodded. He had already seen some of Joshua Cooper's anger, and that was only over a kiss.

## Chapter 9 — Liam O'Connell

Later that week, one midmorning, Paul ran to the yard from the river, his arms flailing wildly. "Pa! Pa! Soldiers!"

Joshua stepped out of the barn and took a few steps in the direction Paul pointed. In the distance, U.S. Cavalry rode slowly but deliberately toward their house. "Go tell your ma."

Paul hurried into the house with his news.

"Soldiers? How many?" May asked as she stepped to the door to look out.

"I dunno. Fifteen, twenty maybe."

"Lana, check the coffee," May ordered over her shoulder as she stepped into the bright sunshine to stand beside her husband. In a few minutes, their dirt yard filled with twenty stamping, thirsty horses and saddle-weary men.

"Dismount!" The men swung out of their saddles and, with their feet barely on the ground, began rolling cigarettes.

"Water detail!" the sergeant called out. Four men gathered up the horses' reins and walked the animals to the river.

A young lieutenant walked over to Joshua, hand extended. "Good morning, sir. I'm Lt. O'Connell. Liam O'Connell." The two men shook hands.

"Lieutenant. Welcome. I'm Joshua Cooper. And this is my wife, May."

"Mr. Cooper, M'am." Lt. O'Connell tipped his hat. He was taller than Joshua by a few inches, but not quite as muscular. His dark brown hair curled past his collar, his face tanned from his time in the saddle.

"Lieutenant, won't you please come in for coffee?" May invited.

"Thank you." He followed May into the house and stopped just inside the door when he caught sight of Lana.

Joshua almost bumped into his back, but managed to step around him. "This is my daughter, Lana."

"Miss Cooper." Lt. O'Connell nodded, but didn't smile as he took off his hat.

Lana straightened up from the fireplace, the coffeepot in her hand, and walked toward the table as she quickly looked him over. "Hello," she said shyly. "Coffee?"

"Yes, please." He sat down and smiled at Paul. "You must be the one we saw running toward the house."

Paul blushed as he grinned.

"I've got two more boys," Joshua explained as he sat beside Liam, "but my oldest and youngest are out hunting right now."

Liam took a sip of the hot coffee and set the cup down.

"I assume you're from Ft. Worth. What brings you out this far?" May asked.

"Yes'm. I'm on a scouting mission, but I saw your place and thought I should stop by."

"A scouting mission? Is there trouble?" Joshua frowned.

Liam glanced at May and Lana, not wanting to alarm them.

"Whatever it is, Lieutenant," May told him, "tell us. My daughter and I live here, too, so we need to know."

Liam sighed, then looked at Joshua. "Apache trouble. They've been raiding all along the Brazos and are getting closer. We almost caught up to them two nights ago, but they got away."

"Exactly what kind of trouble?" Joshua asked.

"Mainly, they're stealing horses, though they've burned out two homesteads in the last month." Liam looked across the room at Lana, staring wide-eyed at this news. He made himself look away. A young woman shouldn't be out here, especially one that beautiful.

May walked over to stand behind her husband and laid a hand on his shoulder. "I'm sure we can handle whatever happens." Then she asked, "Can you stay for a while, Lieutenant? Or do you have to leave right away? We'd love to have you stay for dinner. We don't get much company out this way."

"My troops have been in the saddle for days now. We could use a break, almost as much as our horses could." He smiled at May. "If you can stand us, we'll spend the night by the river. And, please, call me Liam."

"All right, Liam. That will be just fine!" May patted Joshua on his shoulder in her delight.

Liam rose from the table and walked outside, calling for his sergeant.

"We'll camp by the river for tonight. And tell the men that no one — and I mean *no one* — comes over that hill and up to the house without my express permission." Liam pointed toward the river as he spoke.

"Yes, sir." The sergeant wondered at the strange order. But, just as he turned around, he saw Lana walk past the door. It all suddenly became clear. He walked away from the house and ordered the men to move to the river and make camp.

Soldiers repaired tack, washed dusty uniforms, played cards, and slept to pass the time. Inside the house, May and Lana prepared a small feast for their guest. At one point in the afternoon, Lana walked out of the house toward the river, carrying the two water buckets. Liam saw her from his temporary headquarters by the barn and crossed the yard.

"Miss Cooper. Wait!"

Lana stopped and half-turned, wondering what he wanted.

"Better let me," he said as he took the buckets from her.

"There's no need. I do this all the time." She reached to take the buckets back, but he pulled them away.

"You don't do this with the U.S. Army by the river."

"Oh." She stepped back, looked toward the river, and then at him. "I suppose not. But you can't very well fetch the water, either."

Liam smiled at that and then yelled, "Sergeant!" In less than a minute, the sergeant appeared, wondering what the young lieutenant wanted *this* time. "See that these are filled and brought back to the house."

"Yes, sir." He took the buckets and turned away.

While she waited for the water, Lana chatted with Liam. "So, Lieutenant, where are you from?"

"I'm from Georgia. And, please, like I told you in there, call me Liam."

"Georgia. I've never been there before."

"It's beautiful country. You'd really like it."

"How long have you been in the Army, Liam?"

He smiled when she said his name. "Not too long, Miss Cooper."

"No. If it's Liam, then you must call me Lana."

"Lana. All right. How long has your family been out here?"

"Just since June. We've got enough to get through the winter and then we'll plant next spring."

"That's a lot of hard work." Liam shook his head. "Why did your father pick such a far away place to settle? This is no place for..." He stopped himself.

"For what?"

"For a young lady such as yourself."

"Don't worry about me. I'll do just fine."

The sergeant returned with the buckets, stopping their conversation. Liam took the buckets from him and carried them into the house for Lana.

"Thank you, Liam," she smiled.

"Sure. Let me know if you need any more water. I'll see to it."

A little while later, Nathan and Jake came home with three rabbits and six fish, much to May's delight. Now, she could have rabbit pie with wild onions and turnips, fried fish, pinto beans, cornbread, her next-to-last jar of blackberry jam and coffee. No one would leave her table hungry that night.

After dinner, Lana cleaned the kitchen and then stepped outside. She had been in front of that fireplace all afternoon and wanted fresh, cool air. Knowing better than to go toward the river, she walked behind the house. When she heard someone behind her, she turned to see Liam approach.

"Would you mind some company?" he asked.

"No. Not at all." She continued walking. They were silent for a while, neither knowing what to say. Finally, Lana spoke. "Liam, may I ask you something?"

"Certainly. What?"

"Is it true that the Kiowa steal people and sell them into Mexico?"

Her question startled him. That was the last thing he expected from her.

"Well," he stopped walking as he considered his answer. "Yes. It's true. Mainly, they steal children, but sometimes women." He could see her frown in the night. "Why do you ask?"

"No reason. Just something my pa said."

"If you see *any* Kiowa — or Apache — stay away! They are dangerous and they hate settlers, more and more lately."

"Why? Because we're taking their land?"

"Lana. That's a serious subject for a young lady."

"It's a serious subject for anyone. But I'm right, aren't I?"

Liam didn't say anything to that. He simply turned and started walking again. Instead of going with him, Lana stood there. She didn't want to talk to him about the Kiowa anymore. He sounded just like her father.

"I'll say goodnight, now, Liam."

"You're turning in?"

"Yes. It's been a long day and the sun shows up mighty early around here." She smiled and began walking toward the house. He caught up with her and fell into step.

"I've enjoyed getting to meet your family," he said as they neared the house. "And I've especially enjoyed meeting you."

"Thank you. You, too."

He stopped her. "I mean it, Lana. You're a beautiful woman and I'm glad we've met. I just wish Ft. Worth weren't so far away."

"Why?" she teased him. "Would you come courting?"

The boldness of her question surprised him, but he put his hand on her shoulder and leaned down to look closely into her eyes. "You better believe I'd come courting," he said with quiet sincerity.

Smiling sweetly at him for a second, she touched his face. "Goodnight, Liam. Sweet dreams." Without waiting for him to escort her, she found her way to her own front door and into the house.

The next morning, Lt. O'Connell and his troops left at first light. He said goodbye to Joshua briefly outside the barn.

"Tell your wife and daughter that I really enjoyed dinner last night."

"I will. You take care out there." The two men shook hands one last time and Liam rode out.

As the troops continued their patrol, Liam's mind filled with images of his stay at the Coopers. He liked the family and hoped they could survive the rigors of settling such untamed land. Lana, though, filled his mind the most, with her sweet voice and vibrant laugh. He would have to come back soon, if only to look into those amazing eyes one more time.

## Chapter 10 — Scattered Beads

As the cool fall weather chased the heat off the high plains, Two Hawks knew his band would move to their winter camp soon. He needed to see Lana before he left, but didn't want to risk another confrontation with her father.

Two Hawks waited until the day T'on Ma called Sunday, got on his horse and rode out of camp. Making his way to her cottonwoods, he found that she wasn't there. Tethering his horse on the other side of the river from the house, he waited for night and then walked to the barn. He sat beside it, away from the house, and continued to wait. When he was sure the family was asleep, he cautiously crept up to the house, slowly opened the door, and silently made his way over to Lana's bed. Holding his hand over her mouth, he gently woke her.

Startled, she jerked up. Then, realizing who it was, she got out of bed and threw a shawl around her shoulders as she followed him back to the barn. Once there, he grabbed her up in his arms and let his kiss tell her how much he had missed her. When he finally let her go, she stepped back to look at him.

"What are you doing here?" she asked with real concern in her voice. "Pa will kill us both if he finds us together."

Two Hawks placed his forefinger over her lips to quiet her. Then began the task of telling her that his band was leaving for their winter camp and would be gone for months.

Her eyes grew wide. "Oh, Yi Ceŋtas, I don't want you to go."

He drew her to him again, holding her, kissing her, missing her already. *"Come with me,"* he murmured against her hair. *"Live with me."* Even though he knew she couldn't understand all of his words, he began telling her his thoughts. *"I love you, T'on Ma, and I want to marry you. I know you're not Kiowa, but you could learn our ways. I would teach you."* He looked down into her eyes and smiled.

Then he spoke in English, "When we go, come with me."

"I don't know," she shook her head. "I don't know what to do."

He kissed the tips of his fingers and placed his hand over her heart. "I love you. You are my heart." His question filled his eyes. Did she love him, too? Lana looked at the question, searched her own mind, and then, with tears in the corner of her eyes, kissed her fingertips and placed her hand over his heart. Two Hawks closed his eyes for a second as the meaning of her gesture washed over him. She loved him. That's all he wanted to know.

They stood together, underneath the quarter moon, so close that it was hard to tell in the shadows where one of them stopped and the other began. He held her against his body, enjoying how that felt. She wrapped her arms around his waist and simply held him, her head resting on his shoulder.

"I can hear your heart beating," she whispered. "Ba-bump. Ba-bump. Ba-bump." She smiled up at him, only to get another of his kisses, filled with longing and promise. He knew what to do with a woman; how to use his hands and body to bring them both pleasure. He knew what he wanted to do with her. But knowing this wasn't the right time or place, and certain that he would be her first lover, he made himself be content with kisses and embraces.

After a time, she stepped back. "I need to get in," she sighed, regretfully. "But I'll think about what you asked me."

He watched her walk back to the house, determined that when his band moved, she would be with them.

* * *

Two days after Two Hawks' midnight visit, Lana went on another foraging trip along the river. It was gorgeous fall day, the air crisp and cool, the sky beautifully blue. Lana found some interesting plants and, wondering what they were, set her gun and basket down for closer inspection. She had just knelt in front of the plants when someone grabbed her from behind and dragged her forcibly to the river. There, to her dismay, stood a band of five warriors, paint on their faces and on their horses. They didn't look like Kiowa. One of them arrogantly held up her gun. It was his now.

"Let me go!" she yelled as she leapt at the brave closest to her, grabbing at his chest and pulling something from his throat. Beads scattered to the ground like colored raindrops. The brave hit her across the face with the back of his hand, sending her head snapping back. Lana staggered, but didn't fall.

She glared at him, ready to charge again, when a noose was thrown over her neck, choking her. Just as quickly, her hands were tied. The men mounted their horses and headed southwest, forcing her to walk behind them.

Lana spoke what little Kiowa she knew, but none of them responded. She continued in English. "Where are we going? — Do you know that soldiers are looking for you? — My pa will come after me! — You'd better let me go while you have the chance. — That's not your gun, either!"

As her nonstop chatter continued, the warrior who had the other end of her ropes turned on his horse and shook his head at her, saying what she assumed was, 'Quiet.'

But she wouldn't be quiet. She was angry rather than frightened. Didn't they know she knew Two Hawks? After a few minutes of her endless commentary, another of the braves turned his horse around and, riding up beside her, kicked her in the chin, yelling at her. She bit her tongue in the motion, blood running down the side of her mouth. But at last, she was quiet. And, for the first time, she was afraid.

The small band of warriors rode for hours before they stopped. Lana fell exhausted on the ground right where she stood. She had had time to think about who they might be and, when one of them walked close by, she risked another question.

"Apache?" she asked. When he nodded, her heart sank. But she gamely tried again. Pointing to herself, she said, "T'on Ma." That surprised him. He didn't speak Kiowa, but he knew it when he heard it. What was she doing with a Kiowa name? Shrugging it off, he walked away. After a few minutes of rest, the warriors mounted their horses, and the trek continued.

* * *

"Joshua, have you seen Lana?" May asked as she walked out to meet him in the yard late that afternoon.

"No. She's not back yet?"

"No. She left early this morning. I expected her back long before now."

"She's probably out daydreaming again. You know how she gets."

"I know. But she wouldn't stay gone this long. I'm worried."

"All right, May. Nathan and I will go looking while there's still light."

They came back two hours later, empty-handed. It was too dark to continue searching.

"I wonder if she's at the Kiowa camp?" Nathan speculated as he opened the door and walked in.

"If she is, there'd better be a good reason for it," Joshua growled, following him.

Looking anxiously behind them for Lana, May hurried over from the fireplace. "Did you find her?"

"I'm sorry, sweetheart. It just got too dark."

71

"No! Something's wrong. You go back out there and find her!" May commanded as she jabbed her finger toward the door, frantic.

"Honey, we'll have to wait until morning," Joshua explained quietly as he reached for her. "We'll miss her trail otherwise."

Stepping away from him, she cried, "My baby is out there all alone, hurt, or worse. You *can't* quit!" Her husband's sad eyes finally reached her. Her voice softened. "You can't quit." This time, she let Joshua wrap his arms around her while she broke into tears.

"We'll find her, May," he whispered into her ear. "We'll find her."

\* \* \*

By first light, Joshua and Nathan began the search on horseback again. Within two hours, they found Lana's basket. They also found signs in the patches of dirt that someone had been dragged down to the river. At the river, the horse tracks were plain to see. There were also the scattered beads. Nathan picked them up and put them in his pocket.

Joshua's jaws flexed as he studied the evidence. "This is gonna kill your ma."

"Let me go to the Kiowa camp," Nathan volunteered. "Maybe they know something."

"All right. But then you hurry back."

"Yes, sir." Nathan turned north while Joshua turned east, toward home.

Nathan made good time to the camp, cantering most of the way. As he came near, he called for Two Hawks, Broken Man and Crying Fox. They were the only Kiowa he knew.

Crying Fox came out of his lodge, curiosity clear on his face. Seeing Nathan, he nodded and walked over to him.

"I need Yi Ceηtas!" Nathan jumped off his horse.

Crying Fox motioned for Nathan to follow him. In a matter of seconds, they stood in front of Gray Dove's tipi, Crying Fox politely coughing.

Many Deer stepped out, surprised at seeing Nathan.

"Yi Ceŋtas?" Nathan repeated.

Two Hawks followed his father out of the lodge and looked questioningly at Nathan.

"T'on Ma is gone. She's been captured." Nathan gestured toward the southwest and shook his head. He was surprised at Two Hawks' understanding without the need for sign language.

Two Hawks jerked his head around to stare at his father. "Who would take her?"

Nathan pulled the beads out of his pocket, showing them to the Kiowa. After one look at the colors, Two Hawks grabbed some of them out of Nathan's palm and threw them violently in the air.

"Apache! She's been taken by Apache," he growled. "I'm going!"

"Wait!" his father stopped him. "We have a pact with the Apache. Don't start trouble over a white woman. Let the soldiers take care of this." He jabbed his finger at Nathan. "*He's* her brother. Let *him* go. We're moving camp soon. You need to stay here."

Two Hawks looked in disbelief at his father. Many Deer couldn't really expect him to stay behind and let her be taken, could he? In answer, Two Hawks ducked back into the tipi and emerged a few minutes later, ready to travel, light and fast.

As Two Hawks jogged toward the horse herd, Nathan ran up beside him and stopped him. "I'm going, too," he announced as he pointed to himself and then at Two Hawks.

Two Hawks studied him for a moment and then nodded. Within five minutes, they were both mounted and on their way. Nathan managed to convince the impatient warrior to stop by the house to let his parents know what had happened.

* * *

"Pa!" Nathan yelled as they rode into the yard over an hour later.

"Yeah!" Joshua hurried outside along with the rest of the family.

"Yi Centas and I are going after her. He says Apache got her."

"Oh, no! Please, no." May held her apron up to her face, her worst fears realized.

"Why don't you go find the lieutenant, Pa? Maybe he can help, too."

"Why don't I go with Yi Centas?" Joshua countered. "It's too dangerous for you."

"Who is the lieutenant going to listen to? Me — or Lana's father? And, as for dangerous, I don't have a wife and kids. You do."

"All right, son." He conceded to the logic and then turned to May. "Get them some food. I'll get a canteen."

Within ten minutes, Nathan had food, water, a blanket, and more bullets and powder for his rifle. As Two Hawks waited on his horse, May walked over to him and, laying a hand on his knee, looked up into his face.

"You bring T'on Ma back to us. Please."

He understood her words as well as her eyes. Nodding once, he touched his heart, letting her know he would bring her back or die in the effort. "I will find La-nah." May was so upset, she didn't even wonder at his English.

The two young men rode out in the early afternoon, desperate to make up lost time.

# Chapter 11 — A *Very* High Price

Lana spent an uncomfortable first night with her captors. They tied her, sitting up, to a tree. Something in the trunk stuck in the middle of her back, making sleep almost impossible. One of the Apache took pity on her and offered her water and some of the foulest tasting 'bread' (she had no idea what else to call it) that she had ever eaten. But it would have to do. After most of them had settled down to sleep, a second Apache walked over to stand in front of her, staring contemptuously down at her. He took another step closer and leaned over. Lana wondered what he wanted, but someone called him back before she ever found out.

Lana spent the next day in the same fashion as the previous afternoon. Only now, her family and Two Hawks knew she was in trouble. Now, Two Hawks was on the hunt. If she had only known...

Lana trudged behind the horse, walking slightly to one side. Falling once, she was dragged several yards over grass, rocks and thorns before she managed to make it back on her feet. They would not stop for her.

Trying to keep her spirits up, she silently talked to herself, her face and tongue still swollen from the kick she received the day before.

*"You know, it could be worse. This could be August with no water and nothing but a hundred degree heat."* She took a few

steps. *"I wonder if they know I'm gone?"* Tripping, she caught herself and kept walking. *"Of course they know I'm gone! They knew last night."* After a few more weary steps, she thought, *"So, that means Pa is on his way. Goodness, I'd hate to be them when he finds us."* She smiled secretly to herself at that. Pa's temper was rare, but a thing to be marveled at when it erupted.

*"I am so thirsty!"* She licked her dry lips wistfully. *"What I wouldn't give for some lemonade right now!"* Looking at the back of one of her captors, she continued. *"I wonder if he even knows what lemonade is? Probably not."* Then, in order to keep from driving herself crazy, she began designing a new dress — a new dress for a party. No. A dance. Yes, a new dress for a dance. Picking out colors and laces and buttons kept her mind busy for a good long while.

* * *

Nathan expected Two Hawks to slowly track the Apache band and was surprised when, instead, he took off at a steady lope, as if he knew where the Apache were going. They traveled at this distance-eating pace for quite a while before Two Hawks stopped to rest and water the horses.

"You seem to know where we're headed," Nathan said as he slid down from his horse. Two Hawks just nodded once, not understanding everything he'd said. Nathan frowned. They needed a way to talk to each other. Pointing to his horse, he said, "horse."

Two Hawks looked at him and then the animal. When Nathan repeated it, he nodded and told him the Kiowa word for horse. Nathan then pointed to his gun and said "Rifle." Two Hawks gave him the Kiowa equivalent and then admitted, "Your sister teach me English."

"She did? When?" Nathan's brows furrowed as he realized his sister and Two Hawks had spent time together, even after her father's warning.

"Many times," was all Two Hawks would say.

Thus began the rudiments of Nathan's lessons in Kiowa and Two Hawks' continued lessons in English. It helped pass the time while the two men rode in a southwesterly direction, stopping only when the horses needed to. Their first night on the trail was Lana's second.

\* \* \*

At sundown, her captors stopped, but rather than dismount, one of them rode ahead and disappeared into a ravine. A few minutes later, he returned and waved them in. Lana's arms were once again jerked forward, sending her aching, bruised legs into motion. She put her hands against the horse's flank to keep from sliding down the side of the steep ravine. Eventually, though, they made it to the bottom.

Lana surveyed the scene. Several more Apache braves, at least thirty, milled around their makeshift camp. To one side, a white teenage girl sat alone, tied to a stake. Her dress was torn, her light brown hair a mass of tangles. Besides Lana, she was the only other female there. She didn't look up when the latest arrivals came into camp.

Lana's captor led her to a small knot of warriors, where she waited. For what, she didn't know. In a few minutes, the knot broke apart and one of the men walked over to her. Grabbing her chin, he roughly lifted her face to inspect it. His expression held a glint of interest when he saw her blue eyes. Nodding once, he let her chin go and walked around her, closely inspecting her build, height, overall health. Without a word, he pointed to the other girl and then walked away.

Lana's guard led her to the stake and tied her there. It was a relief to sit down. "Hi. My name is..."

"Sshhh!" the girl hissed a warning.

"Lana," she finished in the softest of whispers as she tried to speak without moving her lips.

The girl finally looked at her, her face expressionless. A bad purple-black bruise covered one side of her face. Lana imagined that it matched her own.

"What's your name?" Lana risked asking.

"Christina."

"Do you know where we are?"

"Hell." Christina looked down again in complete despondency.

Campfires were lit as the night fell. The women ate the unpalatable bread again. In spite of her circumstances, Lana was glad that she was no longer alone. She looked over at Christina, wondering why she was so quiet. She had never seen shock like that before.

The brave who had approached her the night before came back again. Looking over his shoulder to make sure no one watched him, he knelt beside Lana. His leer made her skin crawl. Pulling out a knife, he cut the end of her rope tied to the stake and led her out of the camp, up the ravine, behind a large boulder. Lana didn't know if screaming for help would get her killed. Once they were out of sight, he threw her to the ground and said something she didn't understand. But his intentions became clear when he lifted his breechcloth.

Lana took a deep breath and screamed, hoping someone would get there in time. As the brave fell on top of her, she turned her head and closed her eyes, waiting for the worst. He didn't move. When she opened her eyes, she saw four moccasined feet standing beside her. Someone lifted her attacker off. As they did so, she saw the arrow sticking straight out of his back. A pair of hands lifted her from the ground. An Apache grabbed her rope and led her back into the ravine, tying her to the stake again. Drawing her knees to her chest, Lana held her head in her hands and, for the first time since her capture, let herself cry.

"You're lucky," a man's voice said above her. Looking up, she saw the Apache that had "inspected" her earlier, and assumed that he led this madness. "If we hadn't stopped him, you'd be dead by now."

"Why *did* you stop him?" she asked, surprised that he spoke English so well.

"Because you're worth more than ten of him," Dark Fist explained.

"What?"

"You still don't understand?" He laughed derisively. "Those blue eyes of yours will bring a very high price in Mexico. A *very* high price. We'll get twice for you what we get for her." Dark Fist nodded at Christina and then walked away, leaving Lana with that chilling revelation.

"Dear God in heaven," Lana said out loud, "please protect us."

"Pray all you want," Christina murmured. "Won't do no good. Even God's afraid of *him*." She spat in Dark Fist's direction.

Lana looked over at Christina, wordlessly studying her. Lana wasn't ready to give up to that kind of despair — not yet.

\* \* \*

Two Hawks and Nathan rode into the night for a few hours before stopping. They brushed down the horses and hobbled them to graze. Nathan pulled out some of the food his mother had sent and offered half to Two Hawks. The Kiowa took it and sat on the ground next to him.

"Why?" Nathan asked. "Why are you doing this?"

"La-nah. I love La-nah." He spoke in stilted English. He didn't know all the words he wanted. So, he continued in Kiowa.

"*She is my woman.  When we find her, she will live with me as my wife.*"

"*You know trail how?*" Nathan asked in broken Kiowa.

"*It's an old trail to Mexico.*"

Nathan didn't understand all of what was said.  But he knew enough.  Finished with his meager meal, he lay down on the ground and fell into exhausted slumber.  Two Hawks allowed them four hours of sleep before they were back on the trail.

* * *

Lana's second full day with the Apache was a brutal endurance test.  The rough rope left deep, red, blistering sores around the back of her neck.  Stumbling on the uneven ground early in the day, she had sprained her left ankle.  Walking was painful, but better than being dragged.

Besides Christina and herself, the warriors also had a large remuda of horses stolen from raided ranches.  She even saw one horse with a US Cavalry brand.

As Lana studied the band, their faces became more familiar to her.  Some scared her, but there were a few that looked approachable.  Thoughts of befriending one of them kept flitting across her mind.  Maybe — just maybe — one of them would help her escape.

The more she thought about this, the more of an impossibility it became.  She needed a bribe, and she had nothing, not even a locket, to trade.  Even if someone did help her, how far would she get before the Apaches came back for her?  And, then, what would they do to her?

When the raiding party took a rare break, Lana fell down to the ground and rubbed her throbbing ankle.  The guard stood over her, looking down.

"Please," she begged.  "Please."  She pointed to her foot and then to a horse in the remuda.  The Apache pondered over her request. She was only a woman; she should walk. However, how many rifles would they get for a lame woman? Making up his mind, he called over to a compatriot, who roped one of the horses and led it over. When they began moving again, Lana gratefully rode a horse, even though riding bareback was difficult. The rope still cut into her neck. Her hands were still tied. She was still a captive. But in a small way, her life just got better.

When the raiding party made camp that night, she and Christina were staked together again. Lana smiled at her in a greeting, but Christina turned away, angry that Lana got to ride and she didn't. Lana shrugged her shoulders and lay down to sleep, too sore and worn out to care.

## Chapter 12 — Wait For Night

Two Hawks and Nathan repeated their pattern from the day before. During the long hours on the trail, Nathan broached a delicate subject.

"Yi Ceηtas. You love Lana?" When the warrior nodded, Nathan continued. "Does she love you?"

"Yes."

Nathan rode silently for a moment while he thought about this. Two Hawks saw the puzzled concern on Nathan's face.

"She is my woman. One day, my wife."

"Your *wife?*" Nathan shook his head. He hadn't understood the first time Two Hawks had told him that. "Oh, no. Pa won't stand for that."

"Why not? I'm a good hunter. She will never be hungry."

"Why not?" Nathan echoed. "Because you're not... Because she isn't..." He scowled, unable to finish his sentences in English *or* Kiowa. "She'll live with your tribe?"

"Yes."

"And she's agreed to this?"

That stopped Two Hawks. Lana hadn't agreed to anything. He just assumed that she would live as Kiowa. When she hadn't answered him about moving to his winter camp, he thought she was concerned about the timing and about leaving her family. It never dawned on him that she might not want to live as Kiowa. At least, not until now.

In answer, Two Hawks shrugged his shoulders and nudged his horse to a faster pace.

When they finally stopped for the night, Two Hawks lay on his side to try to sleep for a few hours. Before he fell asleep, though, his thoughts went to Lana, worried about her. Knowing why she was taken captive was the only small comfort he got. As long as she did what she was told, they would not harm her. But he had to get to her before they reached Mexico. After that, it would be too late.

\* \* \*

At noon the next day, Two Hawks held up his hand and reined his horse to a stop.

"What is it?" Nathan asked.

"Apache. There." He pointed to the horizon toward Double Mountain. Nathan looked but, at first, he could see nothing. Then he saw movement against the skyline. His frown deepened when he realized how many Apaches there were. And there were only two of them.

Through broken English, broken Kiowa and sign language, the two men devised a plan. Two Hawks would approach the Apaches in a gesture of friendship and ride with them until they camped for the night. Nathan would follow undetected. Then, at night, he would sneak up to the camp and wait for Two Hawks. Between the two of them, they would get Lana out.

Two Hawks rode almost an hour to catch up to the raiding party. He didn't want his horse to be sweaty, or want to look like he had hurried to find them. As he nonchalantly approached them, one rode out to meet him, gesturing with a rifle.

"*Hou*," Two Hawks greeted him, his hand raised in peace. He spoke Apache because he had often traded with them.

"What do you want?"

"Nothing. Just saw your band and thought I'd stop by. See if you have anything good to eat."

The Apache chuckled at that. "No. But come on in, anyway." He knew Two Hawks only had a bow and arrow, no rifle. There was an understanding, a peace, between the two tribes, and Two Hawks would be made welcome.

As they approached the raiding party, Two Hawks scanned it for any sign of Lana. He saw the remuda first. Next he spotted Christina to the left, being led by a rope. As they got nearer, he looked toward the front and saw Lana. His heart leapt, making it difficult to hide his relief.

"You must be taking them to Mexico," he said, nodding to the horses and captives.

"Yes."

"They should bring good money. Enough for new rifles," Two Hawks grinned.

"Yes. If you help us, you might get a new rifle out of it yourself."

Two Hawks nodded, as if he was thinking over this invitation. "All right. I don't have a rifle, but I've always wanted one." The two men laughed. Two Hawks waved, then slowly meandered around the group, taking his time, talking to different braves as he met them. Eventually, he rode up to the brave leading Lana.

"*Hou.* I'm Two Hawks." When the brave only nodded, he continued, "I thought I'd help you get to Mexico. Maybe get a new gun out of it."

"Good. We can use the help. There are a lot of horses this time."

"And some women, I see."

"Yes. But only two of them. One of them has blue eyes, though. She will bring a lot of rifles."

"Blue eyes? Where?"

"This one." The guard nodded over his shoulder.

"Can I see?"

"Why not? She doesn't bite. At least I don't think she does."

Two Hawks dropped back until he rode beside Lana. Reaching across, he took her face in his hand, looking at her eyes. Her captor turned around to watch his reaction.

"They *are* blue!" Two Hawks grinned back at him, relieved that Lana showed no sign that she knew him.

"I told you. Just don't try anything funny. We had to kill a man who tried to rape her. She won't be worth anything if she isn't pure." The man turned back around, concentrating on the path ahead.

At this news, Two Hawks looked at her badly bruised face and wanted to scream his rage while shooting arrows into all of them. But, if he did that, she would be dead for sure — right after they killed him. It took all he had to keep a calm head, to remain expressionless.

Whispering to her in English, he said, "I love you, Lana. Wait for night."

\* \* \*

The third day on the trail found Lana dazed from fear, weariness, and hunger. Her mind wasn't focused. Her back and thighs were sore from riding bareback so long the previous day, but at least she wasn't in danger of falling off the horse any more.

They had been on the trail for several hours when someone rode up to her captor's horse. When Lana heard them talking, she paid no attention, her eyes unfocused on the horizon. But something in one of the voices caught her attention. She did a double take, afraid to breathe, when she realized the newcomer was Two Hawks. The next thing she knew, he was holding her face, looking into her eyes, telling her that he loved her.

She stared at him in disbelief as she whispered, "Yi Ceŋtas?" A single tear rolled down her dirty, bruised face.

Before Lana could say anything more, he rode away. She wanted to scream his name, to make him come back. Why had he left her? Confusion reigned, and she wondered if she had imagined him there. Twisting around, she looked for him. There he sat, laughing with an Apache, as if nothing was wrong. What on earth was he *doing?* She didn't understand. But wait. What had he told her? She shook her head, trying to concentrate. Wait for night?

They covered a quarter-mile while she puzzled this newest development. Finally, Two Hawks' plan began to dawn on her tired brain. They would escape at dark. Until then, they both had roles to play in a dangerous game. She couldn't let on that she knew him. It might even help if she acted afraid of him. That way, whenever the time came, no one would be suspicious of him getting close to her.

They had difficulty avoiding watching each other. Two Hawks worried about how he would get her out with so many guards. Even with Nathan close by, he wasn't sure they weren't all just a few hours away from their deaths.

The afternoon crawled by too slowly to suit Lana. She had no idea what Two Hawks planned to do and hoped, desperately, that her hurt ankle wouldn't slow them down. At least, she reasoned, she would be a little more rested from riding instead of walking. His presence gave her renewed strength and a confidence that everything would be all right.

They stopped for one late afternoon break beside a pond, giving the herd a chance to drink. Two Hawks rode over to Lana under the guise of earning his rifle by watering her horse. When he reached for Lana to help her down, she began kicking and pummeling him with her fists, as if she feared that she was being attacked. Astonished, he put her on the ground and stepped back, while the Apaches around them broke out in laughter. She winced as she put weight on her left leg. Glancing up at Two

Hawks, she winked quickly, and then made a point of glaring at him as she limped away under the warriors' watchful eyes.

Two Hawks turned around, leading her horse to the pond. He understood her little act and now he also knew that she was hurt.

* * *

Joshua Cooper hurried east toward Ft. Worth an hour after Nathan and Two Hawks had ridden off in the opposite direction. He turned once to wave at his wife and remaining two sons. He hated leaving them there alone, but there was nothing else to be done. With every mile he covered, he prayed he would run into Lt. O'Connell before having to go the entire distance to the fort. It would save so much time. And he didn't know how much of that Lana had.

When the sun set on his first day out, he decided to set up camp on high ground. It would give him a better lookout. Climbing wearily down from his horse, Joshua looked around his surroundings, nodding. This would do for his purposes. Turning to his right, he saw the glimmer of a distant campfire. He wondered. Army? Kiowa? Or more Apache? Indecision immobilized him. Then, deciding on a course of action, he got back on his horse and rode cautiously forward.

Whoever they were, there were several of them. He could see silhouettes against the firelight. Their voices carried across the prairie to him. They were speaking English! Joshua called out, making himself known. In a few minutes, a soldier led him to the lieutenant's tent, where Joshua shook hands with Liam.

"Thank God I found you!" he told the astonished officer.

"Why? What happened?" Liam frowned, knowing that it must be urgent.

"Lana. The Apaches have taken Lana."

"When?"

"Yesterday. We found where she'd been captured. Nathan and Yi Ceŋtas left today to go after her and I came for you. Can you help?"

Liam's jaws flexed at the news. "Yes. At least, to some extent. They're probably headed for Mexico, and we can't cross the border. But we'll do what we can."

Liam called his sergeant over. "Miss Cooper has been taken captive by the Apache. We ride at first light for Mexico. Get someone ready to take my message to headquarters."

"Yes, sir."

Once the sergeant left, Liam sat on his campstool and wrote his dispatch. Finishing that, he looked up at Joshua. "Who is Yi Ceŋtas?"

"He's a Kiowa warrior who has befriended us. We've done a little trading with his village. We were hoping he could help Nathan track the Apaches."

"I see." He looked steadily at Joshua in the lantern light. "You know, don't you, that the Apache and Kiowa are friendly with each other. Are you sure he can be trusted?"

Joshua paused before he answered, thinking back briefly on the few times he had seen Lana and Two Hawks together. He hadn't wanted to admit it then, but now, he had to. He had seen genuine emotion, respect, love, even, in the young warrior's eyes when he looked at Lana. Joshua nodded solemnly, "Yes."

"All right. Then I guess all we can do right now is get some sleep. I'll see you at daybreak."

"Goodnight, Liam. And, thank you very much for this. I'm almost out of my mind with worry." With that, Joshua went to get his bedroll and maybe, hopefully, to get some sleep.

Once Joshua left, Liam gave the dispatch to his sergeant and returned to his tent, blowing out the lantern and settling in for the night. But his mind wouldn't be still. Joshua wasn't the only one worried. Liam closed his eyes, only to remember Lana's luscious blue ones looking up at him in the moonlight. Where was she now? Was she all right? Were those blue eyes crying? Scared? Were they still even alive?

## Chapter 13 — Scattering the Wind

Two Hawks desperately needed a plan. Originally, he thought that he would simply sneak Lana out under the cover of darkness, while the camp slept. But now there were two women to rescue. He would have left the other woman behind, but knew that Lana wouldn't stand for it. So he had to come up with another plan, one where two men with two exhausted women, one of whom had an injured ankle, could escape so many warriors. By the time the band stopped and the campfires were lit, he had a solution. Now, he had to wait a little longer and then find Nathan.

* * *

Nathan followed the band as far back as he could without losing sight of them. He assumed that Two Hawks had gained successful entry into the raiding party since he hadn't seen any commotion. So far, so good.

When night came, Nathan could see the campfires in the distance, but he kept riding closer. Almost there, he dismounted and tied his horse to a bush. First he walked and then he crawled closer to the camp. Raising his head, he studied the layout. The remuda stood on the left, guarded by three Apaches. The rest of the band gathered around the two campfires. To the right, just on the edge of firelight, sat two women.

He recognized Lana and, from a distance, she looked to be all right. That encouraged Nathan, but he couldn't see Two Hawks. He lay on his stomach while he kept looking for him.

After thirty minutes, one of the braves walked away from camp in his direction. He stopped a few yards away and called quietly. "Nathan?"

"Yes," Nathan answered softly.

Without approaching him any closer, Two Hawks continued talking in halting English. "T'on Ma hurt foot. Two women."

"I see that. We'll need one more horse, then."

"Yes. Mine tied."

"I'll get them."

"Run horses away. Shoot rifle."

"The Apache will have to chase the horses and then we can get the women out." Nathan said, understanding Two Hawks' plan.

"Yes."

"Wait for my gunshot and then the three of you meet me here."

"Yes."

Two Hawks was about to turn back when Nathan stopped him. "Someone's coming."

Two Hawks looked over his shoulder to see a brave approaching. Nathan flattened to the ground, praying he wouldn't be seen. Two Hawks took a few steps toward the brave.

"Why are you out here so long?" the brave asked.

"Just thinking. It's noisy back there."

"Oh." The brave looked around suspiciously. "What's that?" he pointed at Nathan's supine form.

"What?" Two Hawks followed the direction of his pointing finger. "That? That's your death."

"My what?" Those were the last words the Apache uttered. Two Hawks' bone-handled knife plunged deep into his chest.

"Go!" Two Hawks whispered fiercely to Nathan while he cleaned his knife on the dead man's shirt, resheathed it, and started the walk back to camp.

Once back at camp, one of the Apaches asked him, "Where's Loping Dog?"

"Out there." Two Hawks hadn't known his name. "He has — um — stomach trouble. He may be a while." He grinned as if diarrhea was funny. The others laughed.

* * *

Hunched low to the ground, Nathan first brought his horse to the rendezvous point before he hurried to the remuda. He stopped to look for the guards. Two were on the far side of the herd, talking. The third sat fast asleep beside a boulder, a rifle in the crook of his elbow.

Nathan quietly made his way between the horses, moving slowly so as not to spook them. He found Two Hawks' horse tied with four others. He untied all five and cautiously, slowly led Two Hawks' and two of the other horses back through the herd. It took fifteen agonizing minutes to cover the short distance. His heart stayed in his throat the entire time. Nathan expected to be spotted at any second, putting all of them in danger. But, after giving the camp a wide berth, he eventually made it to the rendezvous point undiscovered. After he tied the horses, he laboriously made his way back to the remuda and looked across the camp for Two Hawks.

Two Hawks finished joking about Loping Dog's intestinal trouble, then nonchalantly walked in Lana's direction. He squatted down by the fire with his back to her.

"Don't get too close," one of the warriors teased him. "She might hit you again."

Two Hawks looked up at him and laughed. "She's just a woman. She can't hurt me."

"You're not married, are you?" the man asked, grinning. "Because they *can* hurt you when they want to."

Two Hawks just shook his head and raised his hand briefly in a gesture of, "*All right, if you say so.*" Then he returned his attention to the fire. When the Apache walked away, Two Hawks looked over his shoulder at Lana.

"Be ready," he said in English. "Both of you."

Christina's head jerked up as she looked at Two Hawks' back and then at Lana. Lana turned to her, squeezing her hand.

"What's going on?" Christina asked, bewildered. "Do you know him?"

"Sshhh," Lana whispered. "Be ready to run."

Christina stared unbelieving at Lana for a second before she nodded, licking her dry lips and swallowing hard. For the first time in days, a flicker of hope sparked in the young woman's eyes.

\* \* \*

At the remuda, Nathan could see Two Hawks squatting close to Lana as he waited for the signal. Nathan crept to the sleeping guard and stood behind him, watching him. He had never killed a man before. It disturbed him that the man didn't have a fighting chance.

Nathan almost decided to simply knock him unconscious. But, as he stood there thinking about what was about to happen — that his sister would be running for her life — this would be one less Apache in pursuit. With reluctant deliberation, Nathan pulled his knife out of its sheath, its blade glinting in the starlight. Gritting his teeth so hard that his jaws hurt, he leaned over and, in one swift, seamless motion, slit the unsuspecting man's throat. There. It was done. As easily as that. He wiped the man's blood off his knife onto the grass beside them, his stomach twisted in a nauseous knot.

With that grisly task done, he stood to his feet, aimed his gun at one of the remaining guards, fired, and began screaming and waving his arms. The horses close to him reared in fright. He picked up the dead Apache's rifle and fired that as well. The horses began to run as he flapped his arms and yelled. Once they were stampeding, he grabbed the two rifles, jumped on the back of one of the horses, and galloped to the rendezvous point.

At the sound of gunfire, Two Hawks jumped up and yelled. "The horses! Someone is stealing the horses!" All attention turned to the remuda at the opposite end of the camp. Warriors scrambled to their feet, running to save the herd.

"Now!" Two Hawks pulled his knife and quickly cut through the ropes holding the two women. "Run!"

He grabbed Lana's hand and pulled her to her feet. They ran out of camp with Christina right beside them.

They hadn't gone very far when Lana saw the horses waiting for them. Then she saw her brother. *"Nathan?"* She couldn't believe he was there.

"There's no time. *Ride!"* he exclaimed.

Two Hawks threw Lana onto her horse, but Christina balked. "I can't ride bareback!" she cried.

Without hesitating, Nathan jumped down, threw her on his saddled horse, and leapt onto another. Within a matter of a few frantic minutes, all four rode for their lives, scattering the wind as they flew.

## Chapter 14 — Find Your People

Even at a gallop, Nathan reloaded one of the rifles, pouring in powder and shot. Instead of tamping down the bullet with a ramrod, he slammed the butt of the rifle against the ground for the same effect before he tossed it to Two Hawks. Nathan loaded the second one as well. Two Hawks had never fired a rifle before and worried about using it correctly — especially on the back of a running horse, in the dark. He preferred his bow and arrows. Lana reached across for the gun, understanding his consternation. He nodded and gave it to her. Now, there were three of them who could fight. Their odds had just improved.

"How long have we got?" Nathan yelled over the sound of hooves.

"Not long," Two Hawks shook his head. They might have an hour head start, maybe two, depending on how far the stampeding horses had run. Recovering them in the dark would take the Apaches even longer than usual. But once the Apache were mounted, Two Hawks and his small, desperate group were in a fight for their lives. If they were caught, there would be no mercy — only slow death.

Forty-five minutes passed and they were riding at a slow lope when Two Hawks veered due north instead of keeping the northeasterly direction they had been taking. The other three followed, hoping he was sure about his choice.

"We didn't come this way," Lana said across her horse's mane at his back.

"I know this trail," he told her over his shoulder. As Lana followed, she wondered how he knew. For that matter, how had he found her so quickly? The only answer was that he had been this way before. With stolen horses? Or captives? She wondered.

They rode for two more hours when exhaustion of both people and horses forced them to stop. Two Hawks found a secluded place and slid off his horse. He walked over to Lana and helped her down. Pulling her to him, he kissed her as she wrapped her arms around him.

"You came for me," Lana whispered.

"Of course. You are my heart."

"I suppose Nathan got you?"

When he nodded, she stepped out of his embrace and over to her brother. "Nathan, I was never so happy to see you as I was tonight." She hugged her brother tightly.

"You scared us to *death*," he told her, and then looked behind her as Christina walked over to them.

Lana turned around and smiled. "Oh, Christina, this is my brother, Nathan." The two nodded at each other. "And this is Yi Ceŋtas."

"Hello," Christina greeted them both. "Thank you for not leaving me behind."

"You're welcome," Nathan told her, "but we're not out of this yet."

"No. We need to rest so we'll be ready for tomorrow," Lana agreed. Nathan had the only blanket, and the night had grown cold. He handed the blanket to Lana, assuming the two women would share it. To his surprise, Lana handed it to Christina.

"You take this. I'll sleep next to him," she nodded toward Two Hawks. "I'll be plenty warm." Christina only smiled tiredly at her as she took the blanket.

Two Hawks had lain down and, when Lana came over, he raised his hand, inviting her to lie down beside him. He put his arm around her as she laid her head on his shoulder and her arm across his chest. She reached up and kissed him once, twice. She felt safe in his embrace, and he felt relieved finally holding her. They both fell asleep in a few short minutes.

Christina lay down a few feet away and settled under the blanket. She was almost asleep when she looked across at Nathan, futilely trying to fall asleep in spite of being cold. Taking pity on him, she called softly. "Nathan?"

"What?"

"I only need half of this." She waved the edge of the blanket to make her point.

"That's all right."

"Would you get over here? You'll freeze otherwise."

After admitting that she was right, he gratefully moved to lie beside her underneath the blanket. The sleeping arrangements would have seemed highly inappropriate, except that everyone was too exhausted to care.

Nathan awoke a few hours later, on his side, snuggled against Christina's back, with his arm across her waist. "Oh, excuse me," he muttered as he hurriedly sat up.

"Don't worry about it. We both kept warm, didn't we?"

At the sound of their voices, Two Hawks and Lana woke up, still tightly wrapped up with each other. Lana sat up, stretching to get the stiffness out of her back.

"I guess we'd better hit the trail," she yawned. "I wish we had some food."

"I might have a little left," Nathan said. He dug through his saddlebag and produced the last of his mother's cornbread. Dividing it up as equally as he could, he passed it around.

"Here. That's all of it."

"We'll be home soon," Lana encouraged him. "Then we can make ourselves sick from eating too much." She got him to chuckle over that.

They mounted up and began a new day of trying to stay ahead of, or possibly even lose, their trackers.

"Christina?" Lana called over her shoulder after they had been on the trail for a while. "Where are you from? I mean, when did you get captured? Are your folks homesteaders, too?"

"The Apache attacked my family's wagon train. They killed my parents and took me captive. They almost brought my little brother, too, but he put up such a fuss at seeing Ma killed that they killed him instead."

"I am so sorry to hear that," Lana sympathized. "How long had you been captive?"

"About three days before you got there."

"A wagon train this late in the fall?" Nathan joined the conversation. "Where were you headed?"

"A new settlement. We were almost there. Just a day or so away, from what Pa said. Others had gone on ahead of us, so we had a house waiting."

"That's unusual," Nathan said. "I mean, to have a house waiting."

"Pa was a doctor. They were giving him a house to move out there."

"I see. A doctor sure would have been good to have around these parts," Lana said.

They had ridden quietly in single file for a few hours when Two Hawks turned northeast again.

"No. Wait," Nathan stopped him. "We need to go east."

"Why?" Lana asked. "Home isn't that way."

"No, but do we want to lead the Apache to our home? Think about it, Lana. We need to go to an Army fort. This spring, the Army built a string of forts down the length of Texas. Ft. Gates and Ft. Graham are two of them. But I think the closest one is Ft. Worth."

It took time before Two Hawks understood Nathan's plan. This decision made Two Hawks uneasy. He didn't want anything to do with soldiers and his deep frown told of his unhappiness.

"Please," Lana asked, reaching across and putting her hand on his arm. "We'll be safe there. All of us."

"No," Two Hawks argued. "My tribe is closer. They will protect us."

"But aren't the Kiowa and Apache at peace? Won't this bring trouble?" Nathan asked.

"No. Not when the Apache know that you are with the Kiowa."

"Are you sure?" Lana asked.

"If we give them many horses, they will be happy."

Lana looked at Christina, who only shrugged her shoulders. She had no home to go to, no family waiting for her.

"Nathan," Lana said, "I think Yi Ceŋtas might be right. His tribe *is* closer and we don't have a lot of time."

Nathan felt as uneasy about putting his fate in the hands of Kiowa as Two Hawks felt about putting his in the hands of the U.S. Army.

"Please?" Lana asked, seeing her brother's hesitancy.

"Well," Nathan conceded, "Pa did ride out to find Lt. O'Connell. If he found him near our place, the cavalry would be closer, too." He looked hard at his sister, hoping they were making the right decision. "All right, Yi Ceŋtas. Let's go find your people."

Two Hawks nodded once in agreement and led them northeast.

# Chapter 15 — I'll Wait

They rode all day, letting Two Hawks guide them. Many times, he waded through creeks or deliberately over rocky terrain, trying his best to hide their tracks. However, he knew the Apache. While his tactics might delay their pursuers for a little while, they would still keep coming. He allowed his small band only three stops during the day, always for water and always for the horses. The pace was brutal. Even when the sun set, he kept them going, trying to buy as much time as he could before they faced the inevitable showdown.

Finding a safe place for a few hours rest, he wearily got down from his horse. The muscles in his back were stiff. He could only imagine what the others must be feeling, as unaccustomed to riding as they were. Lana limped slowly over to him, handing him her horse's reins. He hobbled their two horses while Nathan took care of the other two. With that done, Two Hawks looked for Lana. She was already asleep on the hard ground. He stood over her, watching her sleep. Never a complaint, never a whimper had left her mouth. She would be a wonderful Kiowa wife. Within a few minutes, he was asleep next to her, his arm lying across her.

Nathan held the blanket out to Christina.

"Share?" she asked wearily.

"Yeah," he mumbled, almost too tired to stay on his feet. She nodded once, lay down and spread half the blanket over her. Nathan crawled under his half and then smiled to himself as

Christina snuggled against his back, putting her arm across his chest. He put his hand on top of hers and, like the other couple, they were soon asleep.

All too soon, Two Hawks jostled Lana's shoulder to wake her.

"What!" she snapped.

"Get up."

"Already? I just fell asleep."

"No." He held up four fingers.

"Four hours? Are you sure?" She looked into his eyes for sympathy and found none. "Oh, all right," she sighed. Lifting her hands, she silently asked him for help to stand up. He laughed and pulled her to her feet. Next, he kicked the heel of Nathan's boot.

"Get up!"

"All right, all right!" Nathan grumbled. He rolled onto his side and rose up on one elbow. Gently shaking Christina's shoulder, he whispered, "Time to wake up."

"Hmmpphh."

"Come on, Christina. We've got to ride."

She rolled over on her back and opened sleepy eyes to look at him. "I hate you. You know that?"

Nathan only grinned.

Within a few minutes, the four tired people climbed onto four tired horses and began another arduous day of trying to stay alive.

That day and night passed just like the ones before. The following day, they had ridden for several hours through rolling hills when Two Hawks stopped them. He turned his horse around and rode behind them, watching and listening intently to his surroundings.

"What is it?" Lana asked.

"Apache," Two Hawks answered.

"Where are they?" Christina asked as she nervously looked around her.

Without answering her question, Two Hawks pointed to a low hill a short distance ahead of them.

Nathan nodded. "We need to hurry and make our stand there," Nathan told the two women.

They galloped the distance and dismounted. Two Hawks led three of the horses down the other side of the hill after Nathan pulled his gunpowder and ammunition off his horse.

"Can you shoot?" Nathan asked Christina.

"A little. And I can reload."

"Good." He pulled out his knife and handed it to her. "Just in case."

She nodded and put it beside her as she said, "I still don't see them."

"There," Two Hawks pointed down the small hill covered in prairie grass. Both Lana and Christina looked in the direction he indicated. At first, they saw nothing, but then a movement caught their eye. Someone crawled on his stomach, inching toward them.

"What should we do?" Lana asked. "There's nothing to hide behind."

"Stay low to the ground," Nathan informed her.

Two Hawks led the fourth horse to stand between them and their attackers. With one swift motion of his knife, he killed the animal. It fell to the ground, offering the only cover they had.

"Oh, how awful!" Christina cried as Nathan pulled her to the ground behind the horse.

"You want to live, don't you?" Nathan unsympathetically argued. This was no time to be squeamish. Seeing the sickened look on her face, he felt bad at his tone of voice and reached for her to hold her. "It *is* awful," he murmured against her hair. "But it had to be done."

"They've got guns," Christina said, still alarmed. "How long can we keep shooting before we run out of ammunition?"

"I don't know." Nathan knew they didn't have enough to fend off thirty Apaches. They needed a miracle.

Two Hawks watched the crawling Apache and, as soon as the man was in range, took careful aim with his bow, letting an arrow fly. It found its target, sending the man leaping into the air, only to fall back down, dead. At the sight of their fallen comrade, the rest of the band rose to their feet or rode on horses over the nearby hill. Screams and taunts filled the air as bullets whined past the four desperate people or thudded dully into the dead animal.

"What are you singing?" Lana asked Two Hawks as she lay on her stomach next to him.

"My death song."

She whipped her head around, looking frightened. "Your death song? It's really that bad, then."

He only nodded as he took aim at a warrior.

"What I wouldn't give for another gun!" Nathan grimaced as he hurriedly reloaded his.

The horsemen reached the bottom of the besieged hill, firing relentlessly. They had trouble taking accurate aim, though, as they, too, had to dodge bullets and arrows. One of the warriors made it to the hilltop, leaping off his horse onto Nathan. As the two men rolled, locked in their ferocious struggle, Christina watched, aghast. Then, seeing her chance, she plunged Nathan's knife deep into the Apache's neck. Nathan pushed off the dead weight and retrieved his knife.

"Thanks." He handed the bloody weapon back to her. Picking up his gun, he took aim again, not seeing the tears in Christina's eyes or how badly her hands shook.

"I got one!" Lana announced triumphantly. No one said anything. They were all too busy.

They fought for only fifteen minutes before Nathan looked over at Lana. "We're almost out of powder. Enough for two, maybe three rounds."

Lana closed her eyes. Now what? Looking over at Two Hawks, she told him the news. He only had a few arrows left as well.

Lana reached for his hand. "Don't let them take me. Please." He nodded, his jaws clenching. He couldn't look at her, not wanting her to see how heart-stricken he was.

She turned to her brother. "I won't be taken alive. Yi CenTas will see to it."

"Lana?" Nathan stared horrified at her. "No!"

"Oh, yes, Nathan. They might kill you and Yi CenTas, but they will have a fate much worse for Christina and me. Rape will probably be the least of it. You need to talk to her now, while you have a chance."

Nathan felt sick at his stomach, but his sister was right. The Apache could be cruel. He crawled over to Christina with his gruesome offer.

Lana took careful aim with her last bullet, blinking back tears, and then fired. Her target went down. Two Hawks shot the last of his arrows and, not waiting to see how they landed, pulled her to him, holding her close as he lay partially on top of her. It was time.

"Kiss?" he asked as he looked into her beautiful, trusting eyes. She nodded and offered her lips.

"I love you, Yi CenTas." She touched his dark hair, his handsome face in a gesture of farewell. "Thank you for this."

"T'on Ma, wait for me. I'll be right behind you. Then we can go to our new life together."

"I'll wait." She paused to take one last look at his eyes. "Be quick," she whispered.

As he kissed her with longing and love and sorrow, he pulled his long knife out of its sheath. He could feel her lips trembling against his as she rolled slightly away from him, offering him her breast. Apache war cries filled their ears. This would be last thing they heard. He raised his arm straight up, the knife's blade glinting relentlessly in the sun.

## Chapter 16 — Just Leave Her Be

Nathan reached for Christina, drawing her to him. Killing the Apache guard was as easy as breathing compared to the task that lay before him now.

"I don't know how to say this," he began. "But Lana doesn't want to be taken alive. Yi Ceŋtas has agreed to help her." He looked into Christina's wide, scared eyes for a moment before he went on. "If you feel like Lana does, then I'll help you."

Christina broke into tears. She had never been more frightened or overwhelmed in her life. "What do you think I should do?" she whispered.

"You lived with the Apache as their captive. You'd know more about it than me."

"Will it hurt?"

"No. I'll make sure of that."

"All right. Thank you." She reached for his hand, holding it tightly. "I'm sorry we have to go through this. I really wanted more time to get to know you."

"Me, too." He studied her face, her sweet, bruised, dirty face, and kissed her. She was the first woman he'd ever kissed and now she would be his only. At least, he thought, he would leave this life knowing what that felt like.

As he crawled back to where she had left his knife, he looked at the eastern horizon. "Yeeeeehhaaawww!" he hollered. "Look!"

He whipped his head around to look back at the others. To his horror, he watched Two Hawks raise his knife over Lana's chest. Leaping to his feet, Nathan grabbed Two Hawks' wrist just before the knife plunged.

"No! Wait!" Two Hawks jerked his head up, puzzlement on his face. "Look!" Nathan pointed to the east. Two Hawks stood to his feet while Lana sat up, confused.

Even Two Hawks, with his hatred for the U.S. Army, was happy to see that double column in blue. Lt. O'Connell's scout had reported gunfire a short distance away and that the Apache were attacking a small group of people. The cavalry rode at a full gallop, only a few short minutes away from them.

As he stood beside Nathan, Two Hawks turned, grinning widely, to look down at Lana. His expression changed to one of surprise as he fell slowly toward the ground and into her arms.

"Yi Ceŋtas! Yi Ceŋtas!" Lana cried as she stared at the arrow in his back. He moaned and tried to stand, but Lana held him down.

"No!" she ordered. "Don't move." She looked up at Nathan, her face reflecting her fear and anger. At last, it had looked like they would live through this ordeal, but now — now she didn't know if *all* of them would.

"Keep him still," Christina said. "I've seen my pa pull an arrow out before. I think I can do it."

"Are you sure? We don't have anything to use."

"When the Army gets here, we will," Christina said with confidence. As if on cue, the Army appeared around the hill and charged the Apache, sending them scattering south and southwest. While they outnumbered the Army almost two-to-one, the Apache had used up almost all of their ammunition. They could only hope for a hand-to-hand fight for better odds.

A moment later, Lt. O'Connell and Joshua topped the hill, both men leaping off their horses.

"Lana!" Joshua exclaimed in relief as he ran over to her.

"Pa!" Lana looked up with tears in her eyes, Two Hawks' head in her lap. "He's hurt. Can you help?"

"Sure, we can help." The lieutenant walked over to her and laid Two Hawks flat on the ground. Then, lifting her up by her shoulders, he turned her to face him, looking closely into her eyes.

"Are you hurt, Lana?" She was covered in blood so he didn't know.

"No. I'm fine, Liam. Really."

"That is *such* good news." In spite of their short acquaintance, he held her close. "Such good news. I was so worried."

Stepping out of his arms, she knelt beside Two Hawks. "Will he be all right?"

"If we build a fire and I can boil some water in something, I can get the arrow out." Christina looked at Liam. "Can you help with that?"

"Certainly." He looked down the hill where some of his men were returning from chasing the Apache. Motioning to one, he called out his orders. "We need a fire and some boiling water. Oh, and whiskey."

"Yes, sir," the private said.

In a short time, the orders were carried out. Christina cleaned around the wound as best she could and then poured whiskey over it to sterilize it.

"The arrow is only part way in. If we push it all the way through, we might tear up an organ. If we pull it back out, it will definitely tear up his muscle." Christina gave her assessment.

"What should we do?" Lana looked across at her father.

"I'd recommend pulling it back out," Liam said. "His muscle will heal. You puncture a lung and he's as good as dead."

"All right, then. That's what I'll do." Christina looked over at Lana, who stroked Two Hawks' unconscious face.

As Christina reached for the arrow, Liam stopped her. "Let me. You're too tired."

When she stepped out of the way, Liam took a firm grasp on the shaft, close to Two Hawks' back and, in one strong pull, yanked the arrow out. Two Hawks moaned once and then fell silent. Christina poured more whiskey over the wound, then used water to wash off the blood.

As a final step, Liam cauterized the gash. He had heated his knife until it glowed. Grateful that Two Hawks lay unconscious, he grimaced as he touched the searing metal against flesh. The sound and smell nauseated Lana, who turned her head away, determined not to faint after everything else she had already been through.

"There. It's done," Liam announced as he stood up. "All we can do now is wait."

By then, all of his troops had returned, so he went down the hill for their report. The Apache had scattered and there weren't enough troops to chase them all. Liam decided, now that Lana and Christina had been rescued, to simply let the Apache go.

"Nathan, Lana, I am so glad to find you," Joshua smiled as he finally hugged his daughter. "And who is this lovely young lady?" he asked, trying to lighten the situation.

"Oh, Pa. This is Christina," Nathan introduced her.

"Nice to meet you, Christina," Joshua said.

"You wouldn't have any food, would you?" Christina asked. They all laughed at her request, but the three of them looked hopefully at Joshua.

"Just so happens, I've got a little something." Walking to the saddlebag on his horse, he pulled out some venison jerky and passed it around. "You'll have to chew on it a while, but it's good."

Lana walked over to the fire and put more water in the pot to heat up. When that was done, she put her jerky into the water, making a weak broth.

"For Yi Ceŋtas," she explained. "He needs food worse than all of us right now." Waiting until it cooled, she knelt beside him and lifted his head.

"Yi Ceŋtas? Can you hear me?" When he slowly opened his eyes, she said, "You need to drink this. It will make you strong." Holding the cup to his mouth, she watched as he took a few sips. He lay his head back down, too exhausted to eat any more.

The sun had set and the temperature cooled off. Lying beside Two Hawks, as she had done for so many nights, Lana put her arm carefully across his back.

"Lana? What are you doing?" Joshua asked, shocked.

"Keeping him warm," she replied. "We've slept this way many times now. So have Nathan and Christina. It's how we stayed alive."

"No. He can have my blanket. You and Christina can keep warm together tonight." Joshua tried not to show his dismay.

Lana shook her head. "He'll need me in the night. I'm going to stay right here."

"She can be as stubborn as Ma when she wants to," Nathan said. "Just leave her be, Pa. It'll be all right."

"Well, at least Christina can have my blanket and you and I will share yours."

"Yes, sir." Nathan said with disappointment. In the middle of this nightmare, sleeping next to her had been the highpoint of his existence.

Lana got up and down all night, bringing Two Hawks more broth, or water, or a cloth to wipe his fevered head. He slept fitfully, but at least he slept.

At daybreak, Liam came up the hill. "How is he doing?" He nodded toward Two Hawks.

"I don't know. He's sleeping, but he has a fever. The wound doesn't look infected, though," Lana informed him.

"Well, that's something," Liam said.

"We'll need to get word to his family somehow. I don't know if they've moved to their winter camp yet or not."

"If you didn't seem them on your way here, then they probably haven't yet," Liam reasoned.

"Can you send someone?" Lana asked.

"Not without starting a small war."

"I should go," Nathan volunteered. "They know me."

"That sounds good," Liam nodded.

"Can we make a travois for him and meet them? It would save time," Lana said.

"I suppose we could do that," Liam agreed. He wanted to get the Kiowa off his hands as soon as he could and get back to the fort.

The soldiers soon had a rough travois constructed from salt cedars found by a creek. The slow, painful journey began, Lana walking beside Two Hawks every step of the way. Nathan had already left to find the Kiowa village.

# Chapter 17 — We'll Make Room

By midafternoon on their second day of travel, four riders approached them. One of them was Nathan. The other three were Many Deer, Crying Fox and a Kiowa that none of the Coopers recognized, though he looked like a medicine man.

When the troops stopped, the medicine man, Tall Moon, walked over to the travois and lifted the blanket off Two Hawks. After he inspected the wound's treatment, he nodded once and replaced the blanket. Then he knelt beside Two Hawks and talked to him for a moment. Walking back to the other two Kiowa, he announced that Two Hawks was well enough to continue home.

Many Deer approached his son, touching his shoulder. *"It is good to see you again."*

*"You, too, Father."*

*"We will wait here for the others. They will be here tomorrow, and then we'll go to our winter camp."*

*"All right. I want Water Woman to come with me."*

Many Deer lifted his head to look at the young woman while he considered this request.

"No!" Nathan interjected, understanding enough Kiowa to object.

"What?" Joshua asked, standing beside his son.

"Yi Ceŋtas wants Lana to move to their winter camp with him," Nathan explained.

"Absolutely not!" Joshua added his protest.

"But he needs me," Lana argued.

"Your *family* needs you. Your mother is beside herself with worry over you. His family will take care of him. Much better than you ever could. They know what do to for him. What do you know about living in a tipi during the winter?"

She sighed heavily, knowing that she didn't have the strength to continue this argument. "All right, Pa. All right," she conceded. Shaking her head at Many Deer, she said a few apologetic words in Kiowa. He nodded, feeling relieved at the decision.

Lana leaned down close to Two Hawks' face. "*You go home now,*" she whispered in Kiowa. "*And I go home with them,*" she pointed to Nathan. "*You get better.*"

He reached for her hand, squeezing it. "*Please, don't leave me now.*"

With tears in her eyes, she shook her head. "*I have to. But I'll see you in the spring, won't I?*"

"*Yes.*" He smiled reluctantly. She started to stand up, but he stopped her. "Kiss?" he asked in English.

"Of course. Kiss." She leaned forward and kissed him with great tenderness and emotion. "*I love you, Two Hawks,*" she said in Kiowa. "*You are my man.*"

"*And you are my heart. I will see you in the spring,*" he told her as she stood up. "*Watch for me.*"

"*I will.*" Turning quickly, she walked over to her horse, not wanting Two Hawks to see her cry.

\* \* \*

At first, Liam had watched the whole transaction with disinterest. But when Lana kissed Two Hawks, he became angry and disgusted. In his worldview, as with a lot of the western settlers, to be an "Indian lover" was unacceptable. A "squaw man"

112

was beneath contempt. For a woman of European descent to be romantically involved with a Native American put her beyond acceptance. Her family considered her dead, a social pariah. Even women who had been rescued from capture found re-entry into society extremely difficult because the prejudice of the time ran so deeply.

"I thought you said your family just *traded* with the Kiowa," Liam said to Joshua during the kiss. When he didn't get a response, he looked into Joshua's eyes and saw the same expression of disgusted worry in them that he had.

Liam was extremely glad when his troops, the Coopers and Christina left the Kiowa to cover what distance they could before sundown. As they made their way back to the Coopers' homestead, Liam kept thinking about the kiss he'd witnessed between Two Hawks and Lana. It upset him deeply.

At first, he thought he was only upset because she was white and Two Hawks Kiowa. But, as miles and time passed, Liam realized that he was also jealous. That beautiful young woman should be kissing *him*, should be worried about *his* well being, should be in *his* arms. He kept watching her as they traveled. He'd never felt such a strong attraction to anyone before — not like this. And he was unwilling to walk away without trying to reach her, to make her see reason.

By the end of the second day, the Coopers and the cavalry rode into the Coopers' yard. Paul and Jake raced out of the house, whooping and hollering at the sight of their sister, brother and father. May stepped out of the door, smiling so hard that her face hurt.

"Goodness, let me look at you," she said, holding Lana by her shoulders. "You look too thin." With that, she burst into tears and pulled her daughter close.

"Oh, Ma. I'm all right. Really." Lana hugged her mother tightly and patted her back. "I want you to meet someone." She stepped back and introduced Christina.

"She was taken by the Apache, too," Lana explained. Christina walked over to greet May and was surprised to be pulled into a tight hug herself.

"You poor thing," May exclaimed. "Come into the house this instant. Paul, fill the buckets and keep them coming. We've got two baths to take."

"Make that four," Joshua frowned. "I stink to high heaven and I'm the best smelling one here."

Nathan rolled his eyes at that, but was in no position to argue. Liam laughed guiltily, and then, excusing himself, went with his sergeant to get the troops set up by the river for the night, and to find a bath of his own.

May set up a large washtub in her bedroom. After the first two buckets of water were heated, Christina had the honor of taking the first bath. When she had finished, her black, grimy water was thrown out and fresh brought in for Lana. Soon, the two wet-headed, clean young women were sitting on the edge of May's bed, wrapped in blankets, and drinking hot coffee.

"This is heaven," Christina sighed.

"As soon as you're done with that," May informed them, "you'll need to sit in the other room while the men get cleaned up."

"Yes'm." Lana gulped the rest of her coffee and stood up. "Goodness knows they need it, too." Reaching for Christina's hand, she suggested, "Let's dry our hair by the fire."

They were perched on chairs, their long hair turned toward the fire, when Nathan came in. "Oh, my," he grinned, "Look at you. Those blankets fit you so well."

"Ha. Ha." Christina smirked. "*Very* amusing."

"Get in there," Lana pointed to her parents' room. "You stink."

A lump suddenly appeared in his throat when he looked at his sister and the beautiful Christina, laughing and happy. They were safe now; he had helped save them. Nathan quickly ducked in the bedroom, too tired to fight his emotions and unwilling for anyone to see.

* * *

Once baths had been taken and everyone eaten supper, the three brothers went into their room to sleep. They had barely settled in before they heard loud female voices.

"No, you!" the boys heard through their door. It sounded like Lana and Christina arguing. Nathan frowned, wondering, after all they'd been through, what the two women had found to fight about.

"No. It's *your* bed. *You* sleep in it!" Christina retaliated.

"But you're our guest. I insist. Besides, I'm so used to sleeping on the ground now, I'd probably be uncomfortable."

"Like I wouldn't?" Christina argued.

Nathan pulled a long straw out of the broom perched in the corner of their room. Snapping it into two unequal lengths, he held them out to his younger brothers.

"Short straw gives up their bed," he announced.

"What?" Paul looked alarmed.

"There's no debate," Nathan warned him. "You don't know what those two went through. The least you can do is give them a comfortable sleep tonight."

"Oh, all right," Jake sighed. He carefully studied the straws in Nathan's hand and, finally making a decision, pulled one out. "This one." Paul drew the other one and held it against Jake's. Jake moaned at the sight of his short straw.

"Come on, Paul," Nathan stood up. "Help me carry the bed in there."

The two brothers made it through the doorway with the bed, apparently just in time. Lana and Christina seemed to be on the verge of real anger, neither willing to give in to the other.

"Here you go," Nathan grinned as they sat the bed against the wall. "Compliments of Jake."

"I couldn't," Christina started to protest.

"Oh, yes you could." Nate stopped any further protest by kissing her quickly. Paul blushed at this unexpected turn of events, while May and Joshua exchanged questioning glances.

"Thank you, Jake," Christina called so that Jake could hear her from his room.

"Yeah, sure." Jake didn't sound too happy.

"Goodnight, you two," Nathan said. "See you in the morning." With that, he turned Paul around by his shoulders, and pushed him toward their room.

\* \* \*

Liam joined them for breakfast the next morning, before the Army's planned departure, anxious to see how Lana was doing. Over the meal, May finally learned some of the story. Paul and Jake couldn't believe their sister had killed Apaches with a gun, and that Christina had actually killed one with a knife.

After hearing Christina's plight, May reached across the table, taking her hand. "Don't you worry about it. You'll stay here with us."

"Won't it be too crowded?" Christina asked.

"We'll make room," Joshua told her. "Simple as that."

"Then, I'd love to," Christina smiled brightly. Glancing quickly at Nathan, her heart leapt when she saw how pleased he looked.

"Do you have any relatives at all?" Liam asked. "Is there someone you could write to?"

"I have an aunt in Pennsylvania, my father's sister. I should write to her, I guess."

"If you'll do that before my men and I leave, I'll carry the letter to Ft. Worth and it can be mailed from there."

"That is very thoughtful," Christina said. "I'll see to it right after breakfast."

During breakfast, Lana felt herself becoming detached, withdrawn somehow. Perhaps she was just too tired from her

116

ordeal. She only caught snippets of conversation around her. Maybe she needed a walk. Excusing herself, she grabbed a shawl and headed out the door, the egg basket in her hand.

True to her word, once breakfast was cleared away, Christina wrote her letter. While waiting for it, Liam walked outside to find Lana. She stood by the chicken coop, staring blankly into the horizon.

"I'd like to talk with you before I leave," he told her.

"Sure," she said disinterestedly, not looking at him. "Talk."

"I want you to know how relieved I am that everything turned out all right."

"Well, almost everything," she frowned. "I worried about Yi Ceŋtas all last night."

"I'm sure he's fine." Liam took her hand. "I mean I'm glad that *you're* all right. When I heard you'd been captured, my heart almost stopped beating."

"I'm sorry you had such a fright." She finally turned toward him. "I never did thank you for bringing your troops to look for us. It was a miracle you got there when you did."

Her blue eyes went wide at the recent memory and, now that she had started talking, she found she couldn't stop. Words tumbled from her mouth as if she were trying to explain to herself what she had been through.

"I didn't say inside, but one of them tried to rape me. They killed him and he fell on me, dead. Then, when Yi Ceŋtas and Nathan found us, we ran for so long with no food, very little sleep..." Her voice trailed off before she continued, realizing that she wasn't making sense, but not caring. "And they finally caught us. Yi Ceŋtas sang his death song and I wasn't going to let myself be taken alive. I made Yi Ceŋtas promise. Then we ran out of ammunition and Yi Ceŋtas had his knife out and..."

Something inside of her burst open. Now that she was safe at home, she didn't have to be strong anymore. "...*and I didn't want to die!*" Hot tears ran down her face, carrying her fear, panic, anger, and worry with them.

Liam reached for her, pulling her to him. "Sshhh. Sshhh. I don't want to think about it." He closed his eyes against the picture in his mind. "It's enough that we *did* get there in time and that you *are* all right." Lana clung tightly to his shirt with both hands and buried her face against his chest, sobbing. Not knowing what else to do, he held her while she cried.

After a few moments, she grew quiet and laid her head on his shoulder, feeling safe in his arms. Holding her like that, having her trust him with her raw emotion, being the one who saved her life, pulled her deeper into the young officer's heart. He closed his eyes, relishing the sensation of her leaning against him, taking comfort from his embrace.

Realizing what she was doing, Lana stepped back as she wiped her eyes. "Liam, please excuse me. I shouldn't be crying in your arms like this. You have to know that I have feelings for someone else."

"I know. I saw you kiss him."

"Then you know how I feel."

"Perhaps. But you don't know how I feel." With that, he leaned down and kissed her softly. "That's only a little of how I feel about you," he told her. "There is more. A lot more."

"Oh, Liam, what am I going to do with you?" Lana asked sadly, looking up into his somber eyes. "I can't be mad at the man who just saved my life. But please, don't do that again."

As Lana walked back to the house, Liam watched her with a frown on his face. He had to talk to her again. But not now. There wasn't enough time now, and she was too upset. Within the hour, Lt. O'Connell and his troops headed due east back to the fort, Christina's letter tucked in his top pocket.

## Chapter 18 — Three Women

They had to travel slowly with the wounded brave, but at last, the Kiowa band arrived and set up its winter camp. Gray Dove worried about her son, not just about his physical wound, but about his state of mind. Leaving T'on Ma had made him depressed and despondent. His mother didn't know what she could do for him.

His friends stopped by to visit when they could. That seemed to do some good for a short while. Time passed and, when he was well enough, Two Hawks went for long rides, always alone. It wasn't enough that he knew he loved T'on Ma. The lonely man now discovered just how much he needed her with him. They had endured so much together, had survived impossible odds. And now, this forced separation was unbearable.

"Mother, I need to speak with you," Two Hawks said one blustery afternoon. The two of them sat around the fire as he watched her cut up vegetables for a stew.

"All right," Gray Dove nodded.

"How did you know you wanted to marry Father?"

Gray Dove looked softly into the fire, thinking of old memories.

"How did I know?" she repeated. "I had admired him for a long time. He was such a good hunter. He lived with honor. And, of

119

course, he is very handsome. I never dreamed he was watching me as well." She grinned. "But he was."

"So, you always knew?"

"Maybe not always. But when I was old enough to consider such matters, then, yes. I suppose I knew for a long time."

"That's how it is with me. When spring comes, I am going to bring Water Woman here." He studied her face for a reaction. Seeing none, he continued. "As my wife."

His mother looked at him. "Your wife?"

"Yes. I need you to show her how to be a good Kiowa wife. How to strike the tipi, gather food, make moccasins, and tan hides. Will you do that? Will you ask my sisters to help?"

Gray Dove shook her head. "You know how I feel about this. If you bring her here, there will only be trouble."

"Perhaps not," he argued. "Not if she is here as my wife. I have certain status in the tribe. They will respect her because of me."

"She will be lonely and unwelcome. Do you want to do that to her?"

"Unwelcome? Even by you?"

Gray Dove sighed. "We are only one family. That is not enough. All the others will be difficult. Especially Corn Flower's family. You know that."

She watched her son scowl before she continued. "Has Water Woman agreed to this? Is she ready to become Kiowa? To denounce her people's ways?"

"We haven't had time to talk about all this," he admitted. "But I think she will."

"You'd better make *very* sure about that before you bring her here. You are asking her to give up a lot." Gray Dove could tell by Two Hawks' stubborn expression that he wasn't getting a clear picture.

She tried again. "What if your sister fell in love with a bluecoat? What if she wanted to marry him and live at the fort? Would that be all right with you? With our family?"

"I'd forbid it. Everyone knows that soldiers beat their women."

"No, son. Not all soldiers. And it wouldn't be for you to forbid. It would be your sister's choice, even though it would break your heart." Gray Dove paused, looking somberly at her son. "That's what you are doing to us. That's what you'd be doing to Water Woman's family. For all we know, they may think that all Kiowa braves beat their wives."

"But we don't!"

"Of course we don't, but do they know that? Would they let their daughter go to a life they know nothing about?" She reached across to pat his arm. "Please, don't be so selfish that you hurt people. Think very carefully about this."

"I've done nothing *but* think about this," he grumbled.

\* \* \*

Two weeks after this conversation, the Kiowa band had six Apache visitors. The elders called a general assembly in the late afternoon to hear their news. The men gathered in the center around the council fire while the women and children stood on the fringes, eager to listen to the visitors. Two Hawks had been out riding all day and arrived after the assembly started. Walking through the women and children, he made his way to sit next to his father.

"You!" someone called loudly. Two Hawks looked up and stopped where he stood. There, pointing an accusatory finger at him, stood the leader of the Apache raiding party, Dark Fist, interrupting the delivery of his news of the forts being built in Texas to glare at Two Hawks.

The Apache pointed to everyone in the circle, calling them to bear witness to his testimony. "This man stole from me. I demand my property to be returned!"

A hushed muttering rolled through the tribe. Two Hawks was no thief!

Tall Moon, the medicine man, rose and asked, "What has our brother stolen from you?"

"Two slave women. I was taking them to Mexico."

Tall Moon turned to look at Two Hawks, knowing he had been in the company of two white women, though Tall Moon had never heard why.

"Is this true, Two Hawks?"

Two Hawks walked over to stand in front of Tall Moon. "No! I was not stealing from him. I was taking back what was already mine."

"Already yours?" Dark Fist asked incredulously. He slowly turned around to carefully study the women ringing them. "I don't see her. Where is she? Bring her here so that I can see she is yours."

"She isn't here now," Two Hawks admitted.

"And it wasn't just one woman, but two that you stole," Dark Fist added. "Are they both yours?"

"No. Just one."

"So you admit to stealing at least one."

"I don't admit to anything."

"Then what do you call it?" Dark Fist laughed derisively.

"My woman refused to leave the other behind. So I untied her. She came with us on her own."

"Do you always do what your woman — who *isn't* here — tells you?"

The Apaches snickered.

"And, also, why did you fight beside a white man against us? Do you choose him over your Apache friends?"

Many Deer stood up and went to his son. No one else had heard Two Hawks' entire story of rescuing T'on Ma. His son would need his support now. Gray Dove watched with great concern from her place among the women.

"Apache *friends?*" It was Two Hawks' turn to sound incredulous. Lifting his shirt, he pointed to the scar on his back. "My Apache 'friends' did this!" He slowly turned so everyone could see. "As for the white man, he is brother to my woman."

"So, you are now brother to a white man." Dark Fist's voice was full of arrogant accusation. "Which makes you a white man. Which makes you my enemy!" He pulled his knife, threatening Two Hawks.

"Wait! Wait!" Many Deer took a step closer to the Apache. "There is no need for bloodshed over this. Do not let this break the peace between our two nations. How many horses will you take for the women?"

*"Horses?"* The Apache spit contemptuously on the ground. "The women were worth many rifles. Can you give me rifles?"

"You know we cannot," Many Deer said.

"Then I demand blood!" Dark Fist lunged toward Two Hawks, but Many Deer's hand on his chest stopped him.

"What if my son helps you find two more women?"

Dark Fist lowered his knife as he considered this offer. "One had blue eyes. She is worth at least two women by herself."

"All right, then. Three women?"

"Yes. Help me capture three women and get them to my village. Then I will be satisfied."

"Agreed?" Many Deer looked back at his son.

"Agreed." Two Hawks nodded.

"Good. We leave at first light," Dark Fist informed him as he put his knife in its sheath. "Be ready." With that settled, the assembly returned to the business at hand.

\* \* \*

Early the next morning, Two Hawks said goodbye to his parents and stepped outside to get his horse. He found Laughing Turtle and Crying Fox waiting at the doorway of his tipi.

"What are you doing?" Two Hawks asked.

"We're going with you," Crying Fox informed him.

"That isn't necessary," Two Hawks shook his head.

"Maybe not necessary, but I think three Kiowa with six Apache are better than just one Kiowa. Don't you?"

With that, Two Hawks grinned and leapt on his horse. "Let's ride."

# Chapter 19 — You Earned It

The small raiding party of six Apache and three Kiowa traveled fast for two days, going straight south. Dark Fist seemed to have a specific place in mind as he led the band through the biting wind. By midmorning of the third day, he stopped them and they all dismounted. Leaving one man behind with the horses, the other seven warriors followed Dark Fist to the top of a hill.

From there, they could see the beginnings of a small settlement. There were a few buildings consisting of homes and barns. Several horses were gathered in a corral, tails turned toward the wind. The few people that braved the blustery weather were all men. Several had blond hair and they all had rifles.

Once back down the hill, Dark Fist motioned for Two Hawks, Crying Fox and an Apache to follow him. The warriors crept, unseen, toward a barn on the outskirts of the settlement. Peering inside, they could see one young woman and a boy working there.

"Gretchen, do you think Papa will like the boat I'm carving him?"

"Oh, Helmut, Papa will like anything you make him for his birthday."

"I hope so," Helmut looked up to smile at his sister. His expression turned to one of horror just before he was knocked unconscious by the end of a tomahawk.

Before Gretchen could scream, Crying Fox had his hand over her mouth, holding her against him. When she fought back, Two Hawks sent his tomahawk crashing into her skull, though not as hard as with Helmut. Crying Fox slung her over his shoulder, and the four men made their way back to the others. Throwing the girl across his horse, Crying Fox joined the rest in a mad gallop back the way they had come, buying as much time as they could before their deed was discovered.

Two days later, quite by chance, the raiding party came across a missionary couple with their grown son and teenage daughter. Dark Fist left one guard with Gretchen, and the rest rode hard to chase the missionaries. The small party tried to run, but their wagon was soon surrounded. The father had a rifle, but was so nervous that his first shot missed and, before he could reload for a second shot, they had already killed him. His wife and son were quickly killed as well. The daughter knelt in the back of the wagon and closed her eyes tightly while she prayed. Two Hawks swooped down as he galloped past and lifted her to his horse.

The girl turned to fight, scratch, kick, bite, scream, to do anything she could to get away. With one swift motion, Two Hawks had his knife out of its sheath and the blade pressed against her throat.

"Sshhh," he hissed violently at her. He could feel her trembling in her terror, but at least she grew quiet.

Dark Fist unhitched the two horses from the wagon and added them to his own. When the band rejoined the guard, they bound the captives and put them on horses so they could travel faster.

Dark Fist then turned his band southwest, heading them toward his village, a five-day journey. That night they made a fireless camp by a small creek. The two women huddled together against the cold while Gretchen cried, bemoaning her fate.

"Where are they taking us?" she asked.

"I don't know. But if you don't hush, we won't live to see the morning," Lisa, the missionaries' daughter, warned as she watched the Apache scowling at Gretchen's noise.

"Maybe when they're all asleep, we can untie these ropes and make a run for it."

"And run where? Do you know which way to run? Can you outrun horses?"

Gretchen burst into fresh tears at the hopelessness of their plight. Two Hawks walked over to the two women, standing over them.

"Be quiet," he said in English, to their amazement, "or he will kill you." He nodded over his shoulder at Dark Fist.

"Can you help us?" Gretchen pleaded. "Please. Let us go."

"No!" Walking away, he pulled a blanket down from his horse and, finding a place out of the wind, lay down and went to sleep.

\* \* \*

The next day, the party followed the creek south. They saw a Mexican woman carrying a large basket as she walked away from the creek and up a hill. Behind her, a young girl, about thirteen, stood next to a basket of wet laundry. She wrung out the last of it before joining her mother. Before she knew what was happening, she had a rope thrown around her neck and a hand clamped painfully across her mouth.

Her mother made it all the way back to their small house before she noticed that Carmen wasn't with her. Going back to the creek, she discovered the basket of laundry, several horse tracks, but no daughter. Screaming her alarm, she ran to the house for her husband. But it was too late.

\* \* \*

The raiding party rode well past dark. When they finally made camp, Two Hawks approached Dark Fist. "You have your three captives. I no longer owe you anything."

"Not quite," Dark Fist shook his head. "You have to help me get them to my village."

Two Hawks nodded once, his steely glare matching that of Dark Fist's.

\* \* \*

Lieutenant O'Connell had been put on special detail to escort a political dignitary to San Antonio. He had hoped to spend time close to the Cooper homestead, but orders were orders. Having arrived in San Antonio with his dignitary safe and unharmed, he and his men were given a few days leave before they had to return to Ft. Worth.

On the evening of his third day there, he received a report that a band of Apache was raiding in the area and taking women captives. He and his troops were ordered to retrieve the women. Liam frowned, afraid that he knew who the Apaches were. The next morning, they hurried toward the last place the raiders had been seen.

After two days of riding, an advance scout raced back to the troops, telling the lieutenant that the raiding band had been seen. There were three captive women, all on horseback, and the Apache had Kiowa with them. At Liam's order, the rescue party broke into a gallop.

\* \* \*

Laughing Turtle looked over his shoulder and saw the double columns of blue uniforms approaching. At his shout, the raiders urged their horses into a hard gallop, their hooves thundering across the frozen ground, their breaths in steaming clouds. The Army gave chase and slowly gained ground.

Liam unholstered his gun, ready to shoot at the first opportunity. As they got closer, he squinted, looking hard at Two Hawks, not sure if he recognized him or not. Liam fired at the hostiles and ordered his troops to do the same. At the sound of the guns, Two Hawks turned to look over his shoulder. Catching Liam's eye, the two men glared at each other in startled recognition.

Before the soldiers could reach the raiders, though, an Apache camp rose into view on the horizon. Several warriors swarmed toward their horse herd, getting ready to mount a counterattack. Severely outnumbered, Liam gave the order to cease the pursuit. Frustrated and angry, he watched the raiders thunder away toward safety.

* * *

After reaching his village, Dark Fist ordered that the captives be imprisoned in a lodge, a guard set. Then he looked for the Kiowa, calling them to his tipi.

"Here," he said, tossing each Kiowa a rifle. "I know this wasn't part of the agreement, but you earned it."

Taking the gun, Two Hawks only nodded. Once Crying Fox and Laughing Turtle had received their rifles, the three mounted their horses and headed toward home. With his debt paid, Two Hawks saw no reason to stay any longer with Dark Fist than he had to.

Dark Fist waited a few days before setting out for the border. When his band arrived, several days later, he had them wait on the outskirts of a small village while he road ahead. He returned shortly with a stranger.

The stranger was round with dirty, black hair and a thick moustache. His shirt had originally been white, but now had stained to a dull gray with brown streaks down it. His pants had been mended several times. His yellow teeth chewed on the end of a cigar and he reeked of liquor and an unwashed body.

"So, *amigo*, what do you have for me this time?" Miguel asked.

Dark Fist led the three women out by the ropes around their necks.

"Oh ho!" Miguel exclaimed. *"Tres señoritas. Muy bien!"*

He walked over to Carmen and lifted her face with his stubby, tobacco-stained fingers. "She's young. This is good."

Nodding once, he then turned his attention to Lisa. She crossed herself and began silently praying. "It won't do you no good," he laughed. "But pray if you want to." He turned her face to the left and then the right. "She's kind of skinny, but I'll take her, too."

Stepping over to Gretchen, he broke into a wide grin. "Ah. A blonde. This is very good." He nodded approvingly. Grabbing her ample breasts with both hands, he laughed at her embarrassment and discomfort. "Get used to it, *chica.*"

"Rifles," Dark Fist demanded. "Many rifles." He jerked the ropes, pulling the women back.

*"Sí.* Wait here." Miguel started to walk away, but Dark Fist joined him. He had learned long ago never to turn his back on Miguel.

Within the hour, the women were in the back of Miguel's cantina, safely stashed away until their journey to Mexico City and a life of slavery began. In exchange, a cache of rifles set on the ground at the raiding party's camp.

## Chapter 20 — Mail

Life at the Cooper homestead had fallen into a routine now that Christina settled in. With her arrival, Joshua had planned to add an extra room onto the back of the house for the two girls. However, watching Nathan watch Christina, Joshua decided he should plan ahead and build two extra rooms: one for Lana and the other for the newlyweds, if it came to that.

Lana enjoyed having a new 'sister' who was close to her own age. Neither had ever been to a proper dance and were aching for the chance. They'd never been to a quilting bee, or a church picnic, so the two young women talked and dreamed and planned all types of things together.

Even though difficult, Nathan managed to find time alone with Christina. He would wait until the girls went to gather eggs and then make an excuse to go outside. After a few minutes, he would pull Christina into a horse stall in the barn. Lana could hear the giggling and cooing and soft voices, even though she tried not to listen. Watching them together made her miss Two Hawks even more.

She missed his kisses and lying beside him at night, wrapped in his arms. No matter how bleak their situation had gotten, his eyes still lit up when he looked at her. How was he doing, she wondered. Was he thinking of her? Did he miss her as much as she did him?

Shaking her head at the futility of these questions, she turned to finish gathering the eggs, but it didn't help her melancholy. Nothing she did to keep busy helped — not sewing or quilting or doing daily chores. She had difficulty keeping her spirits up in the small, crowded house.

Late one afternoon, just before sunset, Lana snuck away to the barn for a little privacy. Paul and Jake were in a restless mood and tore up the house as they wrestled with each other. Their shrieks of laughter got on her nerves.

She walked up to one of the horses and, picking up a brush, began grooming the animal. Her mind filled with thoughts of Two Hawks and her heart filled with loneliness for him. Before she could stop them, tears flowed down her face as she gave in to her sadness.

"Hey, sis." Nathan's voice startled her.

"Oh, Nathan. I didn't hear you come in." She brushed the horse more briskly as she refused to face her brother. Walking up behind her, he took the brush from her hand and turned her around.

"What is it? You've been so sad. Even when you're smiling, you're sad."

Her bottom lip began quivering again as she looked into his eyes. "I miss him so much," she finally whispered. "So very much." She didn't have to say who.

"I'm sorry." Nathan murmured. "I know how you feel about him. I know how he feels about you."

"You do?" She was surprised at that.

"Sure. How do you think I learned Kiowa so well? I was dying to know what he said."

"And what did he say?"

"That he loves you."

Searching his eyes to see if there was more, she finally looked away at his silence. "I know. I feel it, even now."

"Lana," Nathan's tone changed. "You've got to know this isn't good. He expects you to give up everything you know, give up your family, and live as a Kiowa squaw. Did you know that?"

"Yes. He's asked me to live with his people."

"And what did you tell him?"

"That I'd think about it. But I was captured shortly after that and everything changed. Since then, I've realized that I want to be with him, no matter what."

"Lana, be careful. 'No matter what' covers a lot of territory. No matter that it kills Ma or breaks Pa's heart? No matter that you turning Kiowa means you never get to see us again?"

"Why wouldn't I still see you?" she asked, truly puzzled.

"Lana, the Kiowa travel all the time. They have summer camp and winter camp and follow the buffalo. You'd never be in one place very long. And do you want to shame your family like that? You know what people think."

"I don't care what people think!" she said stubbornly.

"All right, Lana. All right. But before you do anything rash, talk to Pa. Please." When she wouldn't answer, Nathan shrugged his shoulders and walked back to the house, worried.

\* \* \*

One cold, bright winter afternoon, a knock on their door announced a visitor. Paul opened it and grinned as he stepped back to allow their guest to enter. "Liam! Come in!"

Liam stepped through, greeting everyone as he walked to the fire to warm himself. "Hello, Cooper family."

Joshua emerged from his bedroom and shook Liam's hand. "This is a welcome surprise. Sit down and tell us what brings you all the way out here."

May poured the two men coffee.

"I came with some mail," Liam announced as he sat down. Reaching into his coat pocket, he pulled out a well-worn envelope. "I believe this is yours." He made a point of presenting it to Christina.

"It's from my aunt!" she exclaimed as she hurriedly opened it and read out loud.

*"My dear Christina, I am extremely sorry to hear of the loss of your family. These times of sorrow must not be easy for you. I am glad to hear you have found such a wonderful family to live with. My brother always was foolhardy and I warned him against moving to the wild, lawless frontier. But he would not listen and has, unfortunately, paid the ultimate price. It's too bad that his wife and son also had to pay it.*

*You are aware, I am sure, of my limited means in supporting myself. I would offer you a place to live here with me, but simply cannot do so, economics being what they are. You are a very bright and talented young woman and I'm sure you will be able to make your way through this life with some measure of success.*

*Best Regards,*
*Lydia Perkins"*

Christina stared at the letter for a moment and then carefully folded it. She hadn't known what to expect from her one remaining relative, but certainly not this. Slowly standing up from the table, she laid a hand on Liam's shoulder.

"Thank you for bringing this all the way out here," she said quietly. Without waiting for his remark, she picked up her coat and walked outside, Nathan following closely behind her.

When he caught up to her, he took her hand and led her to the barn. "Come here, honey," he said as he held her once they were inside. "Don't cry. Please don't. Everything is going to be just fine."

"How can you be so sure?" she asked, with tears in her eyes. "Aunt Lydia doesn't want to hear from me again. I could tell from the sound of her letter. I've got no one. Absolutely no one."

"No one?" Nathan countered. "Then who am I?"

"Oh, you know what I mean. Family. I've got no family."

"You would if I was your husband. Then you'd have more family than you could shake a stick at."

"Funny." She rolled her eyes, thinking he was joking. But his kiss that followed told her otherwise.

"Please, Christina. You've got to know by now that I love you. Marry me."

"Oh, Nathan," she sounded unsure. "Marry you? Really?"

"Yes, really."

"Where would we live? There's no room in that little house."

"Why do you think Pa and my brothers and I have been working on two new rooms? One of them is for us. Pa hasn't said exactly, but I know."

Nathan watched her as she considered this new information. "Then, this summer, we can build our own place close by," he added. "How about that? Will you marry me? Will you?"

Christina wrapped her arms around his neck and smiled up at him. "Yes, Nathan Cooper. I will be more than happy to marry you and be your wife."

"That's what I wanted to hear." He leaned down and kissed her with deep emotion.

"Nathan!" his father barked at the barn door.

"It's all right, Pa," Nathan turned Christina around and put his arm around her shoulders. "She just said she'd marry me!"

"Oh. Oh." Joshua's eyes lit up at the news. "Well, you'd better get in there and tell your ma before too much more time passes. News like this just won't wait."

"Yes, sir." The happy couple walked back into the house. Their faces told the news before their words did, but May waited for them anyway.

## Chapter 21 — The Feast

"This is wonderful!" May gushed as she hugged first Christina and then Nathan. "A wedding! We'll have to celebrate tonight. Of course, Liam, I hope you can stay for a few days before you have to go back." She turned to study the larder, wondering what they should have.

"I'd like that very much," Liam agreed. "But is there room for one more in here?"

"Sure," Paul said. "You can bunk in with us."

"Well, all right then." Liam stood up. "I brought a few things with me." Motioning to Jake, the two went outside and quickly returned bearing two bulky burlap sacks tied off with string.

Setting them on the table, Liam opened the first one. "Let's see. There's some canned peaches." He sat four cans down on the table while May cooed over them. "I've got some smoked ham, five pounds of butter, some apples. They're a little worse for wear, but I bet they'll make a fine pie." Each item he produced was met with oohs and aahs and the sound of smacking lips. Everyday fare at the fort was luxury for the homesteaders. "There's some light flour and cinnamon. And, Joshua, for you I got some really fine tobacco. Oh, yes. Here is a little bit of whiskey. Enough for a celebration, I believe."

Liam looked around at the beaming faces. He rarely got to be the beneficiary of so much largesse, and he truly enjoyed himself — even though the food cost him almost a week's wages, and he took all of his accumulated leave to bring it to them. He looked at Lana, but, to his disappointment, she refused to meet his gaze.

"I've got to hug your neck," May warned him, just before she hugged him tight enough to take his breath away.

"I'm glad you like this," he laughed as he stepped back. "I'd have brought more, but my horse couldn't carry all of that *and* me."

"Don't you worry about it," May smiled. "This will do just fine. Just fine."

May shooshed the men out of the kitchen, telling them to find 'something to do outside' while the women fixed the feast. Stepping through the door, Liam untied his horse and led it to the barn for a well-deserved rubdown. The others followed him.

"So, Nathan, when do you figure on getting married?" Liam asked as he slipped the saddle from his horse.

"The sooner the better, I reckon," Nathan grinned.

"Where are you getting a preacher?"

Liam's question stopped Nathan. He hadn't thought that far ahead. "I don't know."

"You could always come to the fort and have the chaplain marry you."

"That's a good idea!"

"We'll have to wait till it warms up a bit before we travel that distance," Joshua interjected. "Maybe March or April."

"That long?" Nathan frowned.

"Steady, boy," Joshua grinned. "That long."

\* \* \*

In the kitchen, amidst all the cooking, the three women chattered about the wedding. "I wish we had material to make you a new dress," May sighed.

"That would be nice," Christina agreed. "But it's not necessary. It's not what I'm getting married in that matters. It's who I'm getting married to."    Looking at Lana, who seemed a little distracted, she asked, "Isn't that right?"

"Oh, yes. Absolutely right," Lana looked across the table and smiled. "We might come up with something between now and then. You just never know."

Christina waited until May's back was turned and walked over to Lana. "What's the matter? Aren't you happy for us?"

"Christina, I am so happy for you." Lana hugged her neck. "This talk about weddings has got me missing Yi Ceŋtas. That's all."

"Oh. I'm sorry."

"Don't be. I'll be fine." With that, the two young women turned their attention back to the feast.

And what a feast it was! May had outdone herself with a pheasant pie. The apples had been cored, lightly buttered, and covered with molasses. They were then tightly covered in a Dutch oven, which was set in the hot embers. The lid was covered with coals to bake the apples to a bubbly sweetness. Lima beans simmered with chunks of smoked ham and wild onion. Melted butter made the inevitable cornbread even more delicious.

During dinner, the conversation continued to be about wedding plans. Christina was delighted to learn that they were to be married at the fort. When Liam found out that her one wish was to have a wedding dress, he suggested that one of the wives at the fort could make her dress for her. Liam would make sure it would be waiting for her when she got there.

"But I have no way to pay for it," Christina explained. "I have nothing."

"Let that be my wedding present to you, then," Liam offered.

"Oh, I couldn't," Christina started to protest.

"Please. The winter can be very boring at a fort. The women will enjoy having a wedding to plan for. Especially if they make the dress."

"Thank you," Nathan chimed in and then winked at Christina. "We can't deprive all those people of that much fun, now can we?"

"No. I suppose not," Christina agreed. "Thank you, Liam, for everything."

"My pleasure."

"How will they know what size to make it?" Christina looked worried at May.

"You leave that to me, dear," May smiled. "That's no problem."

After dinner, the whiskey appeared and Joshua and Liam filled their pipes with the aromatic tobacco. Everyone — even Jake — got at least a sip of the whiskey. It made for a very lighthearted group. As Lana walked by the table, Liam stopped her and pulled her by the wrist down to the chair next to him.

"You've been flitting around all day," he said. "Sit here and keep me company while I smoke this pipe."

"Liam, please." Lana looked down at her hands, suddenly feeling awkward.

Joshua studied the two. "*So, that's how it is,*" he thought to himself. "*Liam's interested and she's not. That can be remedied.*"

"Please what?" Liam asked Lana. When he didn't get an answer, he continued. "I've been meaning to ask you how you've been doing since the last time I saw you."

"Me? I'm doing fine. Why?"

"Oh, I don't know. You just seem kind of lost. I've been worried about you."

"There's no need to worry. Really." Giving him a small smile, she stood up and walked across to her new room. "I'm turning in now. Goodnight."

"Goodnight, sweetheart," Joshua called after her. Once her door closed, he announced that Paul and Jake needed to turn in, too.

"I suppose you men want to sit and jaw," May smiled. "Christina, why don't you and I call it a day as well?"

"Yes'm." Christina stood up but, before she could walk away, Nathan pulled her down to give her a quick kiss.

"Goodnight, bride-to-be," Nathan whispered. She blushed all the way to the room she shared with Lana. She wasn't used to Nathan kissing her in front of his parents.

Joshua and Liam continued smoking their pipes and Nathan nursed a shot of whiskey while they listened to the sounds of the house settling down for the night. Once it grew quiet, Liam spoke, keeping his voice low.

"I want to ask you about Lana," he told Joshua. "I wasn't simply making conversation when I said I've been worried about her."

"I know." Joshua knocked the ashes out of his pipe. "I've been worried about her, too."

"We all have," Nathan added. "She hasn't been herself ever since the Apache took her."

"I know she was almost raped," Liam told them. "That's probably part of her trouble."

"*What?*" Joshua spoke louder than he intended. Quickly lowering his voice, he repeated. "What? She never told me that."

"Last time I was here, she fell apart and told me quite a bit. More than she meant to, I imagine. I don't think she told you a lot about what happened. Nathan knows more than the rest of us, but I don't think even he's aware of everything."

"I know more than I want to," Nathan shook his head. "She really thinks she's in love with that Kiowa, Yi Ceṇtas. And he says he loves her. He intends to marry her."

"Over my dead body," Joshua growled. "That girl has no sense whatsoever!"

"I've tried talking to her, Pa. But I don't think it did much good. She's too sad to listen."

"She'll listen by the time I'm finished with her," Joshua said angrily.

"No. Wait a minute," Liam interrupted. "Maybe it would help if I said something." His eyebrows raised in speculation. "I mean, I'm not her father."

"Yeah. Maybe," Joshua conceded. "But if she doesn't listen to you, then I'm next."

## Chapter 22 — Outrun the Truth

With breakfast over, Nathan and Paul went hunting, hoping for venison.  May and Christina disappeared into May's room to discuss more wedding plans and to measure Christina for her new dress.  Joshua took Jake to the barn to exercise and groom the horses.  That left Liam and Lana in the main room, Lana trying desperately to keep busy.

"Sit down," Liam invited.

"No.  I've got some mending to do."

"So do your mending here."  He patted the spot on the table next to him.

"Liam, please."

"You know, you said that last night.  Please what?"

"Please leave me alone," she sighed wearily.

"Why?  Am I bothering you?"

"No.  I just don't want to have a certain conversation with you again.  That's all."

"I see."  Liam pushed back from the table and began filling his pipe.  "By 'a certain conversation,' I assume you mean Yi Ceŋtas."

"Yes."

"All right.  I won't talk to you about him.  But I do need to talk to you."

"And not about how you feel," she warned.

Liam was starting to get perturbed. "No, Lana. Not about how I feel, either."

"All right, then." She picked up her mending basket and carried it to the table, where she sat beside Liam.

"Do you know how worried your family is about you?" he opened.

"Worried about me? Why?"

"You're too sad and withdrawn. I know you told me some of what happened with the Apaches, but you haven't told them. Have you?"

"No, not everything," she admitted.

"It might help if you did. You know. Get it all out."

"Liam, some of that is too awful. I don't want to remember it, let alone talk about it."

"You might not want to," he agreed, "but you need to." He paused for a moment, watching her hands as she sewed. "After everyone else had gone to bed, I mentioned last night about the Apache who tried to rape you. Your father and Nathan had no idea. They about fell out of their chairs."

"You did *what?*" She looked up, alarmed.

"I'm sorry. I thought they already knew. But that's what I mean. They don't understand what you survived. If they did, they could help you get through all of this."

"I don't mean to worry them. I really don't." Her eyes were wide in their sincerity.

"I know you don't, Lana, but you've got to help them help you. If that makes any sense."

"A little." She finished with one shirt and picked up another.

"There's something else, too." Liam said.

"What?"

"I need to tell you about how the Kiowa live."

"No. You said we wouldn't talk about Yi Ceŋtas."

"And we won't. This is about the Kiowa in general. It's what I know from living out here. I wonder if you realize what they are

143

like, how they reason, how their women are treated. That type of thing."

"I know quite a bit."

"Granted. But do you know enough?"

"Like what?"

"They have a reputation far and wide for stealing horses, women and children. They attack settlers on a frequent basis. They are ferocious and dangerous with very little regard for human life."

"Ferocious and dangerous?" She shook her head. "I haven't seen that, and I've been to their camp."

"One camp. Once. On a trading mission where they knew you," Liam countered. "You walk into one where you *aren't* known and see what happens."

He could tell from her expression that she didn't believe him, so he went on. "Did you know they can have more than one wife?"

"No, I didn't."

"Kiowa women have no say in anything, either." Liam continued pressing his point.

"And that's different from my life? My mother's?" She watched his face, knowing he couldn't refute that. "No. It isn't," she continued. "However, unlike my mother, Kiowa wives own their own homes and property. Not the husbands. That's how the power is balanced out. In my world, the women have nothing unless their husbands choose to give it to them."

Liam frowned and then tried another tack. "Their religion and yours are very different, too."

At that, she simply shrugged her shoulders. "We *all* pray, Liam."

"Maybe, but to whom?"

Lana clenched her jaws and stared down at the floor, refusing to be drawn into an argument on religion and faith.

Gamely, Liam tried again. "You can't be blind to the prejudice that the settlers have against them."

"I know it's there, but I can't do anything about that."

"No. But it will hurt you if you become Kiowa."

"Now you sound like Nathan."

"Do I? Has he told you what it will be like if you live with the Kiowa? How you will be an outcast among your own people as well as theirs? How your children will be half-breeds and live a life even worse than your own?"

The stubborn set of her jaw made him angry. "Lana, don't be naïve! For a white man to live with a squaw pushes him to the very fringe of society. But you let a white woman *choose* to be a squaw," he stopped for a minute, trying to find the right words. "Lana, in many ways, she'd be better off dead."

"Stop! Just stop!" Lana sprang to her feet, angry, her hands over her ears. "I've heard enough." She took a few steps away from the table, but then spun around to face him, her hands making enraged gestures.

"I can't help it that I love Yi Ceŋtas. It doesn't matter if he's Kiowa or the King of Siam! Do you hear me? The Kiowa may have a ruthless reputation, but he is kind and gentle and he loves me!"

"I wasn't going to talk about him, but since you've brought him up, there's something you need to know about your 'gentle' Kiowa," Liam growled as he, too, stood up.

"I recently got back from an escort detail to San Antonio. While I was there, a band of Apache was stealing women in the area to sell in Mexico. I was ordered to give chase. We didn't catch them, but we got close. Very close. Guess who was with the raiding party."

He took a few steps to stand in front of her.

"Don't want to?" he snapped. "Well, then, I'll tell you. Yi Ceŋtas! Capturing and selling women."

"No!" Lana shook her head. "No! You just thought it was him."

"Oh, it was him, all right," Liam spit his words at her. "I saw his face!"

Lana gave a cry of pain and denial as she ran to the door and escaped outside, trying desperately to outrun the truth.

Liam watched her go, shaking his head, his jaws flexing. This hadn't gone well at all. Deciding to give her a little time before he went to look for her, he sat back down at the table to clean out his pipe.

* * *

Lana headed for the river, furious at Liam, furious at her life. If she had known where Two Hawks was, she would have left for his camp that very minute. But she didn't know. So she walked and walked, trying to get her emotions and her mind to settle down and make some kind of sense. All of Liam's arguments could easily be refuted and dismissed. All but one. If Two Hawks really was involved in selling women, what was she going to do? She *couldn't* believe that report. And yet, something in Liam's eyes and voice told her that he wasn't lying.

She walked aimlessly along the river for an hour when she saw Liam approaching. Frowning, she turned to face him, her arms across her chest, her chin set defiantly.

"What do *you* want?" she snapped.

"To make peace," he said quietly, all trace of his earlier anger gone. "I don't want to fight with you, Lana. I just need you to hear me, to really listen, before you make a decision you'll regret later."

"It's my decision to make," she retorted.

"Yes, it is. But it affects so many people you love. So many people who love you." Liam reached out and put his hands on her shoulders. "Even people who aren't born yet."

"Oh, for goodness sake! Quit being so dramatic," she fussed.

"Only if you quit being so stubborn and at least *admit* that I've given you something to think about." He shook her once in frustration and then softened his tone. "At the very least, girl, tell your folks what happened while you were captured. All of it." He frowned. "Please."

She sighed, looking away and then back at him. "All right. I'll talk to them. And, I'll admit that you *have* given me something to think about. But that's *all* I'm promising."

"That's enough. Thank you." He pulled her to him. "Please, Lana. Keep talking to me, too. Don't shut me out."

## Chapter 23 — One Man, One Woman, One Love

The next morning, Liam got up early and packed. Christina's dress measurements were carefully tucked away in his saddlebag, along with food for his journey. His horse was rested and ready to go. Liam took a moment alone with Joshua, and told him about his conversation with Lana.

"Hopefully, she'll talk to you and Mrs. Cooper soon. And, when she does, just listen. Don't overreact."

"I'll try. But it might not be easy," Joshua admitted. "Thanks for speaking with her. I'm not sure what I would have said. It probably would have ended up in an argument."

Liam laughed at that. "It did, anyway." He said goodbye to the others, saving Lana for last. He took her by the elbow and walked her away from the house. "Are we still friends?" he asked. "We were both pretty mad yesterday."

Much to his relief, she laughed. "Yes, Liam. We're still friends. It couldn't have been easy telling me some of those things."

"No. It wasn't. And I knew I risked your friendship by saying them."

Smiling, she said softly, "Liam, I think we'll always be friends." She kissed him on his cheek. "Have a safe trip."

Looking deeply into her eyes for a moment, Liam fought back the urge to kiss her lips. Instead, he mounted his horse, turned to everyone, and waved. "I'll see you for the wedding." Among the chorus of 'goodbye' and 'see you,' he rode away.

\* \* \*

For several days after Liam's departure, Lana found herself thinking about what Liam had told her. Combined with what Nathan and her father had already said, she knew they all worried about her feelings for Two Hawks. His involvement with capturing women needed to be addressed. But when? She wouldn't see him until his return from his winter camp.

Lana kept reminding herself that she had promised Liam she would talk to her parents about her time with the Apaches, but the time never seemed right. Everyone was too tired in the evenings and too busy during the day. At least, that's what she kept telling herself.

One particularly gray day, the skies opened up with a cold rain in the afternoon, sending the Cooper family indoors for the rest of the day. The fireplace was warm and inviting. May sat in her rocking chair, knitting. Joshua planned which crops to plant where in the next few weeks. The rest of them were scattered around the room.

Lana sat at the dining table with a fresh cup of coffee. "I promised Liam I'd talk to you," she said to the room. "Now's as good a time as any."

"Talk to us about what, dear?" May asked, looking up from her handwork.

"About my time with the Apaches."

"Oh." May put her knitting down and turned to say over her shoulder, "Jake, Paul, maybe you ought to go to your room for a while."

"No, Ma," Lana stopped her. "They need to hear this, too. This didn't just happen to me. Christina was there as well. And Nathan. So this affects the whole family."

Joshua nodded for his two youngest sons to sit back down.

Lana began her story at the river and told how angry and indignant she was at being captured. Except for keeping her tied, the Apaches had left her alone until they joined up with the rest of their band. Her account of the near-rape and of having the dead man fall on her shocked them all.

She then told them how Two Hawks found her. "I didn't know at the time that Nathan was with him," she explained. "I thought the stampeding herd was a coincidence." Turning to Nathan, she asked, "How did you do that, anyway?"

Nathan told briefly of killing the guard and using both their guns to stampede the horses. "It was Yi Ceŋtas' plan," he finished.

Lana nodded and then continued. "So, while the Apaches were distracted, Yi Ceŋtas cut Christina and me loose. We ran for the horses and then rode for our lives." She shook her head at the memory. "We ran forever, it seemed. We'd only stop to sleep for a few hours before we'd start out again. There was only one blanket, so I gave it to Christina. I slept next to Yi Ceŋtas to keep warm. Nathan slept next to Christina."

Christina blushed deeply at that revelation.

"We were very hungry and *beyond* tired. When the Apache finally caught us, we made our stand on a small hill. Yi Ceŋtas killed a horse to give us what little cover there was. We fought as best we could, but we ran out of ammunition and arrows too soon."

She stopped here, finding the next bit difficult to confess.

"So I told Two Hawks that I didn't want to be taken alive. There was no way I was going back to the Apaches."

"What?" May was horrified.

Lana raised her hand to stop her. "I asked Yi Ceŋtas if he would help me with that, and he said he would. I knew Nathan was making the same offer to Christina."

150

Lana stood up and walked toward the fireplace, her back to the rest of them. "I thanked Yi Ceŋtas and kissed him goodbye. My eyes were closed, but I could hear his knife scraping the leather as he pulled it out of its sheath. I could feel him raise his arm. The Apaches were screaming all around us."

Her trembling hand wiped a tear away from her cheek. "Yi Ceŋtas asked me to wait for him in the next world. He told me he would be joining me quickly and that we would start our new life together there. I kept that picture in my mind while I waited for the knife. But it didn't fall. When I opened my eyes, Yi Ceŋtas was standing next to Nathan, looking behind us. I suppose that's when they saw the cavalry. Then Yi Ceŋtas fell to the ground, shot by an arrow."

Lana turned to face her family now, studying their expressions. "That's what happened to me out there. That's the hell I went through. Yi Ceŋtas saved me from that. I owe him my life."

"Oh, sweetheart," May stood up and hugged her daughter. "I had no idea it was that bad. I am so sorry."

Lana returned her mother's hug and then stepped back. "Now do you understand why I love him? He did all of that for me — even risking death."

"Lana, I understand that's how you feel now," Joshua spoke, "but that doesn't mean you'll always feel this way. Time will change how you feel. You'll find some young man who will sweep you off your feet. Just see if you don't."

"Time will change how I feel?" Lana echoed in disbelief. "I don't see you telling that to Nathan and Christina. Did time change how you feel about Ma? You loved her once, but that disappeared?"

"Lana, that's different," he argued.

"How? One man, one woman, one love."

"Enough! I will not have this discussion with you right now. We're all too upset by what you've just told us." Joshua stood up and went outside. To where? He didn't care.

## Chapter 24 — Don't!

A few days after Lana's revelation, Joshua knew his family needed something else to focus on, and the upcoming wedding provided that. He calculated that the road to Ft. Worth would be dry and passable in two weeks. There would be just enough time to get there and back before planting. Already March, Nathan grew impatient for the wedding. Nathan and Christina enthusiastically met Joshua's announcement that they would leave in two weeks.

The day after Joshua's announcement, Lana began her day by going to the river, her two water buckets in hand. She crested the small rise to start her descent to the water. There, on the other side, sat Two Hawks, straight and proud, on his black horse. He sent his horse trotting through the river as Lana set her buckets down in anticipation. Two Hawks jumped from his horse before it stopped and wrapped his arms around Lana.

"Hello, my heart," he smiled as he looked into her eyes. "Beautiful woman."

"You're here!" she cried and then, holding him tightly, reached up for his kiss. They stood like that for a few moments, happy to be together, hungry for each other.

"Come." He led her to his horse and, once she was on, jumped up behind her. They rode to her grove of cottonwoods where they dismounted and he tied his horse. Turning to Lana, he kissed her once, then released her and gathered wood for a small fire. Lana spread his blanket next to the fire and, when the wood was burning brightly, sending its warmth to them, Two Hawks sat next to her.

Lana reached out to touch his face. "I missed you so much, love," she said softly. Kissing her fingertips, she placed them over his heart.

He returned the gesture and then, wrapping his arms around her, he laid them both down. He had waited all winter to be with her, and today he would take her to his village as his wife. But, now that she was in his arms, he couldn't let go, not yet.

"I love you." Strong emotion filled his voice as he stroked her cheek and touched her hair. Lana's hands were clasped behind his neck as she smiled up into his handsome, brown eyes.

"Did you miss me?" she asked, already knowing the answer.

"Yes. Too much."

Her hands slid down his chest and around his waist. She provocatively slipped them under his shirt, but stopped suddenly when she felt his scar.

"Oh, Two Hawks. I should have asked. You are all right now from the arrow?"

"Yes. I'm fine."

"You were so hurt when I saw you last that I've been worried about you."

"You have? Then that must be why I healed so fast. My woman's thoughts made it so."

"Yes. Your woman made it so." She smiled again, but then grew serious. "I never had a chance to thank you for saving me from the Apaches on our last day together. You were so powerful and so brave."

"If I am powerful, it is because of you," he murmured as he leaned down to kiss her again. Taking her hand, he put it suggestively under the front of his shirt, enjoying the sensation of her touch on his skin.

She studied his face for a moment and then closed her eyes while his lips went from her mouth to her throat and his hands went from her waist to her breasts. At his touch, her eyes flew open. This was new for her, but she saw his passion and desire for her, and she couldn't deny him what she wanted so badly herself.

In spite of the cool morning air, she slowly raised his shirt. Two Hawks sat up and lifted it over his head, tossing it aside. She ran her hands across every inch of his chest and stomach, up his arms and across his shoulders.

Sitting up, she pulled her hair to one side and turned her back to him. He had never undone buttons before and, at first, they frustrated him. By the time he had the second one undone, he nodded in satisfaction. By the fifth, he smiled in anticipation. With the last one undone, he pushed her dress off her, revealing her lacy camisole and beautiful shoulders.

He kissed her back and her shoulders as his hands slid beneath the lace to touch her soft skin. Her camisole soon joined her dress beside his shirt. He pulled her back against his chest, his strong hands around her waist. As she leaned her head to one side, he kissed her exposed throat while his hands moved up to caress her breasts. She put her hands on top of his, encouraging him.

Lana didn't notice the cold. She was in his arms, being loved by her man, being shown how to make love. She sighed as he laid her down again, his lips sensuously kissing her breasts. His hands drove her wild as they moved to her hips and started pulling down her petticoat. Lana arched her back and turned her head to one side. As she did so, she caught sight of his rifle. It had been there all along, but she just then noticed it. The rifle's significance took a minute to sink in.

"When did you get a rifle?" she asked, still under his spell.

"What?" He looked up, confused at first. "Rifle?"

"Yes." She pointed to his horse.

"Oh. I traded for it."

"Traded? What? Horses?" She was fully alert now.

"No. Not horses." The young man scowled. He didn't want to talk about trading right then.

"Then what?" When he didn't say anything, she went on. "Someone told me that you were taking captives. Is that where you got the rifle?"

"Yes," he nodded. Lana pushed away from him and, grabbing her clothes, quickly dressed.

Two Hawks' consternation showed in his face. "I owed a debt of three women to Dark Fist because I took two women from him. One for Nathan's woman and two for you." He grinned. "Two for your beautiful blue eyes. But I didn't take them to Mexico. I just helped him catch them and take them to his village."

"Wait a minute!" she exclaimed as she sat back down beside him. "You were with the band that captured me? You helped *them* capture more women?"

"Yes. What is wrong?" he asked, genuinely puzzled. Two Hawks put his shirt back on, realizing that the lovers' tryst was over.

"What's wrong? You were selling women! Just like the Apaches wanted to sell me! How could you *do* that?"

"How could I sell women? Easy. I catch them and take them to Mexico. We do it all the time."

"But why?" Lana almost wailed her question.

"To get things we need. Rifles."

"Don't you think it's wrong to take captives? Don't you think it's wrong to sell them into slavery?"

"No. Why is it wrong?"

Thoroughly exasperated, Lana could hardly speak. "You mean that you didn't think it was wrong when I was captured?"

"No. I didn't like it. It made me very angry, but it happens all the time. Only a strong man who can take you back is worthy of you."

"Oh. So the strongest man gets the woman?"

"Usually. What woman wants a weak man?"

"What about her family, her home? What if she doesn't want to be captured?"

Two Hawks shrugged. "She will get used to her new home. All our captives have."

"All your... You mean there are captive women living in your village *now*?"

"Yes. Four, maybe five. All with husbands and children. One even has grandchildren. They are very happy with us. They are lucky to have Kiowa men."

"For heaven sake!" She shook her head, looking skyward. "Then, is it true you can have more than one wife?"

"If my brother is married and he dies, I have to marry his widow."

"You have to? Why?" She didn't sound angry any more, only confused, in desperate need to hear the truth.

He looked at her, frustrated at how much she didn't understand. "Who else will care for the woman or her children? Without a hunter, they will starve. It is a brother's duty to care for them."

"Do you have a brother?"

"No. Only sisters."

"So, if we were married and you died, what would happen to me?"

Frowning, he took a moment before answering. "You would either return to your family or perhaps another man in our village would want to marry you. If not, you would starve."

"If I marry you, I can't go home. My family will disown me." She returned his frown. "What are the chances another Kiowa would want me?"

When he didn't answer, she nodded. "I thought so. No chance at all. The color of my eyes scares them. So if I marry you and you die, then I starve."

Again, he didn't answer. Lana stood up, feeling like a rock had just rolled onto her heart. All the debate over the winter, all the voices that had been talking to her, suddenly focused into one unmistakable conclusion. Knowing what she had to do, she held her hand out toward him. Taking it, he, too, stood.

"Yi Ceŋtas." The serious look on her face scared him. "I — I can't do this. I can't be your wife. Too many things are against us."

"No, my heart. No! Do not say this. I am strong and will not die for many, many years."

"You can't promise that. There are buffalo hunts and raiding parties and soldiers. You almost died once already. That was too close."

"But I did not die," he argued. He could tell from her expression that his words made no difference.

"I am so sorry. So terribly sorry." Two tears trembled on the edge of her lashes before they rolled down her face. "I love you so much, but I can't do this. There's too much I don't understand. I'm afraid we'd wind up hurting each other, or, worse, hating each other."

"T'on Ma — Lana, no! Do not leave me."

"Then you come live with me."

He jerked his head back, as if he'd been stung. She might as well have asked him to live on the moon.

"And there it is," she whispered sadly, with heartbreaking resignation. "You can't live in my world any more than I can live in yours."

Looking up into his woeful face, she kissed him quickly once, turned and walked away. He took a few steps after her, but, without turning around, she held up one hand.

"Don't!" she ordered.

The further away she walked, the more the young warrior's heart bled. How could this be happening? She was his life! This was their wedding day. When she was almost out of sight, she heard the most heart-stopping cry. It filled the air with its grief and her conscience with guilty sorrow.

## Chapter 25 — Follow Her Wisdom

Halfway home, Lana ran into her father and Nathan, out looking for her.

"Where have you been?" Joshua demanded. "We thought you'd been captured again."

"No, Pa."

The sadness in her voice and expression made Nathan take a guess. "Yi Ceŋtas? Was he here?"

"Yes," she said quietly.

"Lana!" Her father grabbed her arm and started to scold her.

"Please, Pa. I told him to leave." She wriggled loose from her father's grasp. "I'm not going to live with him or marry him or anything." With that announcement, she burst into tears. Nathan reached for her, understanding some of what she felt. He had seen how much they loved each other. Lana cried in her brother's arms, not caring what her father thought.

Joshua surprised himself with his own reaction. Instead of being happy, he saw his daughter torn apart, and couldn't stand watching her grieve. "Come here, sweetheart," he murmured as he pulled her to him.

"Oh, Pa! This hurts so bad!" she cried just before she buried her head against his chest.

He wrapped his arms around her, his little girl no longer. "Sshhh, honey. Sshhh. It'll be all right. Everything will be all right. It's all for the best." Waiting a few minutes, he then turned her by her shoulders, and the three of them started back home.

\* \* \*

That night, after everyone had gone to bed, Joshua and May had a few quiet minutes together. May brushed and braided her hair for the night and got settled under the covers. Joshua blew out the lamp and then, once in bed, pulled her to him.

"I suppose we ought to be happy about Lana's decision," May said.

"We should be," he agreed. "And I *am* relieved. But happy? No." He kissed the top of May's head as it rested against his shoulder. "For the first time, I realized that she didn't just have a crush on that boy. That was a woman's love. That was a woman's heartbreak I saw today."

"Poor Lana." May ran her fingers sympathetically across his chest. "But honey, she'll recover. She's strong like her pa."

"And stubborn like her ma." Joshua finally smiled and then kissed his wife goodnight.

\* \* \*

Two Hawks rode into camp feeling more lost than he ever had in his life. Returning his horse to the herd, he went looking for his grandfather, Red Flint. He found him walking along the river, looking the land over now that winter was over.

"Grandfather," Two Hawks called as he hurried to catch up with him.

"Yes?" Red Flint stopped and turned around to wait.

"Can I walk with you?"

161

"Certainly." He resumed walking as Two Hawks fell into step beside him. They walked quite a distance with neither saying anything.

"You know," his grandfather finally broke the silence, "whenever a young man is this quiet, he's got something on his mind. And, whenever a young man wants to spend this much time with his grandfather, it's because he needs advice."

Two Hawks looked sideways at him and sighed heavily. "You're right," he admitted. "I do need your advice."

"A woman?"

"Yes."

"With blue eyes?"

"Yes."

"Have you seen her yet?"

"This morning."

"I thought you were going to bring her here. Where is she?"

"She wouldn't come."

"Hmmm." They took a few more steps.

"She's killing me!" Two Hawks exclaimed with more emotion than he wanted to show.

"Really?" Red Flint looked at his grandson's chest and then his back. "I don't see a knife or arrow sticking out. Did she feed you poison?"

"No." Two Hawks sounded exasperated. "She's broken my heart."

"Ahhhh. Because she wouldn't come here with you?"

"It's more than that. Because she doesn't want to see me again."

Red Flint looked closely at Two Hawks, seeing the pain on his face as clearly as he would have seen war paint. "What were her reasons?"

"She doesn't understand our way of life. For some reason, she thinks taking captives is wrong. And having more than one wife seemed to bother her. I tried to explain everything, but it didn't do any good."

"The white man has a funny way of looking at things," Red Flint commented. "I can understand why she might be confused. They are very illogical."

"But what can I do?" Two Hawks looked forlorn. "I love her, and I need her here with me. She would lack for nothing."

"Except maybe acceptance from the rest of the tribe."

"I don't understand that. We have people living with us who aren't Kiowa. Everyone accepts them."

"Yes, but none of them are white — with blue eyes. And, they've all had to earn their acceptance. You want to bring her here as an equal to all the other women. The tribe won't stand for that. She'll have to prove herself. Can she strike a tipi? Does she know which roots are good to eat and which will kill you? Can she even tan a hide?"

"None of that matters to me," Two Hawks argued. "I want her."

"And that's it?" Red Flint asked with some sarcasm. "You want her, so that's the way it must be."

Two Hawks became irritated. He had hoped for sympathy and advice on what his next step should be to get Lana there. Instead, he only heard the same thing over again, except this time from his grandfather.

"You know," Red Flint continued, "I believe that, in this matter, she is wiser than you. Follow her wisdom and let her go. You'll both be happier."

Two Hawks scowled at Red Flint. He didn't want to show disrespect to his elder, but he couldn't continue walking with him either.

"I have to go," Two Hawks said tersely.

"Then go."

Two Hawks stalked away, leaving Red Flint contemplating the river.

* * *

That evening, Two Hawks sat outside his mother's tipi after dinner. The pleasant evening starkly contrasted his black mood. But it was a good evening for smoking his pipe and thinking. As he watched the smoke drift upward and disappear into the evening sky, he went over his argument with Lana, adding what he *should* have said and *wished* he'd said. But it was too late. All winter he had planned this time to be with Lana. Without her here, he didn't know what to do with himself. He didn't know what to do with the overwhelming heartache. His sorrow turned into anger.

Corn Flower walked by with her brother, Laughing Turtle. "Hello, Two Hawks," she greeted him with a friendly smile as they stopped to talk with him.

"Hello." He nodded once and, wishing to be left alone, continued to smoke.

"I suppose you know about the dance in a few days to celebrate our new summer camp."

"Yes. I know."

"Will you be there? I'm going to wear my new dress."

Two Hawks stared at her for a moment, angry at her flirting. But her question helped him make up his mind. "No," he said gruffly. "I won't be here."

"You won't?" Laughing Turtle asked. "Where are you going?"

"I think I'll head north to see if there are any good horses to steal."

"By yourself?" the younger man asked.

"Maybe. Unless anyone wants to come with me."

"I will."

"Good. We'll leave day after tomorrow."

"Humph," Corn Flower snorted. "Horses! Don't you have enough already?"

"Never!" Two Hawks stood up and unceremoniously went into the tipi, leaving her standing there, feeling slighted.

* * *

Word spread quickly through the camp of Two Hawks' horse raid. Four men, anxious to get out and 'do something' after a long, boring winter, eagerly joined him. Besides Laughing Turtle, Six Hands joined the band. He had been married just over a year and already regretted his choice of wife. Spotted Horse was the youngest at fifteen, and eager to prove his valor and worth as a warrior. The oldest at 26 and a widower, Many Rivers' wife had died in childbirth that winter. He needed something to distract him from missing her. In some regards, he and Two Hawks had the most in common. They both wanted to forget about the women they loved.

Early dawn saw the small band of five Kiowa warriors ready to ride north, northwest. Two Hawks and Six Hands both had rifles with enough powder and bullets for a few rounds each. Fresh arrows filled everyone's quiver. Their axes were honed to lethal sharpness, their parfleches full of food.

Under the guise of seeing her brother off, Corn Flower stood next to Two Hawks' horse, her hand on its mane.

"Take care of my brother," she said, looking up at him.

"Of course."

"Take care of yourself, too."

As Two Hawks looked at her, he understood her message underneath her words. "Corn Flower, don't wait for me."

"What?"

"Don't wait for me," he repeated. "If I come back, it won't be to you."

Without waiting to hear her protest that she didn't know what he meant, he prodded his horse into a trot and then a lope as he led his band out of camp.

## Chapter 26 — Flowers

Two weeks passed quickly, and the day to leave for Ft. Worth arrived. The loaded wagon carried clothes, food, and cages with all the hens, since no one would be home to feed them. Besides, the Coopers hoped to trade eggs for things they needed.

They took turns riding, two at a time, while the rest walked. It was hard to tell who was more excited, Nathan or Christina. Christina and Lana had worked hard to get the newlyweds' room ready. A new quilt covered the new bed. A braided rag rug lay on the dirt floor. They had even scrounged enough wood for Nathan to make a rough washstand. Christina hoped, while at the fort, that she could find a basin and pitcher to put on it.

They traveled several days, but at last, the wall-less fort rose into view. Over an hour later, the Cooper family reached the first outlying building.

"You're here!" Liam grinned when he saw them. He shook first Joshua's and then Nathan's hand. "Come to the Officers' Mess," he invited. The small band of weary travelers followed him in and, after yelling for the cook, Liam soon had them drinking hot, bitter coffee.

"The wives are going to be so excited that you got here," he laughed. "They've been working like crazy folk ever since I told them about the wedding. They won't let me see the dress. You'd think *I* was the groom!"

Nathan laughed at that. Christina just blushed.

"So, when will this all take place? Tomorrow? The next day?" Liam asked.

"Probably the next day," May said. "We need tomorrow to get a few things ready."

"All right. I'll spread the word. The cook is willing to help with anything you need, Mrs. Cooper. And I've already told the chaplain you'd be coming, Nathan, but I'm sure he'll want to meet you and Christina tomorrow."

"Just say when," Nathan answered, "and we'll be there."

"I don't know if there's room to put everyone up," Liam warned.

"We didn't plan on staying at the fort," Joshua said. "We brought a couple of tents. One for the men and one for the women."

"Why don't I get a room for the two young ladies? Then, you and your lovely wife can have a tent all to yourselves, and these young bucks here can share a tent. After the wedding, Lana can move out and Nathan can move in with Christina."

Again, Christina blushed. "Thank you," she managed to say.

In short order, the two young women were deposited in guest quarters, their clothing and personal items brought in from the wagon. The two tents were set up some distance away. The horses were allowed room in the stables, where they received oats as a treat with their dinner.

\* \* \*

The next day went by in a hectic flurry. Lana and Christina's morning began at a knock on their door. After donning her robe, Lana answered the door to find several military wives outside. One held a large box, another a cloth-covered tray.

"Is the bride awake?" one woman asked cheerfully. "We've brought the dress to try on her."

"Of course. Come in." Lana stepped back and smiled as they entered one-by-one.

The women surrounded Christina in a matter of seconds, as she tried to learn everyone's name.

"We know it's still early," one of the wives smiled, "so we brought you some breakfast. I hope you like pancakes."

"We *love* pancakes," Lana peered eagerly at the tray the woman carried. Soon, Lana and Christina were eating delicious buttermilk pancakes made with light flour, drenched in butter and syrup. There couldn't have been a better way for them to start the day.

With breakfast over, and knowing that she would only be in the way, Lana quickly dressed, wanting to see the chapel. She wondered if she could find enough flowers for decoration.

The Cooper's also rose early. Nervous about his appointment with the chaplain, Nathan spent many careful minutes getting shaved and dressed.

May wanted to speak to the cook about arrangements for the bridal supper and, more importantly, for the wedding cake. After feeding her family oatmeal and coffee for breakfast, she made her way across the compound.

"Excuse me," she poked her head through the mess hall doorway. "I'm looking for the cook." One of the soldiers pointed toward a door at the back of the room. Thanking him, May followed his direction and soon stood face-to-face with a redheaded man.

"I'm May Cooper. I believe Lt. O'Connell informed you about my son's wedding," she introduced herself, her hand extended.

"Hello," he shook her hand. "I'm Sergeant Billings. How can I help?"

"I'd like to talk to you about the wedding supper and the cake, if you've got the time. I don't have all the ingredients I'll need, but I do have fresh eggs."

With that, the cook poured them each a cup of coffee while he shouted orders over his shoulder to the privates who had pulled KP duty. The sergeant and May quickly ensconced themselves at one end of the long worktable with menus and ingredients and deal making.

Joshua, Paul and Jake found it diplomatic to simply stay out of the way. They spent their day exploring the fort, the smithy, the prison, the stables, and the barracks. Joshua also kept an eye out for trading after the wedding. He hoped to return home with a dairy cow and, possibly, a calf.

* * *

Lana walked to their wagon after lunch, looking for a basket and knife. Once she found those, she headed out on foot searching for wildflowers. She had gone a mile from the fort when a column of soldiers came riding in. The one at the head broke away and rode over to her.

"Lana," Liam greeted her. "Picking flowers, I see."

"Yep. I'm hoping to get enough to decorate the chapel."

"That will be nice." He dismounted to walk beside her.

"Shouldn't you be with them?" she asked, looking over her shoulder at the disappearing soldiers.

"They know how to get back. At least, I *hope* they do." He laughed at his own joke. Ignoring his attempt at humor, Lana knelt to cut some Johnny–jump–ups and Sweet Williams. Liam watched her a few moments and then broke the silence. "So, how've you been?"

She looked up at him, squinting against the sun. "I've been fine."

Reaching for her elbows, he pulled her up. "No, Lana. How have you been? Honestly."

Sighing once deeply, she frowned. "Well, I had that talk with my folks like I promised."

"Good. How'd that go?"

"They were shocked, just like I thought they'd be. And I was a mess having to remember all of it again."

"So, it didn't help to talk about it? Even a little?"

"Yes," she admitted. "It *did* help. I just didn't like it at the time. But it helped." Spying a patch of showy primroses and bachelor buttons, she walked over to them, leaving Liam and his horse to follow.

"I'm probably gonna get in trouble asking you this," Liam said as Lana knelt again. "But have you thought any more about our talk?"

"Our talk about the Kiowa?"

"Yes."

"I've thought a lot about that." Placing the flowers in her basket, she stood up. "Yi Ceŋtas came for me a few weeks ago." Trying to sound as nonchalant as possible didn't help. She still felt the pang in her heart.

"I see." Liam wasn't sure how to proceed. "It's obvious you didn't go with him. What happened?"

"I asked him about taking captives for the Apaches." She winced. "And he admitted it. What's worse, he doesn't see anything wrong with it." Lana looked over her shoulder under the pretense of finding more flowers, but, in truth, she hid her trembling chin. "So I told him I wasn't going to marry him."

"Oh." Liam and his horse followed her to a patch of bluebonnets and corn poppies. "Well, for what it's worth, you made the right decision."

At those words, Lana whirled around to face him, her angry eyes brimming with tears. "*The right decision*? It just about killed me. And I know it just about killed him! There's nothing *right* about it!"

"I'm sorry," Liam backed up a step when he saw how upset she was. "I was just trying to say something comforting."

"I know, Liam. I'm sorry." She reached across and touched his shoulder. "Please, forgive me?"

"On one condition," he said seriously.

"What?"

"That you dance with me at the wedding."

"Of course I'll dance with you! I was counting on it." She finally smiled, bringing a smile to Liam's face as well.

"There. That's my girl. Then all is forgiven," he grinned. "That's a much prettier face, by the way."

"Oh, please!" she rolled her eyes. Then, changing the subject, she asked, "Do you think I've got enough flowers?"

"Probably. Besides, I know for a fact that one of the officer's wives grows irises behind their quarters. If I ask real sweet, she might let you have some."

"Oh, for the bridal bouquet," Lana said happily.

"Have you seen the bride's dress yet?"

"No. Christina didn't want me to see it until it was finished. I'm hoping to after dinner."

Liam laughed. "I thought there was going to be a small war among the wives over who was going to make the lace."

"Liam," Lana hooked her arm through his as they headed back to the fort, "it's awfully sweet of you to do this for my brother and Christina. Especially the dress. She's talked of nothing else since you offered it. Curiosity just about killed her, wondering what it would look like."

He patted her hand contentedly as he explained, "I've come to think of your family as my own. I'd do just about anything for you." Her response of a kiss on his shoulder surprised and delighted him.

## Chapter 27 — The Wedding

The day of the wedding dawned with the promise of beautiful weather. The Coopers had breakfast eaten before the sun was fully up. The wedding would take place late that afternoon, and the entire fort buzzed with activity. Everyone had been invited, from the lowest ranking private to the fort commander.

May and the cook outdid themselves preparing the feast. Not only was the cake made out of light flour, eggs, butter and fresh milk, but there were bits of shaved chocolate in the batter *and* a chocolate frosting, *and* it was a triple layer cake. May had never heard of using chocolate in a frosting and learning a new recipe thrilled her.

Beef roasted on a spit beside the Mess Hall, its mouth-watering aroma filling the compound. New potatoes were ready to be boiled and buttered. Running the risk of encountering the Supply Sergeant's wrath, the cook made a huge batch of buttermilk biscuits entirely of light flour. Smoked ham, roasted turnips, creamed onions, spiced peaches and fresh greens filled out the menu.

The wild flowers Lana had gathered and arranged brightened the chapel. The chaplain's eyes lit up when he saw her work.

"You know what would make this even lovelier?" he asked. "Candles. Lots of candles." Leading Lana to a back storeroom, he showed her dozens of yellow candles.

"Oh, you're right," she exclaimed. "These will be perfect!"

The chaplain picked up two tall candelabra and placed one on either side of the pulpit. Lana put the candles in and then carefully straightened them so they were in perfect alignment.

"Lana," Jake came running in. "Christina needs you."

"Oh, all right." She turned to the chaplain. "Thank you for your help. But if you'll excuse me?" At the wave of his hand, she hurried out the door.

Lana burst into Christina's room and stopped. Christina stood there in her wedding dress.

"What do you think?" Christina asked.

"Oh, my," Lana said breathlessly. "You are so beautiful!"

The Army wives had done themselves proud. One of them had sacrificed her own wedding dress to be altered for Christina. In the style of the time, the dark brown satin shimmered in the light. Some of the most intricate lace Lana had ever seen adorned the high neckline and bodice. Lace also trimmed the long flowing sleeves. Dozens of tiny satin buttons went down the back. The scalloped hoop skirt revealed a beautiful black underskirt, also covered in lace.

"Nathan is going to be so proud," Lana said as she sat on the bed to admire the dress up close.

"I hope so. You know, I love him more than life itself."

"I know. I can tell. You don't seem nervous. Are you?"

"Maybe a little," Christina admitted. "But only a little. I know I'm doing the right thing." She touched Lana's shoulder. "I don't love just your brother. I love his whole family." Christina teared up from the emotions of the day. "I don't know what would have become of me if your family hadn't taken me in."

"Oh, don't talk like that!" Lana fussed as she wiped her own tears away. "Of *course* we'd take you in. I've always wanted a sister. And now, I've got one!"

The two young women hugged each other.

"Where's Ma?" Lana asked. "I thought she'd be in here with you."

"She was, but I think she went to make sure the cook was doing everything just right."

"That sounds like Ma," Lana laughed.

"Oh, I almost forgot. Liam sent this over for you."

"Sent what?" Lana followed the direction Christina pointed. On the wall hung something covered in a blanket.

"What on earth?" Lana asked as she walked across the room and took down the blanket. There, to her amazement, hung the most beautiful dress she'd ever seen. "This is for me?"

"There's a note pinned to it," Christina informed her.

Lana found the note close to the hem. Taking it off, she read:

"*My dearest Lana, I know the bride is supposed to be the most beautiful woman at her wedding. But, as true as that may be, I know you'll be the most beautiful to me. With my compliments, Liam O'Connell.*"

"Try it on," Christina urged. "He had the wives make it so you could wear it to the wedding."

"I don't know," Lana shook her head, but the light in her eyes belied her curiosity.

"Oh, come on!" Christina walked over and took it down. "Here."

"All right, all right." Lana quickly took off her own dress. "I won't be able to wear my camisole with this," she said, noting the dress's design.

"So? It's for a wedding and a dance. It's *supposed* to be a fancy dress. Haven't you and I dreamed and dreamed about getting to go to a dance and about what we'd wear?"

"Yes," Lana admitted. She hesitated only a moment before she slipped it over her head. Once it was on and the sash tied, Lana turned to face her reflection.

The creamy, light blue silk dress fit her perfectly. The off-the-shoulders bodice trimmed with plum satin ribbon accentuated her graceful throat and shoulders. A plum sash encircled her waist and tied in the back to form a graceful bow. The skirt fell in layers of light blue over a dark purple petticoat that peeked out flirtatiously as she swirled. "Oh! Oh my goodness," she cried. "I look like a fairy princess."

"You do. You really do!" Christina agreed. "You be careful dancing tonight. Those soldier boys are gonna hurt themselves trying to be the first one to get to you." They both broke out in giggles at that.

A light knock sounded at the door. When Lana cracked it open to peek out, Joshua stood there, his face still pink from the scrubbing he had given it. He wore his best clothes.

"Is the bride ready?" he asked.

"Just about. Did you bring her flowers?"

"Right here." He handed them to Lana.

"We'll be right out." Lana closed the door and turned to face Christina. "No bride can be without a bouquet," she explained as she held out the yellow and purple iris bouquet tied in yellow satin ribbon.

"They are beautiful! Wherever did you get them?"

"One of the officer's wives let me chop down her flowerbed this morning," Lana laughed.

"Tell me which one and I'll thank her later."

Lana walked to the door and, stepping back, opened it so that Joshua saw Christina first.

"Oh, my," he said without smiling. "You're much too beautiful for Nathan," he teased her. Then he grew serious. "Your folks would be so proud of you right now. And I am very proud to have you as a daughter." He kissed her cheek and then offered her his arm.

Looking behind to Lana in her new gown, Joshua stopped. At the questioning expression on his face, Lana volunteered, "Liam had it made for me."

"You look beautiful, daughter." He stared at her for a moment as his mind flashed back twenty years earlier to her mother, who had looked just that beautiful, just that sweet. A pang filled his heart. Time went by too fast. His baby girl had grown up too fast. Forcing himself out of his reverie, he escorted the two young women to the chapel.

The chapel overflowed with people. Several enlisted men stood outside the entrance, wanting to at least hear the wedding. Seeing the bride approach, they respectfully made a path until she, Joshua and Lana passed. Lana hurried inside and sat by her already sniffling mother. The chapel had no organ or piano, so there was no music. On cue from the chaplain, the congregation stood up, and the bride and Joshua walked down the aisle.

Nathan stood at the front, next to the chaplain. When the groom saw Christina in her sumptuous satin dress, with her hair so beautiful and her eyes shining, he caught his breath. This was it. This was really it. He was getting married to the most wonderful creature he'd ever seen! Smiling softly, he wondered if she was as nervous as he was.

The simple ceremony held timeless vows. May had loaned Nathan her ring for the wedding. When he could, he would get Christina her own ring, but there were few places on the frontier to buy one.

In a few short minutes, the groom kissed the bride and the world was introduced to Mr. and Mrs. Nathan Cooper. People they had never met pounded Nathan on the back and kissed Christina. From there, all went outside to the feast and the dance!

At first, the fiddle, banjo and guitar sounded like screeching cats, but after a few bars, the musicians agreed on a rhythm and key, and a song broke out. In no time, what few women there were were quickly grabbed up and whirled around the dance floor.

Liam had been unable to take his eyes off Lana from the moment she stepped into the chapel. Now, as she stood there in the light of the setting sun, he was completely lost in her. He had hoped she would like the dress. What he hadn't counted on was how beautiful she looked wearing it, and how deeply the sight of her affected him.

Cutting through the throng of admirers surrounding Lana, Liam reached his hand out. "You promised me a dance," he smiled.

"Why, so I did," she said coyly. "Excuse me, gentlemen." Lana had never been the belle of the ball before, and enjoyed herself immensely.

Liam whisked her away in his arms, twirling her around, making her skirt swish. "You are so beautiful."

"Thank you," she said, suddenly feeling self-conscious.

"No. I mean it." Liam drank her in. "I've never seen any woman this beautiful."

"Oh, now. It's just the dress. Anyone would look beautiful in *this* dress. Thank you, by the way. You really shouldn't have."

"Lana. It isn't just the dress. And don't thank me. Thank *you* for wearing it." The young officer paused for a moment before he admitted in a quiet voice, "I don't know if I can stand it."

"Stand what?" she asked, confused.

"Stand how you look right now."

Lana didn't say anything to that. She didn't know what to say.

They had gone twice around the dance floor when an outranking officer cut in. "May I?" he asked politely.

"Of course," Liam mumbled, trying to be gracious. But looking around at all the men staring predatorily at Lana, he knew he needed to get her away from the dance if he hoped to spend some time alone with her.

## Chapter 28 — I Need Your Answer

Liam stepped back and watched Lana dance away. He then walked over to Joshua and shook his hand. "You must be proud."

"I am. This is a happy day." Joshua watched the dancers for a moment. "You and Lana look good dancing together. She told me you gave her that dress."

"Yes, I did. I figured she didn't have anything new to wear, and this was as good a reason as any."

"You have feelings for her, don't you, son?"

Liam looked at Joshua, studying him for a moment. "Yes, sir. I do. She knows it, too."

Joshua nodded as he continued watching the dancers. "You know she told Yi Ceŋtas goodbye."

"Yes. She told me yesterday."

"Good." Joshua watched the dancers for another moment before he added, "In case you haven't figured it out, now's your chance." He winked at Liam and then looked around. "Where's my wife? I feel like dancing!" With that, he walked away, leaving Liam grinning at the go-ahead he'd just received.

Liam watched the dancers, or rather, watched Lana as she danced. He knew that he loved her, that he had been in love with her for some time. But he wouldn't be stationed at Ft. Worth for much longer. He needed to decide what his next step should be: let Lana go without saying anything to her, knowing he would be leaving in a few months — or risk speaking his heart on the hopes of taking her with him as his wife? If he let her go, if he walked away, where would he be? Alone — still — and lonely.

Two hours passed before Liam could finally lead Lana away from the dance and, by then, it had gotten dark. Her admirers were legion as well as persistent. Fights almost broke out between men waiting for the next dance with her. Lana stepped out of one pair of arms and directly into another, all of them turning into a blur of Army blue.

"Excuse me," Liam deliberately cut in. "But someone needs her."

"Yes, sir," a sergeant said. He stepped back and bowed at the waist toward Lana. "Thank you for the dance, m'am."

"You're very welcome," Lana smiled and then looked up at Liam as he led her away. "Who needs me?" she asked, worried.

Leaning close to her ear, he whispered, "I do."

He led her past the Mess Hall, past the barracks, and behind the stables. It was quiet there, safe from the sentry's watchful eyes.

When they stopped, she turned to face him. "Thank you for rescuing me back there," she smiled. "I always wondered what a dance would be like. I dreamed about what I would wear, who I would dance with, what we'd talk about. But never, in my wildest imagination, did I ever dream up something like tonight!"

"You *were* slightly outnumbered, weren't you?" he grinned.

"Just a little," she giggled. "I think my feet are going to fall off." She looked around her and then up at him. "What are we doing back here?"

"I wanted to talk to you alone, and this was the best I could come up with on short notice."

"I see."

He stood there quietly for a moment, not sure where to start. The rising moon sat low in the horizon, its soft light dancing across her shoulders. Caressing them, searching her face, Liam began talking in a low voice.

"If we lived in a city, I would do things so differently. But we don't. We live in this great expanse called Texas. Since we see each other so rarely, I have to make the most of every opportunity." He paused for a moment and then said, "I want to hold you, Lana. And kiss you. I want you around me, close by. Not days away. You've captured my heart."

"Liam, I..."

He didn't wait for her to finish. Leaning down, he kissed her, hard at first, as if he was afraid of changing his mind and not kissing her at all. Lana tensed under his hands, but as his kiss grew softer and his lips more expressive, he felt her relax. Pulling back to look at her, he saw her confusion.

"I — I don't know what I'm doing," she murmured as she shook her head.

"You're letting me love you. Finally, you're letting me love you." He drew her against his body and kissed her again, long and slow. After a moment, he felt her hands glide up his chest and around his neck; the sensation left him breathless. He *felt* her make up her mind as she molded her body to his and returned his kiss with a passion he had been afraid to hope for.

Nuzzling her hair, he whispered in her ear, "Do you mean this? Because, if you don't..." he pulled back to look seriously into her eyes, "...don't kiss me like that again. I can't take it."

"And if I do?"

"I'd be a fool not to ask why, knowing how you feel about someone else."

"I told that 'someone else' goodbye, Liam. And I meant it. I have to start over. And *I'd* be a fool to pass you by."

"So, does this mean you know what you're doing now?"

"Yes." She reached up and kissed his right cheek, then his left, and then, looking deeply into his eyes, kissed his lips. "I'm starting over — with you, if you want me."

"If I *want* you?" Liam raised his head, looking skyward, and then back at her. "I want you so badly, I don't know what to do." Pausing for a moment, he continued. "I've kept this to myself for a long time, but I'll tell you now. I love you, Lana. There. I said it and now you know. I'm in love with you and want you to marry me."

"This is all moving too fast." Lana stepped back, trying to take it all in.

"Yes. It *is* moving fast. But Lana, when will I see you again? I don't know. It could be next week, or next month, or never, if the Army reassigns me soon. I have to tell you *now*." Then, in a quieter tone, he added, "I need your answer now."

"Oh, Liam, give me a minute to catch my breath. I don't know what to say."

"Certainly. I didn't mean right this minute. Just before you leave to go home."

"All right. I'll have an answer before then."

"Good. Then let me continue making my case for why you should accept." Pulling her to him, he kissed her, and then kissed her again, and then kept kissing her until Jake came around the corner of the building, looking for her.

"Ma's wondering where you are," Jake explained. At the sound of his voice, Lana turned to look at him, but she stayed in Liam's arms instead of guiltily jumping back. For some reason, that simple gesture convinced Liam that she really did mean that kiss — and all the ones that followed. She really was starting over.

"All right," Lana said. "I'll be right there."

"I'll walk with you," Liam offered.

"No. That's all right. I need to talk to my mother alone. I'm sure you understand why." She smiled coyly at his handsome face and winked.

"Yes, I understand completely." He smiled down at her. "Then, Miss Cooper, I'll say goodnight here." After kissing her one more time, he watched her walk away with Jake. A jumble of emotions filled the young lieutenant: excitement, happiness, fear that she would say no, and then fear that she would say yes. Was he ready for a wife? Whatever her answer, his life would never be the same after tonight.

* * *

"There you are!" May exclaimed when Lana joined her at the dance. "I wondered where you'd gotten to."

"I was with Liam." Lana picked up a crumb of cake and ate it. "Ma, I need to talk to you about something serious."

"Let me guess," May smiled. "The lieutenant has asked you to marry him."

"How did you know?" Lana was astonished.

"I didn't. It was just a hunch. But I saw how he's watched you ever since we got here, with his heart on his sleeve. And getting you this dress. That is one love-sick man."

"Then, what am I going to do?" Lana looked at her mother, her worry and indecision clear in her eyes.

May led her daughter away to a quieter place. "Lana, child, you know you've worried the fool out of both your pa and me over Yi Ceŋtas."

"I know, Ma."

"And when you told him goodbye, I know it broke your heart. It's still broken. You still love him."

"But..."

"I'm right, aren't I?"

"Yes, Ma. You're right. I do love him. I probably always will, at least a little. But I have to start over. Liam has been so good to me, to all of us. I thought this is what you and Pa wanted."

"That really doesn't matter," May said. "Is it what you want? Really deep-in-your-heart want? Because, unless it is, you'll be doing that boy more harm by marrying him than if you turn him down now. Don't take vows you can't keep, Lana. Don't do it."

"What's going on over here?" Joshua asked, walking up to the two of them. "I'm at a dance and my two favorite women aren't there."

"Liam's asked Lana to marry him," May explained, "and we're just discussing her options."

"He has!" Joshua broke into a wide grin. "That's wonderful. Of course, you said yes."

"No, Pa. I don't know what to tell him. That's what Ma and I were talking about."

"You'd be foolish not to say yes," he said, frowning. "An officer in the Army? Why, that's steady work and solid housing. He's a fine young man."

"I know all of that." Lana looked at her mother for help.

May, in turn, looked at her husband. "Honey, what if she doesn't love him? This is all very sudden for her."

"Sudden? No. It's not like they just met. She's known Liam long enough to know what he's like. And, not love him? Love grows. If she respects him and likes him, that will turn to love."

"So you think I should say yes," Lana said quietly.

"I sure do. I know he loves you. And I know he'll take good care of you."

Lana sighed. "I need to sleep on this. If you'll excuse me, I'll say goodnight now."

"Goodnight, honey." Joshua watched Lana walk toward the tent she now shared with her mother.

When she was out of earshot, May turned to Joshua. "I hope you don't live to regret that advice, Joshua Cooper."

"Oh, dear. 'Joshua Cooper,' huh? I must be in trouble." Grinning, he pulled May to him by her waist and kissed her hard. "It's going to be fine. It really is."

"How can you be so certain? If they marry and the Army reassigns him, we may never see her again."

"I know," Joshua grimaced. "But I'd rather have her safe with Liam than living as..."

He didn't finish his sentence, but they both knew what he meant. Kiowa.

# Chapter 29 — Are You Sure About This?

The next morning, the Coopers were having breakfast around their campfire when Liam walked into their camp.

"Good morning," he greeted them.

"Morning. Sit and have some coffee," Joshua invited.

"No, I can't stay. I'm bringing an official invitation for you and your family to have dinner with the colonel in the Officer's Mess tonight."

Joshua looked at May, who nodded. "That's very kind," Joshua said. "We'd be honored."

"Good. I'll tell him."

Before he left, Joshua stopped him. "Say, do you know where I could get a dairy cow? I've got a little cash money set aside for one."

"Hmmm. Talk to the Supply Sergeant. He might know."

"All right. I will. Thanks."

Liam turned again to leave, but, as he did, he winked at Lana. "Morning, beautiful."

"Morning," she answered cheerily.

"Sleep good?"

"Oh, I had the *best* sleep."

"So, nothing on your mind or anything? Just a good sleep?"

"Like I said. The best sleep ever." She smiled guilessly at him. In truth, she had tossed and turned all night, keeping her mother awake for a good part of it. But she wasn't going to admit that to him.

Shrugging his shoulders, he said, "Well, I'll see everyone this evening." With that, he left.

"*Have* you made up your mind?" Joshua asked.

"No. And, please, let's not talk about it." Lana stood up and walked into the tent, ending that discussion.

\* \* \*

The Coopers spent the day productively. Joshua spoke to the Supply Sergeant, as Liam had suggested, and managed to wrangle a deal for a dairy cow. May bartered with some of the Army wives, trading her fresh eggs to get sewing needles, canned fruit, candles and anything else of value she could find.

Nathan and Christina made a brief appearance at lunch, but then disappeared again until dinner.

\* \* \*

After clearing up the breakfast remains and tidying up camp, Lana strolled through the compound, wondering if she should drop in on Nathan and Christina. Her stroll was short-lived, though.

"Miss Cooper!" a soldier called as he sprinted toward her.

"Yes?"

He stopped in front of her and smiled. "I wanted to thank you again for dancing with me last night. I had such a good time."

"You're more than welcome," she smiled in return, and started to resume her walk, but he stopped her.

"I also wanted to tell you how beautiful you looked in that dress. I've never seen anything that fancy."

"Thank you." Trying once again to walk away, once again, the soldier stopped her.

"One more thing," he hesitated. "Um — well — would you care to have a picnic with me this evening? I get off at four. We could go to the river."

"Excuse me, but what's your name?"

"Oh, I'm sorry. I'm Sgt. Mark Kensington."

"Sgt. Kensington, I'm flattered. I really am. But, I have to decline your kind invitation. I'm sorry." Lana finally escaped his attention, but only got three yards away when another soldier walked up to her, offering the same type of conversation she had just shared with the sergeant. Seeing the futility of staying on the compound, Lana walked a mile away from the fort, and from the ever-attentive, woman-starved soldiers.

Once on her own, surrounded by countryside, solitude, and her thoughts, Lana found shade under a knot of cottonwood trees and sat down. At first, she chuckled at the soldiers she had just encountered. They had been so sweet and polite and nervous as they talked to her. But her thoughts turned to Liam and his proposal. What should she do? Liam wanted her to marry him. Her pa wanted her to marry Liam. Her ma? Well, her ma wanted her to follow her heart. The question was — what did her heart want?

Her heart wanted Two Hawks! Tears fringed her eyelashes as she felt the fierceness of that desire. Closing her eyes, Lana recalled the last time they'd been together, before the argument. They had lain together by the river, lost in loving each other. His dark brown eyes filled with his love for her, with his desire for her body. His hands taught her delightful secrets. And his kisses — oh! Lana sighed and wiped an escaping tear from her cheek. She *loved* his soft, warm kisses.

"Stop it!" she fussed at herself. "You can't be with him, so quit thinking like this!" Standing and straightening her skirts, she resumed her walk, determined to figure this out.

"Liam. What am I going to tell Liam?" After hours of meandering aimlessly, she finally sorted through her concerns and confusion. Liam loved her. Of that, she was certain. Did she love him? Her answer surprised her. Yes. In many ways, she did.

* * *

At the Officer's Mess for dinner, the long table had been laid out with its finest appointments. A white, heavily starched tablecloth lay beneath slightly chipped china. Wine glasses of unmatched design formed an uneven line down both sides of the table while several candles sputtered and dripped yellow wax onto their holders.

Once again, Lana shone as the belle of the ball, even though she had on her old dress. It didn't seem to matter. After a few glasses of wine, even some of the married officers flirted with her. Liam sat across the table and one chair down from her, watching and listening to everything that was said to her. In spite of some of the more obvious remarks, she handled herself well, able to turn them into a joke.

"If I were twelve years younger," one of the married men remarked suggestively to her.

"Then I would only be six," she smiled.

"Would you care to go for a morning ride with me tomorrow?" another queried hopefully.

"Oh, my brothers and I would *love* to go for a ride. Wouldn't we, Paul?"

"You were the most beautiful girl at the dance last night," a third tried his luck.

"Seeing that I was the *only* girl last night, that's hardly a surprise."

Liam couldn't help but grin, proud of how she kept them all in line. But, through all of this attention, other conversation flowed around the table. Conditions with the Kiowa and Apache were discussed at length. Growing unrest between the north and south got a lot of attention. Much of the conversation bored Lana, and,

188

after a while, the men took sides and argued simply for the sake of arguing. There was no debate, no quest to get at the truth. They all insisted on being right.

After the meal, Lana sent Liam an unspoken signal of needing to be rescued. When he nodded, she stood up.

"Colonel, excuse me, please. But I have a slight headache and wish to lie down."

"Certainly." The men at the table stood up in a respectful gesture.

Liam walked around the table to Lana. "Miss Cooper, may I escort you back?"

"Yes, please." Turning to her mother, she added, "I'll see you later. Please, don't hurry on my account."

"All right, dear. Feel better."

Liam escorted Lana out, his hand in the middle of her back. Once they were outside in the cool spring night, she smiled and stretched her arms out. "This is so much better," she sighed.

Liam watched her, simply enjoying the sight of her. As they walked across the compound, she took his arm and fell into step with him. They didn't speak until they reached her tent.

"So," he said, "Do you have an answer yet?"

"Stir up the fire while I get us a blanket to sit on. Then we can talk."

In a few minutes, they were seated next to the fire, Lana facing him. "Before I answer your question, I have to ask a few of my own."

"Of course. What do you want to know?"

"I'm not quite sure if I'll say this right," she began nervously, "But here goes. As much as I feel for you, I think you have stronger feelings for me right now."

"Granted. I've known for quite some time now that I love you."

"You don't mind that it's uneven between us?"

"No, because I am sure that your feelings for me will grow deeper, just like mine will for you. That doesn't worry me at all."

"All right. Good." She turned to watch the fire for a moment. "Do you want children?"

"Yes. I do."

"Me, too." As she looked back at him, she added, "I don't know anything about your family. I know you're from Georgia, but where in Georgia? Do you have any brothers or sisters? Tell me about yourself."

"All right." He smiled and reached for her hand. "That's easy enough. My family lives in Atlanta. I have two sisters and one brother. I'm next to the youngest. The oldest is my sister, Colleen. The next oldest is my brother, Patrick, Junior. The youngest is my sister, Mary. My father is Patrick, Senior and my mother is Maeve. In case you couldn't guess, I'm Irish. My grandfather came over in 1804.

"I am a West Point graduate and, after the military, plan to make politics my career. I love dogs and hate cats. I'll eat lima beans, though I don't particularly like them. Don't, under any circumstances, try to feed me liver. I hate the stuff." He stopped to listen to her giggle. "Let's see. What else? Oh, my birthday is September 14. How's that for a start."

"That's plenty," she laughed. "What's West Point?"

"That's an Army college."

"You've graduated from college?" Lana's eyes went wide at that. "I only got as far as the eighth grade and I was proud to get that far. There were only two other girls in my class." She paused before she asked, "Don't you want someone with more of an education?"

"Lana, honey, there are book smart people and then there are naturally smart people. You are naturally smart, and I'd rather have that in my wife than all the book smarts in the world."

"Promise?"

"Promise. So, any more questions? Or will you answer mine now?" He grew serious as he waited, watching her face in the flickering firelight.

"No. No more questions." Lana, too, grew quiet. "Liam, are you sure about this? You really want to get married? And, of all people, to me?"

"I've never been more sure about anything," he reassured her. "And especially to you. Only to you."

"Well, if you're sure, then, yes. I'd be honored to be your wife."

"Yes? You said yes?"

She laughed and nodded. Liam stood up quickly and reached to pull her to her feet.

"Come here, woman," his handsome face smiled, "I have to kiss you now. I think that's an Army regulation or something." He quit smiling as he looked into her beautiful blue eyes. "You have just made me the happiest of men. And I intend to make you the happiest of women." With that, he leaned down and kissed her.

"When?" she asked when he finally let her go.

"When?"

"Yes. When do you want to get married?"

"I don't know. I mean, the sooner, the better. What do you think?"

"Don't you have to go through the Army? Get permission from someone? Do you have a place for both of us? How long will it take to get a place?"

"I don't know any of this," he sounded perplexed. "I'll have to ask in the morning."

"Then we won't know until you get some answers, so we'll just have to wait to decide."

"You're a very logical woman," he pointed his finger at her. "This is going to work out great!"

## Chapter 30 — A Little Overwhelmed

Liam waited with Lana until her parents came back from dinner. At the young couple's news, Joshua was ecstatic.

"Welcome to the family," Joshua said as he pounded Liam on the back. "This is such good news!"

May hugged her daughter and whispered, "Are you sure about this?"

"Yes, Ma. I'm sure."

"Well, then, I'm happy for you." Turning, she gave Liam a hug as well. "No need to call me Mrs. Cooper any more. I'm Ma now."

"Yes, Ma," Liam grinned at her.

\* \* \*

Liam hit the ground running the next morning. He first stopped at the commander's office. Obtaining permission to marry Lana proved much easier than he had expected because the commander had already met and liked the Coopers. Next, he saw the Quartermaster about housing. Liam and Lana could have their choice of the two places available.

Liam then went looking for the Coopers and found them in the mess hall. "I think I've got some answers for us," he said after he kissed Lana good morning.

When he told her of his news, she turned to her father. "So, Pa, I'm wondering when the best time would be to get married. Do we wait till after planting? Or till after harvest this fall?"

"Or do we wait at all?" Liam chimed in. "I don't know if I'll still be here this fall."

"Goodness!" May sat with a concerned expression on her face. "This is all so fast."

"It is fast," Lana agreed. Turning to Liam, she asked, "How long do we have to choose quarters?"

"Two weeks."

"Two weeks!" May looked dazed. "That's all?"

"Yes, m'am. We're expecting replacements in soon, and some of the new officers will have families with them."

"I suppose we ought to go look at our choices," Lana suggested.

May stood up to go with them, but Joshua put his hand on her shoulder, shaking his head. "No, Mother," he said gently. "This isn't your decision. Besides, they need a little time alone to talk."

"You're right." She patted his hand. "But two weeks!"

"Want to know what I suggest?"

"What do you suggest?" she echoed.

"They should get married now, while we're all still here. I'm not going to have time to travel back across the country, and still get our crops in. It's either now or after planting, and I'm wondering if there will be any housing available for them then."

May frowned. She had always looked forward to helping her only daughter plan her wedding and to making the dress and meeting Lana's in-laws. Her dream wasn't going to happen, and her disappointment was too big to hide from Joshua.

"Fuss and fume at me all you want to, May," he offered, "but please, don't let Lana see you like this. It will tear her up."

\* \* \*

The young couple looked at their choices for housing. Each living quarters was one part of a triplex. One sat at the end of a triplex on an east-west line with the front door opening to the north. The second sat in the middle of its triplex, on a north-south line, opening to the east.

As Lana and Liam stepped through the door of the second place, they found it almost identical to the first. The kitchen set to the right and a larger living room in the middle, with a bedroom on the left. The living room had a window on the back wall and the kitchen and bedroom had a window on the front and back walls. The stove, even though small, was more than Lana had at home. The floors were wood, not dirt, and real glass filled the windows.

"What do you think?" Liam asked.

"They're pretty much the same," she answered as she turned slowly in the middle of the living room. "Why don't we take this one? It faces east. If I plant flowers in the front, they'll get the morning sun. Plus, we'll have the sunrise in our bedroom window. *And*, during the winter, the blue norther won't blow the door in."

"My goodness," Liam grinned. "You ought to ride scouting missions for us. You're a natural!"

"Why, thank you, sir." She reached up to him and gave him a sweet, happy kiss. "Now, back to our original question. When?"

He contentedly wrapped her up in his arms as they talked. "If this is only available for two weeks, the wedding needs to be before then."

"Then it needs to be now," Lana added, reaching the same logical conclusion her father had. "While we're all still here."

"That suits me just fine. You've got your wedding dress."

"My party dress?"

"The very same. Or you could borrow Christina's. And, like you said, your family is all here."

"But yours isn't." She frowned when she looked up at him. "Shouldn't they be here?"

"I know they'd like to be," he agreed. "But they'll understand. Army life doesn't give me much room to accommodate other people's schedules."

"Oh, Liam, I just thought of something!" She sounded dismayed.

"What? What's wrong?"

"I don't have any dishes or quilts or anything to set up a home."

"Don't worry about it," he laughed. "We'll have fun getting those things together. That's one good thing about Army families. They're good at helping each other find what they need."

"I hope you're right."

"I just have to say the word, and by tonight, we'll have more quilts than we could ever use in a hundred years. And dishes, too. They might not match. They might even be chipped or cracked, but we'll have dishes." He smiled down at her. "Besides, I'm not broke. I'll take you to the supply store, and you can buy some new things. A skillet. A coffee pot. Oh, definitely a coffee pot." He felt her sigh in his arms.

"It's going to be all right, Lana. It's going to work out perfectly. A lot of people have started out together with a whole lot less than we've got right now standing in this empty house."

"You're right. I'm just a little overwhelmed thinking of all the things I need to do."

"A *little* overwhelmed?" He laughed at that and then grew serious. "I love you, Lana. And I am so proud that you'll marry me." Kissing her once, he then led her to the door. "We ought to tell your folks what we've decided."

"And the Quartermaster. And the Commander. And the chaplain." She chattered at him all the way across the compound.

After a family council, they decided the wedding would be held the next day. This time, there would be no large dinner or dance. This wedding would be a quiet ceremony with just the family and Liam's friends present. After that, Joshua simply had to get back home and start planting.

The rest of the day was busy. May instructed Lana to go through the things they had brought and pick out what bare necessities she would need to set up housekeeping. Joshua went to tell Nathan about the impending wedding. May insisted on a wedding cake and, with that in mind, she hunted down the cook.

"It's me again," she smiled brightly when she found Sgt. Billings in front of the cookstove.

"Good morning, Mrs. Cooper," he nodded. "Coffee's on."

"Thank you. I wanted to tell you how fabulous the meal was for the wedding. Especially the cake!"

"You liked the chocolate? I thought you might." He grinned, pleased with himself.

"You're never going to believe this," May said as she carried her coffee to the kitchen worktable and sat down. "But my daughter, Lana? You might remember her from the dance."

"Do I ever," he nodded. "The whole fort is talking about your daughter in that dress."

"Yes, well. It turns out that Lt. O'Connell proposed to her, and she has accepted."

"Really?" The sergeant stopped stirring the beans he planned to serve for lunch and sat next to her.

"Yes, and the wedding is going to be tomorrow."

"Oh." Sgt. Billings knew what was coming next, but still he waited for it.

"I was wondering..."

"You need another wedding cake, m'am?"

"If you would be so kind," she smiled with pleading eyes.

"I'm out of chocolate," he warned.

"It doesn't have to be chocolate. Lemon crumb would be very nice."

"I could manage that," he nodded and stood up, returning to the stove.

"What can I trade for the ingredients? I'm all out of fresh eggs," May asked.

"Consider this my gift to the officer and his bride."

"You really are too kind. Thank you." With her mission accomplished, May returned to their camp.

\* \* \*

That afternoon, Lana was sitting on a blanket by their tents when Christina walked up. "*There* you are. I've been looking everywhere for you!"

"Well, you found me." Lana smiled and patted the blanket next to her. "Sit down and talk. I want to hear all about married life."

"I guess you do. I just found out you're getting married yourself tomorrow! I can hardly believe it."

"I can hardly believe it, myself."

"How did this all happen?" Christina asked. "Why didn't I know about it sooner?"

"You were too busy getting married," Lana teased.

"I suppose so." Christina pulled her knees up and wrapped her arms around them. "Can I ask you something?"

"Of course. After all we've been through together, you can ask me anything."

"I don't want to upset you, but — I thought you loved Yi Centas and that he loved you. What happened? I mean, I know you had a fight, but to marry someone else so quickly just doesn't sound right."

"Oh, Christina, it's such a mess. I wonder if I'm going to wake up and realize this has all been some kind of crazy dream. I don't know where to start."

"At the beginning. What happened with Yi Ceŋtas?"

"We had a real eye-opener of a conversation about the differences between the way he and I live. I don't understand his ways, and he'd rather die than live in my world, so I told him goodbye. It was the hardest thing I've ever done. I know I hurt him deeply."

"So you don't love him anymore?" Christina didn't understand how feelings that deep could change so quickly.

"Of course I still love him. Like I told Ma, I probably always will, at least a little."

"Then why Liam? That's hardly fair to any of you." Christina's pretty face wore a deep frown.

"There are so many reasons why." Lana sighed deeply before she went on. "We're from the same type of world. He loves me so much, I can feel it. My pa is crazy about him. He's got a college education and a good career with a real future. I think the world of him."

"Well, you've said a whole lot, but I haven't heard the most important reason. Do you love him?"

"In a way. And, before you fuss at me, he already knows how I feel. He's willing to give me time."

"He'll give you time to fall in love with him *after* he marries you? Isn't that a little late?"

"Christina, who else is out here? More Kiowa, a few buffalo hunters, homesteaders like us scattered over hundreds of miles, and soldiers. If you danced with any of them at your wedding, then you'll know what slim pickings those are."

"I didn't mean to make you mad," Christina apologized.

"I'm not mad. Not really. Just frustrated and scared." She picked at a loose thread on the blanket. "Were you scared when you got married?"

"A little. But I knew I was in love with your brother."

"Speaking of whom," Lana changed the subject, "how is your husband?"

"Grinning like a possum," Christina laughed, shaking her head. "He is so happy."

"Can I ask you something?" Lana looked over her shoulder at her.

"Yes. What?"

"What was it like the first time that, uh, that you slept with him?"

"What was it like?"

"Yes. Did it hurt? Does it hurt? Were you miserable or did you like it?"

Christina turned bright red and burst into laughter again. "Oh, dear! I don't know what to tell you. It's all so, so private and personal."

"I'm sorry. I shouldn't have asked. It's just that I'm worried about that, too."

"Have you talked to Ma?"

"No."

"Well, let me try to answer you, then. Did it hurt? Only a little, at first. Does it hurt? No. Did I like it? I *love* it. Maybe I'm not supposed to. Maybe I'm wicked or something, but I truly love it."

"Oh, good." Lana let out a long sigh, not realizing she had been holding her breath. "That makes me feel so much better."

"You know, it's funny, but I'd always just assumed that you and Yi Ceŋtas had already — well, you know."

"Nope. Almost, but no."

"Well, then, that's good. I mean for you and Liam."

"Yes. For me and Liam." Lana looked across the horizon as a sadness passed over her heart.

A group of women walked up, interrupting their conversation. "Excuse me," one of them said, "Is Mrs. Cooper here?"

"Which one?" Lana laughed, glad for the interruption.

"I think she means your mother," Christina poked Lana in the side.

"Ma!" Lana yelled over her shoulder.

"What?" May stepped out from one of the tents where she was sorting through the bedding and smattering of dishes Lana had chosen to keep with her.

"Mrs. Cooper, hello again," the woman smiled. "We just heard that there is to be another wedding tomorrow."

"Yes, but on a much smaller scale," May nodded. "It's going to be very simple."

"Even so," the visitor turned to indicate the women standing with her, "we'd like to offer a potluck supper tomorrow night for the bridal party."

"You don't have to do that," May shook her head.

"We'd like to. We're all fond of our bachelor officers and we'd like to send Lt. O'Connell off right."

"Lana," May turned to her daughter. "It's your wedding. What do you want?"

Lana stood and straightened her skirts before she approached the small group. "I know Liam would appreciate that very much. So do I. Thank you for your kindness."

The spokeswoman stepped up to Lana and hugged her. "It's the least we can do. Welcome to the Army, Lana."

## Chapter 31 — Cuss The Barn

"Liam, son." Joshua knocked on the door of Liam's quarters late that night.

"Mr. Cooper, come on in." Liam smiled and stepped back so Joshua could enter.

Joshua looked around the small room. It held only four pieces of furniture: a bed, a desk, a chair, and a bureau, yet it was cramped.

"Please, have a seat," Liam gestured to the chair. "Whiskey?"

"Sure. We might both need it."

Liam filled up a shot glass, handed it to Joshua, and then splashed some into his tin coffee cup. Sitting on the edge of his cot, he looked at Joshua.

"I'm surprised you're stopping by so late."

"I apologize for the hour," Joshua said. "But this is something I need to talk to you about privately."

"All right. What is it?"

"I just had this talk with Nathan a few days ago, but that doesn't make this any easier," Joshua chuckled and then grew serious. "When I got married, my father never told me what to expect, but I was very fortunate that my father-in-law did. He sat me down the night before my wedding and gave me quite a talk." Taking a sip of whiskey to clear his throat, he then continued.

"Since your father isn't here, I was hoping maybe you'd let me tell you what he told me."

"Of course. I'd welcome any and all advice about being married." Liam grinned, trying to hide how nervous he had just become.

"I don't know if you've ever lain with a woman," Joshua said, looking directly at him, "and I don't need to know. But I'm going to assume that you know the basics."

Embarrassed silence met his statement, so he bravely plunged ahead. "When a woman takes a man for the first time, there's going to be some blood."

"I've heard about that," Liam tried to sound casual.

"Don't let it frighten either one of you. It's just nature. But in order to — to make it — well..." Joshua stumbled around for the words, "In order to make it easier for her, take your time. Move slow. She'll let you know when she's ready." He took a large gulp of whiskey, draining the glass, and then handed it to Liam. "More, please."

"Yes, sir." Liam was glad to have something to do. After he refilled both the glass and mug, he handed Joshua his drink and sat back down.

"All right. Where was I? Oh, yeah. Getting ready. We men, well, all we need is a wink and a smile, and we're good to go." They both chuckled at that. "But women, they're put together differently. To make sure she's ready, you've got to excite her here," he touched his forehead, "and here," he touched his heart, "before you'll ever excite her physically.

"I know most men don't understand that, or don't care to. They think a woman is there for them and for what they want. They're missing out on the best part of loving a woman."

"What do you mean?"

"If you take care of your woman in bed and see that she's happy, she will certainly take care of you. There is nothing finer

202

in this world than having her explode in your arms, lying with you, loving you for all she is worth. Nothing. It fills you up with pride and love and a connection that you'll never have with anyone else."

Joshua's candidness amazed Liam. Even if his father *had* been there, he wouldn't have talked to Liam this way.

"There's something else I'd like to point out," Joshua said. He took a sip and then continued. "We men are providers, but women are multipliers."

"What? I'm not following."

"We provide a bill of groceries. They take that and make a meal. We give them four walls and a roof. They give us a home. We give them our seed. They give us children."

"Oh. I understand."

"But the reverse is also true," Joshua shook his head, one eyebrow raised. "You give them a harsh word or a hard look, and it's gonna come back to you with a lot more potency. So, whatever you want in your marriage, you're gonna have to put it there."

"I'd never thought of it like that before."

"Most people don't. I think that's why we don't seem to figure women out. They surprise and confuse us. I've wondered many a time, 'Now where'd *that* come from?' when arguing with my wife. But when I thought about it, it was something I'd said or done four days earlier. She'd taken it, multiplied it, and given it back to me, but good!" He chuckled at that.

"Which brings me to Lana. She is very intelligent, which I like to think she gets from me." He grinned. "But she is also extremely stubborn and thinks she already knows most of the answers. You two are going to have some be-u-ti-ful fights."

"Oh, now..."

"I mean it, Liam. Some real humdingers. Whenever you do, though, keep respecting each other during the fights. No name calling or hitting or shoving. Say what you've got to say, and, if you're *that* mad, go out and cuss the barn. But not each other."

"All right. If that's the case, then I pity the barn."

They both laughed at that and then finished their whiskey.

"Is there anything else?" Liam asked.

"No. Only that I am proud to have you in this family. Real proud." Joshua nodded once at Liam without smiling. "Do you have any questions? After all that I've just said, you know you can ask me anything."

"Not at the moment. You've given me a lot to think about, though. I know who to ask if I do have questions."

"Good." Joshua stood up and they shook hands. "I'll say goodnight, then."

"Goodnight. I'll see you tomorrow."

Once Joshua left, Liam sat at his desk and began writing a letter to his family. After a few lines, he crumpled up the paper and started again. This time, it was a telegram.

"*Dear family. Am getting married tomorrow to Lana Cooper. Wish you were here. Love, Liam.*"

Even though it was late, he stepped outside and crossed the compound to put his note in the communiqué folder. It would be taken the next morning to the nearest fort with a telegraph, which was several days' journey away. But his news would reach his family quicker this way than by letter.

* * *

When the Quartermaster signed off on the housing Liam and Lana had chosen, the couple moved their few possessions into the triplex the morning of the wedding. The Coopers also packed most of their things so they could make an early getaway the next morning. The wedding would be just before dinner, and then the family would have one last meal together.

As they had planned, the ceremony was simple but beautiful. Christina returned the favor and made Lana a bouquet from wildflowers. Lana had also borrowed Christina's wedding dress, preferring the traditional satin to the blue silk.

Joshua didn't realize how hard it would be when the Chaplain asked, 'Who gives this woman away?' He managed to speak around the lump in his throat. But Joshua realized, when they left in the morning, Lana wasn't going to be with them. For the first time in her life, they were leaving her behind, and they might never see her again. Joshua put his daughter's hand in Liam's and then, through blurred eyes, found his seat next to May. Putting his arm around her shoulders, he could hear her softly crying. In spite of his resolve, tears shimmered in his own eyes. He was going to miss his baby girl.

After the vows were repeated and Liam and Lana were announced to be husband and wife, they led the bridal party to their new home. Liam's friends brought whiskey for a toast. Some of the officer's wives had left a few gifts, along with the potluck supper, much to Lana's undying gratitude. The gifts were all things the newlyweds desperately needed.

During the potluck meal, one of Liam's friends rose and held his glass. "A toast to the new couple," he announced. Looking around the room to make sure all glasses were raised, he continued, "Now we know why Liam kept volunteering for missions due west of here!"

The room filled with laughter and everyone drank to the toast. At May's nod, Lana took Liam by the hand and stood in front of the lemon crumb cake to cut it. After the meal was over and the dishes reclaimed by the wives, people began leaving one or two at a time until only Joshua and May were left.

"We'll say goodnight now," May hugged her daughter.

"All right. We'll see you in the morning before you leave."

"Honey, it's going to be very early."

"I know. We'll be there just the same."

"We certainly will," Liam added as he put his arm around Lana's shoulders.

As her parents left, Liam closed the door behind them and turned to Lana. "So, wife, let's look at those presents."

One by one, Lana set them in front of Liam at the table. "There's a bread bowl. It looks new, too!" Setting that to one side, she reached for the next item. "Two pillows. That is so nice. I'll have to find out who gave us those." Putting the pillows down, she said, "And, last, two coffee mugs."

"Great! Now all we need is coffee and a coffee pot," Liam teased her.

"I'll put that on my list for shopping tomorrow."

As they sat at the table and looked at their gifts, an uneasy silence filled the room, neither knowing what to say next.

"I suppose we ought to turn in," Liam finally spoke. "Especially if we're getting up early to see your folks off."

"All right." They both remained seated, neither moving.

"Lana, I'll tell you, I'm kinda nervous about tonight."

"Are you? I am so glad you said something. I'm beyond nervous."

# Chapter 32 — Doubly Wicked

"Oh, honey! Don't be nervous. Everything is going to be all right." Liam took her hand and pulled her over to sit on his lap. "I might not be real smooth with this at first, but we'll figure it out. Besides, your pa had a good long talk with me last night."

"You talked to *Pa* about this?" Lana hid her face in her hands, blushing deeply.

"No. He talked to me. Your pa is a smart man who loves you very much. He was just making sure I don't do anything to hurt you — now or ever." Filling two glasses with the remaining whiskey, he handed one to her.

"Here, drink this. It will help you relax."

Lana took a careful sip, not wanting to choke on the strong liquor. "I guess I should tell you that I talked to Christina yesterday about her first time."

"You did? What'd she have to say?"

"That she liked it." Lana burst out into giggles and then drank more whiskey.

"Why is that so funny?" Liam asked, a smile playing around the corners of his mouth.

"She was afraid she's wicked because she likes it. If that's so, I'm probably going to *love* it, and then what does that make me?"

"Well, do you want to find out?" he asked, a gleam in his eye.

"Yes, I do." Lana drained her glass, the whiskey taking its effect. "But let me get ready for bed first. Please?"

"Sure. I'll wait right here." He lifted his half-empty glass and kissed her shoulder. "Just don't take too long."

"Yes, sir." She hopped off his lap and walked into the bedroom, carrying the two pillows with her. When she lit the lamp, she stopped. There, on the bed covered with the quilt May insisted that she keep, someone had left her a nightgown and the smallest bottle of perfume she had ever seen. Its sweet aroma filled the room when she dabbed some tentatively behind her ears and on her wrists. She'd never worn perfume before.

Next, she took her hair down and brushed it until it shown. Then, when she was undressed, she slipped the gown on and, with a sly grin, put a small dot of perfume between her breasts. There was no mirror to see her reflection, so she looked down at herself.

The champagne-gold satin gown had elegant lace around the low-cut bodice. Lace formed the shoulder straps and trimmed the empire-waist. The gown's long, full skirt swept and swirled gracefully around her ankles as she walked to the bedroom door.

"Oh, husband," she called softly.

Liam looked over his shoulder at her and then slowly stood up. "I..." He took two steps toward her, wonder in his eyes. "You..." Taking two more steps, he stopped where he stood. "Never in my life have I ever seen anyone more beautiful."

"So, you like it?" She stepped out of the doorway and twirled around once.

Grabbing her up in his arms, he murmured, "Do I *like* it? Your pa told me to take it slow, but I don't know if I *can*." He looked down into her shining, blue eyes. "Woman, you are driving me wild. Absolutely wild." With that, he picked her up in his arms and carried her back into the bedroom where he laid her on the bed.

"Don't move. Not one muscle," he ordered as he blew out the lamp. The eager lover took less than a minute to undress and lay down on his side next to her. Looking at her in the moonlit shadows, he laid his hand on her stomach and slid it across the satin, enjoying the fabric's cool smoothness.

"Have you ever done this before?" she finally got the courage to ask.

"Now that I'm here with you, I'm ashamed to admit it," he answered truthfully. "But yes. In college, on weekend leave, I've done this a time or two. No. That's not quite right. I've never done *this*, making love to *my* woman. But I've been with women."

Looking seriously at her, he asked, "Does that bother you?"

"Not really. That's in your past." Smiling up at him, she added, "I'm glad at least one of us knows what we're doing."

Liam kissed her, softly. "I love you so much, Lana." He kissed her again, encouraged by her response to him. Sliding his hand to her breast, he looked down at her. "You let me know if I'm hurting you, or if you want me to do anything, or stop doing something, or..."

Lana stopped him. "I trust you, darling. You won't hurt me. You'd never hurt me. Now, please, kiss me some more."

Liam smiled at that and relaxed. Following Joshua's advice, he took his time. His hand caressed her breasts and then slowly moved down her arm, down her hip and across her thighs while he murmured lovers' secrets in her ear. Seductively, he raised her gown higher and higher up her legs until the hem reached her hips.

"This is in the way, isn't it?" she asked as she sat up. "Help me."

He raised the gown above her head and turned to toss it on the floor. When he turned back, she lay beside him, waiting.

"Oh," he moaned, looking at her nude perfection. "I don't think I can breathe."

"Kiss me," she whispered. When he leaned down to do as she asked, she stopped him. "No. Kiss me here." She held her breast, offering it to him. For a second, a question flitted across his mind as he wondered how she knew to ask him to do that. But it was forgotten as soon as he thought of it. Without a word, he began sensuously kissing her breasts, first one, then the other, and then back again, each kiss taking longer than the one before.

Shyly, she began caressing him. Raising his head, he had a surprised, pleased look on his face. This must have been what Joshua meant. She was taking care of him now. Liam gave her an encouraging smile and continued preparing her for him. After a moment, he could hear her breathing change. Still kissing her, he moved on top of her.

"Oh, yes, please," she said breathlessly as she wrapped her legs around his waist. Not able to wait any longer, he took her, rocking gently at first, afraid of hurting her. But her passionate, eager response vanished his concerns. He made love to her with an abandon and forcefulness that pleased them both. To his delight, she exploded in his arms, wrapped tightly around him, moving with him. In a short time, he gave her all that he had, loved her with all that he was.

This was it. This was the passion he had been hoping for in his marriage. She was his heart and he would die for her without even blinking.

"Woman, what you do to me," he gasped as he rolled onto his back. Pulling her to him, he stroked her hair as she lay against his chest, her arm across his stomach. "That was better than I imagined. And I've got a vivid imagination," he chuckled softly.

"That *was* pretty amazing," she sighed contentedly.

"So, did you like it?"

"No. I *loved* it. I guess that means I'm doubly wicked." She reached up and kissed him. "I guess you'd better hand me my gown now, please."

"No."

"No? Why ever not?"

"Because I'm going to want some more of you in a little while and that will just be in the way again."

"Oh, you'll want more, will you?"

"You'd better believe it."

"Good. I want some more, too."

"My goodness," he purred, "you *are* doubly wicked. What a lucky fellow I am."

Later — much later that night — Liam finally rolled over on his side, falling asleep quickly. Lana turned her head to look out the window that faced west. For the smallest of seconds, she wondered where Two Hawks was.

## Chapter 33 — The Palomino

The newlyweds were dressed and out the door before the sun came up. Hurrying through the compound, they saw that the Coopers were also awake and were breaking camp.

"Good morning," Lana called out to her family.

"Hi, sis." Nathan walked over to her. "I guess we're both old married folk now."

"Yes, I suppose we are," Lana laughed. Watching everything be packed away brought a frown to her face.

"This is going to be so hard." She turned to Liam and leaned her head against his shoulder.

"I know, sweetheart. I know." He put his arms around her, trying to comfort her.

Christina walked up and tapped her on the shoulder. Stepping out of Liam's embrace, she turned to Christina.

"Here's your wedding dress." Lana handed the carefully folded garment to her. "Thank you, again, for letting me borrow it."

"You are more than welcome," Christina smiled, hugging her.

"You all ready?" Lana asked.

"Yep. Everything is loaded up." The two young women walked closer to the wagon while Liam went to help Jake with the team. "So," Christina continued. "How was it?"

Lana cut her eyes to look at her sister-in-law. "It was amazing. I mean, I don't want to leave our bed."

"I know!" Christina grinned. "Isn't it great?"

"We should be ashamed of ourselves. We're just two hussies. You know that?"

"Probably," Christina agreed. "But I don't think our husbands would have it any other way."

"What are you two grinning about?" May asked as she stepped from behind the wagon.

"Just newlywed stuff," Lana explained. "Oh, here's your ring back, Ma." Lana pulled it from her finger and handed it over.

"This ring has been really busy the past few days," May laughed. "From me to Christina to you and now back to me." Putting it on her own hand, she looked at the two girls. "You'll both have your own rings soon enough. And they'll be prettier than this old thing."

"Ma, you wouldn't take for that 'old thing' and you know it!" Lana teased her.

"You're right. It was all your pa could afford at the time, but it means more to me than the world."

"We're all packed," Paul announced as he put the last of their things in the wagon and Jake tied the new dairy cow to the back.

"Then I guess it's time to say goodbye." Lana began tearing up. While she and Liam made the rounds, saying goodbye to everyone, she managed to keep her emotions in check. But, when she stood in front of her father, she began crying.

"Oh, Pa." She buried her face against his chest. "I'm going to miss all of you so much. I don't know if I can stand it."

"Sshhh." He patted her back, that dangerous lump in his throat again. "It's going to be just fine. Besides, we'll see you soon enough, whenever the crops are in. We'll be back to trade. And you come see us as often as you can."

"I will." Lana wiped her eyes. She hugged him tightly one last time and then stepped back.

Shaking Liam's hand, Joshua looked him straight in the eye. "You be good to my little girl."

"I will, sir. I promise."

"All right, then." Joshua turned to survey the wagon and the horizon and then turned back to study the fort for a moment. "All right, then," he repeated, trying to hide his sudden panic at leaving Lana behind. "I guess we'd better make tracks."

Nodding once to Nathan, who started the team, Joshua fell in step by the rolling wagon just as the sun peeked over the eastern horizon.

"I love you! All of you!" Lana called out after them as she waved. "Bye!"

"Bye, Lana." Christina turned from her place on the wagon and waved back. "Bye!"

In a few minutes, the wagon rolled behind a hill and the Coopers were out of sight. Lana turned to her husband with the most woeful expression he'd ever seen.

"Come here, beautiful." He pulled her to him. "I know just the thing that will cheer you up."

"What?" she asked, knowing that nothing could cheer her up right then.

"It starts with a good breakfast and then we'll go shopping."

"Yes, sir." They turned back and walked into the fort, heading for the Officers' Mess and hot coffee.

* * *

Quietly, slowly, the Kiowa warriors crept up to the grazing herd. The horses belonged to the Cheyenne and were poorly guarded as they ate the rich spring grass. The camp sat further back against a low hill. If they moved quickly, the raiding party could have the horses away and across the river before an alarm sounded.

Two Hawks slunk up behind one of the four guards, killing him instantly with a sharp thrust of his knife. Laughing Turtle also reached a guard, but wasn't as adept at his task. The man lay on the ground, blood gurgling from his mouth, as he stared accusingly at Laughing Turtle. Grimacing, Laughing Turtle stabbed him again, this time, making sure he hit the heart. The man's head fell back, his eyes still open.

With all the guards dead, the five Kiowa herded the horses toward the river without causing too much commotion. They had successfully crossed it when they heard a cry go up in the village. Shouting and waving their arms, they brought the herd to a gallop and disappeared into the distance.

It took several days to return to their tribe, but they arrived to a hero's welcome. The horses were divided up between the five men, making each one wealthier. Horses meant status and power, rifles and wives. Two Hawks now had eighteen horses of his own. But he wanted more. Driven by Lana's rejection and his own anger, he wanted so many horses that he could buy *ten* Lanas if he wanted to!

Three days hadn't passed since his return before he was on the raiding trail again. Only this time he traveled alone, heading northwest.

* * *

T'on Ma had her arms wrapped tightly around his waist as she lifted her head for his kisses. He leaned down, touching her sweet lips with his own, when she burst like a raindrop, splashing on hard earth, and turned into a stream of water flowing toward the east. Two Hawks turned to look east, but it sat in total darkness, and he could see nothing. Peering into the inky black, straining to see any shred of light or form, he heard a cry, a woman's cry, a heartbroken cry that pierced him with its sorrow.

Jerking straight up from his blanket, the warrior looked around him in the night. There was no one with him. There was no one crying. He held his head in his hands, clenching his eyes against the dream. Again. This dream, again. Slowly, reluctantly, he lay back down for a few more hours sleep before the dawn and another day's journey north.

* * *

In a week's time, Two Hawks had ridden many miles, finding nothing of interest. However, late one afternoon, he came across a small band of Osage hunters. They had made camp for the evening and were busy with fires and food. Looking over their horses, Two Hawks saw a magnificent palomino stallion. Its owner tied the horse close to the camp so he could keep an eye on it.

Slipping back from his outlook, Two Hawks tethered his horse and settled down to wait for night. There were seven Osage warriors, so he needed to be quick as well as quiet in order to escape with the palomino. Once night fell and several hours passed, Two Hawks crept back to his outlook. It surprised him that the Osage had not set a guard. All seven men were asleep.

Creeping cautiously toward the camp, Two Hawks watched the horses. One sound of alarm from them meant trouble. A few flicked their ears back as they listened to his approach, but none whinnied. Taking a few more cautious steps, he stopped and watched again. One of the horses stomped its foot and shook its head. His owner turned, mumbling in his sleep, and then grew quiet again. A few more steps brought Two Hawks to the palomino's flank. Reaching out steadily toward the horse, he began gently stroking its side. Its ears flicked, but it made no other move.

The Kiowa untied the rope from the rock next to the horse's owner. Two Hawks looked carefully at each sleeping form. None had moved. Pushing against the horse's chest, he moved the horse back two steps. After waiting a moment, he repeated his action. He went through this process several times until they were several feet away from the camp. Two Hawks turned the horse around and led him away at a slow pace, trying to stay as quiet as possible.

Finally, carefully, he had just made it back to his own horse when he heard a shout from the camp. Two Hawks jumped on his horse and galloped into the night, leading the palomino by its rope. The Osage warriors heard the hooves and began running and shooting in that direction. Just when Two Hawks thought he was safely away, something stung his right shoulder. He could feel warm blood running down his back as he lurched forward. Clinging to his horse, he sent them galloping faster, not able to stop, knowing the mounted Osage were in hot pursuit.

By switching every few miles from horse to horse, he outran the Osages' exhausted horses, though it took a long time to do so. Once safe, he stopped to tend his wound as best he could, but he couldn't reach the bullet in his shoulder. His only hope was to travel quickly to his village for help.

Several days later, Two Hawks rode into camp and fell from his horse. A high fever and infection ravaged his body. Tall Moon came immediately and treatment began as he dug out the bullet from Two Hawks' infected shoulder. Gray Dove, her two daughters, and Corn Flower took turns tending the sick man for days. Many times, Gray Dove feared for his life, but the four women kept bathing in him with cold water and Tall Moon forced him to drink cup after cup of willow bark tea. Once the fever broke, the patient slowly began to mend.

* * *

Two Hawks had just awakened from a nap when Corn Flower came in carrying a bowl of food.

"Good. You're awake," she said, stepping over to him. "Laughing Turtle caught some rabbits this morning. I've made you a stew from them." Kneeling beside him, she held out the bowl. He took it and began eating. She watched him, grateful that his appetite had returned.

"We were so worried about you. There were many nights we thought were going to be your last." Reaching out, she touched his shoulder. "But you are too strong to let a bullet stop you."

Finished, Two Hawks handed the bowl back to her, expecting her to leave. When she didn't, he looked at her, frowning. "What?"

"I want to ask you something."

"All right. Ask."

"Why are you so angry? Why are you trying to get yourself killed?"

"Get myself killed?" That puzzled him.

"Yes. Why else would you keep raiding, even when you're alone? Why are you so angry?" she asked again.

The expression on his face told Corn Flower that he didn't want to talk about it.

"I can guess," she filled in the silence. "Water Woman has done something to hurt you. Perhaps even told you to go away."

"She is none of your concern," Two Hawks snapped.

"She is if she's your concern." Corn Flower moved her hand from his shoulder to his chest. "Is she your concern?"

Two Hawks shook his head once. "No. Not any more."

"I see." She paused for a moment before continuing with her confession. "You told me before you left that I wasn't to wait for you. But I did. I have had many suitors, but I have always waited for you." Leaning over, she kissed him as sweetly as she knew how. He didn't respond, didn't move. She might as well have kissed a rock. It would have been less cold.

Sitting up, she frowned. "I don't understand! What's wrong?"

For a moment, Two Hawks felt sorry for the beautiful young woman. "Don't you understand yet? My mind and pride might be at war with her, but my heart still needs her. Go to one of your suitors. Marry him. Waiting for me will be wasting your life."

"So, your heart needs someone you are at war with? You will die a lonely old man if you don't change."

Two Hawks had no argument for her, so he simply turned his back to her.

"Oh, you are impossible!" Picking up the bowl, Corn Flower stormed out of the tipi, refusing to give up on Two Hawks, much as he refused to let go of T'on Ma. Somehow, though, she didn't see the similarities. It might have helped her understand him if she had.

## Chapter 34 — The Telegram

As soon as he grew stronger, Two Hawks made plans for another raiding party.

*"What?"* Many Deer exclaimed. "Why? You're barely on your feet."

"Please," his mother begged. "Don't go again so soon. You still need to heal."

But Two Hawks only turned his face from them, unwilling to listen to their words, unmoved by their concern.

"Why is he doing this?" Gray Dove asked her father, Red Flint, later that day. "It's as if he had a death wish."

"Perhaps he does," Red Flint acknowledged. "He hasn't been the same since Water Woman refused him."

"Her!" Gray Dove scowled. "I wish he had never met her. She's brought nothing but trouble. He should have married Corn Flower last summer. I'd be a grandmother by now."

"Wishing won't make it change," the old man shook his head. "Not for you. Not for your son."

"I don't understand why he won't take Corn Flower. She's perfect."

"Daughter, you've married the man you loved, so perhaps you *don't* understand why he won't take Corn Flower. Water Woman is in his heart, in his mind. Asking him to replace her with another woman is like asking a starving man with buffalo steak to trade it for a meal of dirt."

"So he's trying to get himself killed?"

"He might not realize it, but yes. I think so." Red Flint paused for a moment. "Once, many years ago, when you were too young to remember, I saw another brave lose his woman. He deliberately went out starting trouble with other tribes. Eventually, he got what he wanted and was killed."

"Then what shall we do for your grandson?"

"I'm not sure there is anything we *can* do."

Frustrated at his answer, Gray Dove shook her head and walked away.

\* \* \*

Several days later, Two Hawks was hunting when he came across Nathan working in the field. While they disagreed over Lana, they still had a mutual respect for each other. Riding up to Nathan, Two Hawks dismounted and lifted his hand in a sign of friendship.

"Hello," Nathan said in Kiowa as he leaned on his hoe. "Are you well?"

"Yes. And you?"

"I am well. Christina is my wife now."

"Oh? That is good. I thought perhaps she would be one day." The warrior looked around at the plowed earth in its straight rows, green shoots pushing their way through the soil. "What have you planted?"

"Corn. Beans. Wheat."

Two Hawks only nodded. After a period of silence, he then asked the question burning in his mind. "How is your sister?"

"Lana? She's doing well. She got married, you know."

That news hit Two Hawks in the gut. "No. I did not. Who?"

"You might remember him. Lt. O'Connell from Ft. Worth."

"The soldier who rescued us from the Apaches?"

"Yes. The same."

"So she lives at the fort now?"

"Yes. We don't get to see her now, but hopefully, when the crop comes in, we'll travel up there."

"Hmmm." Two Hawks didn't know what else to say. News of her marriage left him stunned. Even though she had said they were through, he always thought that somehow they would be together again. "I must go now."

"All right. It was good seeing you again."

"You, too." Two Hawks jumped on his palomino, waved once, and loped away. By the time he made it home, he'd finalized plans for his next raiding excursion.

* * *

*"Dear Son, Excited about your news. Will arrive at Ft. Worth in late May. Love, Father"*

Liam read the telegram to Lana over the supper table one night.

"Late May," Lana repeated. "This *is* late May. They could be here any day now!"

"I suppose so," Liam's smile slowly faded as he looked at her. "What's the matter?"

"Your parents are coming here! *Here!*" She stood up and motioned to their humble quarters. "We've no place to put them. There aren't enough plates for meals. I don't even have curtains up yet. And, just *look* at this dress!" She held the mended skirt out in evidence of its shortcomings.

"Whoa, girl. Stop." Liam laughed as he stood up and took her in his arms. "First of all, they aren't coming to see where I live. They are coming to meet my beautiful wife. Second of all, they can eat at the Officer's Mess and stay in guest quarters while they're here. And third, we can get you a new dress. Two, if you want."

Lana looked up into his handsome face. "Two? Really?"

"Absolutely. Nothing is too good for Mrs. O'Connell." He kissed her quickly and then sat back down.

"I wish my roses were blooming," she pouted.

"Would you stop worrying?"

"Make me," she said with a mischievous twinkle in her eyes.

"Make you, huh?" Liam rose, grinning, and chased her into the bedroom. He trapped her in the far corner of the room, where she stood breathless and giggling.

"Aha!" he laughed. "Got you!"

"Yeah, me and this ratty old dress."

"Oh, dear. Whatever shall we do?" he asked in mock concern. "I know," he snapped his fingers. "Let's take the dress off you. My wife can't be wearing a ratty old dress, now can she?"

"No, I suppose not," Lana agreed. "But then, what shall I put on?"

"Me."

"Oh, lieutenant, I like the way you think." Reaching up, she kissed him, and then turned so he could undo her buttons. Something in his movement sent her memory back to the cottonwood trees and Two Hawks fumbling with these same buttons. She was glad she faced the wall so Liam couldn't see her eyes right then. Two Hawks. She missed him.

\* \* \*

Four days after the telegram, a wagon drove into the compound late one afternoon. Liam had just gotten off duty and turned to look at the newcomers. Recognizing them, he hurried across the grounds.

"Dad! Hello!" The two men hugged and then stood at arms length, studying each other.

"You're looking well," Patrick said. "Marriage and Army life agree with you."

"Thanks. You look like you've gotten a little thin."

"Trying to find decent food to eat is impossible while traveling." The two men walked to the wagon where two white women, two black men and one black woman were seated.

"Mary, Mother. Hello." Liam helped his mother down first and then his sister, each one kissing him on the cheek.

The youngest black man jumped down from the wagon.

"Jason!" Liam pounded him on the back. "You've sure grown since I saw you last."

Jason just grinned and then turned to help the older black woman down.

"Becca, how have you been?" Sweet natured and observant, Becca served as personal maid to Mrs. O'Connell. Streaks of gray ran through Becca's neatly combed hair.

"And Toby. My, oh, my." Liam nodded to the older black man. "I bet you never thought you'd travel this far west."

"No sir, I never did," Toby agreed.

Liam turned back to his family. "Lana is so anxious to meet you. Let me show you to the house and then I'll put the team and wagon away."

"No. Jason can put the team away. Just point him in the right direction," his father instructed.

"All right. Jason, see that long building over there?"

"Yes, sir"

"That's the stable. Just tell the soldier there that you're with me. He'll show you what to do. Then come to the house, the middle one over there."

"Yes, sir." Jason and Toby jumped back on the wagon and drove the team to the stable.

Liam led the small entourage to his quarters and stepped through the door. "Guess who I found wandering around outside?" he smiled at Lana and then stepped back. First his mother, Maeve, then Mary, and then Patrick, walked in.

## Chapter 35 — A Wall of Disapproving Looks

Putting his arm around Lana's shoulders, Liam introduced his family.   Lana shook hands with her father-in-law and then awkwardly leaned forward and kissed Maeve and Mary on the cheek.

"Please, come in and sit down," Lana invited them.   She mentally rejoiced that she wore one of her new dresses that day.

A single horsehair sofa offered the only seating in the sparsely furnished living room, so Liam carried kitchen chairs into the room.

"You must be thirsty after your travels," Lana said, trying to break the ice.  "I have some fresh lemonade.  Would you care for any?"

"That would be lovely, dear," Maeve accepted.  Maeve struck Lana as a serious woman, prim in her attire, her posture and her attitude, well-kept and used to being obeyed.  She loved her children fiercely and thought she knew what was best for them at all times.  Learning of Liam's marriage without her consent, or even prior knowledge, had greatly upset her.  Lana inherently sensed she would have to earn her mother-in-law's approval.

As Lana went into the kitchen, she saw Becca sitting on the porch.  "There's someone outside," she sounded worried.

Leaning to look out the window, Mary explained, "Oh, that's just Becca."

"Becca?"

"Mother's maid." Mary looked a lot like her mother, though slightly taller. As strong-willed as Mary was, she wouldn't defy her mother, which explained why she still lived at home, unmarried.

"Oh." Lana frowned at the mention of a maid. She'd never known anyone with a maid before and suddenly felt out of place in her own home. Once everyone had their lemonade, Lana said, "Perhaps Becca would like a drink. Shall I take her some?"

"Goodness, no," Maeve shook her head. "You don't serve slaves. They serve you. Just tell her it's here and she can get her own." Lana's naivety went down as a second black mark against her in Maeve's book. Lana already had one for marrying Liam without Maeve's consent.

"Yes, m'am." Lana barely heard Maeve past the word 'slave.' Slave! *Here?* She shot a look of concern to Liam, who quietly gestured for her to be still.

At the knock on the door, Liam rose and answered it. Jason and Toby stood there with the O'Connell's luggage.

"Where do you want this, Mr. O'Connell," Toby asked, looking at the floor.

"I don't know yet. Liam, where are we staying?"

"I've arranged guest quarters for you. I'll show Toby and be right back."

"Hurry," Lana tried to keep the panic from her voice. She didn't want to be left alone with her in-laws any longer than necessary. When Liam left, Lana stood up and walked to the door. "Becca?"

"Yes'm?" Becca looked over her shoulder at Lana and slowly stood; the trip had been especially hard on her rheumatism. Lana winced watching the elderly woman's pain.

"There's some lemonade in here if you'd like. Please, help yourself and, if the others want any, they're welcome, too."

"Thank you, m'am." Becca nodded. Lana wished she could bring her a drink. Instead, she dutifully returned to face her new family.

As she sat on a kitchen chair, Lana wrapped her hands around her lemonade glass to keep them from fidgeting. "So, did you come by wagon all the way here?"

"No, child." Maeve answered as if that was the silliest thing she'd ever heard. "We took a train as far as we could. Then we caught a stagecoach as far as that went. We only hired a wagon when we came to the end of civilization."

"I see." Lana looked around the bare room, trying to think of a question that wouldn't sound stupid. She took a sip of lemonade to stall for time. "I guess you saw a lot of pretty country, then," she gamely tried again.

"We couldn't see much from the train window. It all went by so fast," Mary answered. "And, of course, that's where the best scenery was. Once we got out here, it never changed. Quite boring, actually."

"Dear, me. I'm sorry you found it boring." The small group fell quiet, the silence growing more awkward with each passing second. Lana straightened in her chair when she *finally* thought of a subject, and smiled at her father-in-law. "When was the last time you saw Liam?" *Where was Liam?*

"Shortly after he graduated from West Point. The Army gave him some leave and then sent him out into the wilds." Patrick sounded proud of his youngest son.

"So it's been a few years then."

"Yes, dear." There was that tone in Maeve's voice again. "Tell me. Did you ever go to finishing school?"

"No, m'am. I don't even know what finishing school is. I got through eighth grade, though." Lana received her third black mark.

"Eighth grade. How wonderful for you." Mary smiled, but Lana didn't believe her words.

"I'm back," Liam announced as he walked through the door. "Sorry it took so long, but I forgot about getting quarters for the servants."

Becca came in behind Liam, and led Toby and Jason to the kitchen to pour them all lemonade.

"When you're done," Maeve called out, "we could use some more in here, too, Becca."

"Yes'm."

Lana bit her lip. Didn't Maeve know how much Becca hurt? Instead of just sitting there, Lana stood up and walked into the kitchen.

"Let me." Lana took the pitcher out of Becca's gnarly-jointed, painful hands. Winking at her, she poured them all a drink and then took the pitcher to the living room, where a wall of disapproving looks met her.

"What?" she asked innocently. "I don't want my only good pitcher chipped." There! That ought to keep the snoots quiet.

* * *

Dinner at the Officers' Mess that evening went better. More people were there to diffuse the conversation. Liam's father was enamored with the romantic ideal of military life and almost sparkled while talking to captains and colonels and majors.

Mary kept flirting with one of the young officers across the table from her. Lana watched with great interest. Mary would last about five minutes in the rigors of military life and only about three in Texas. She was the type of girl who needed theater and church and schoolgirl friends and new dresses from Paris every season.

Lana learned that the O'Connells were wealthy foundry owners and had been for several generations. The oldest son, Patrick, Jr., had stayed at home to oversee the business while his parents were away. Their married daughter, Colleen, lived in New York with her financier husband.

"What does your father do?" Maeve asked Lana during a lull in the conversation.

"My father? He's a homesteader a few days west of here."

"Oh. A farmer, then."

"Yes'm. He moved us here after he got out of the Mexican-American War a couple of years ago."

"So he fought in the war, did he?" Patrick's estimation of Lana went up half a notch, but her answer turned the conversation back to military topics, and the trouble the Kiowa and Apache were giving homesteaders and the military.

"Lana knows all about that," the commander said. "She was captured by the Apache last year."

"*What!*" Maeve almost dropped her wine glass. "Captured?" She looked alarmed. Truly alarmed. "For how long?"

"Only a week or so," Lana explained somberly. "Liam helped rescue me."

"How fortuitous." Maeve nodded her head, but her tone was curt. *That* was why he married this little slip of a farm girl. He had fallen for the 'damsel in distress'. Maeve wanted to change the conversation to something more socially acceptable.

"Tell me, Colonel, where do you recommend we go for a morning ride?"

The talk turned away from Lana, who looked worriedly at Liam. Something had just gone horribly wrong, but she didn't know what, or why. He squeezed her hand under the table.

After dinner, Liam and Lana said goodnight and walked back to their home, Lana quiet the whole way. She worried that she didn't fit in with the O'Connell family.

"What are you thinking about so hard?" Liam asked as they walked in the door.

"Nothing. I'm just tired. I think I'll turn in early."

"All right, sweetheart. I'll be in in a little while."

Lana dressed for bed and opened the windows to let the evening breeze through. After she crawled under the covers, she lay there, staring at the ceiling as she thought about the conversation over dinner. There were so many things Liam hadn't told her about his family. She didn't know he was wealthy or that his family had slaves. That bothered her most of all. First Two Hawks and now Liam seemed to think slavery was all right. Maybe *she* was the one who was wrong.

Turning over on her side, wishing her mind would hush, she heard footsteps outside on the porch. There was a soft knock on their door, which Liam answered.

"Dad, come in."

"No. Come outside where we can talk."

"All right." Liam closed the door behind him and the two men stood beside the bedroom window, unaware that it was open.

"Are your quarters all right?"

"Yes, son. Everything is fine. Your mother and sister have turned in for the night."

"Good. You sure you don't want to come in?"

"No. I don't want to disturb your wife."

"What is it, Dad? Something's on your mind."

"Yes, there is." Patrick looked steadily at his son for a moment before he began. "You know how very proud I am of you. West Point. Army officer. I don't have any buttons left on my shirts. Someone says your name or asks about you and I just pop them off."

The two men chuckled at that. "But your mother and I are concerned — very concerned — about your choice for a wife."

## Chapter 36 — Are We Clear?

"Concerned? Why?" Liam asked, sounding perplexed.

"She's not the type we'd hoped you'd marry."

"Not the type? What type was I suppose to marry?" Liam scowled.

"Someone with more than an eighth grade education. Someone raised around culture and society who could help you further a political career once you left the Army."

"Oh, for goodness sake!" Liam looked across the compound and then back to his father. "Does the fact that I'm so in love with her I can't breathe make any difference at all to you?"

"So, you love her. Good for you. But you didn't have to marry her. Have your fling here in Texas and then, when you get home, marry the right woman."

"My *fling!*" Liam was past irritated and now at full-bore angry. "How *dare* you talk about her like that!"

"Liam, face it. She was with the Apaches for over a week. You know she was raped. Had to be." Patrick knew the shame and stigma that people — voters — would attach to his son over this.

"I know for a fact that she wasn't. *I* am the first man she's ever had."

"If you say so."

"You sound like you don't believe me."

"I think you'd say anything to defend your choice," his father countered heatedly.

"I need to go in now, before I say something we'll both regret," Liam snarled.

"Son, I'm just looking out for your best interest."

"Good night!" Liam stepped into his house, slamming the door behind him. Cursing under his breath, he came into the bedroom only to see Lana sitting up, knees to chin, arms around knees, sobbing.

"Oh, *damn!* Did you hear that?" he asked. She nodded and pointed to the open window. Liam threw his head back, furious at his father. Walking over to her, he sat on the edge of the bed and drew her to him.

"Honey, I am so sorry. So terribly sorry. My father can be such an insensitive, belligerent bully. He had no right to say those things about you. And I promise, I will get this all straightened out in the morning."

He lifted her chin so he could look into her eyes. "Please, Lana, please don't let them make you cry. I can't stand it."

Grabbing his shirt with both hands, she jumped into his arms, sobbing. "They hate me. They all hate me. Your mother — Mary — all of them. I'm not good enough for you. I wish I was dead!"

Liam rocked her back and forth, holding her while she cried. His family would pay, and pay dearly, for hurting her like this. No one made her cry. *No one.*

"Sweetheart, baby, if you die, then kill me, too. Because I can't live without you. Do you hear me? I love you so much. And *they're* not good enough for you. I'm sorry they ever showed up!"

"You shouldn't say that," she huff-huffed against his chest. "They're your family. They love you."

"*You're* my family," he whispered. He laid her back on the bed and began loving her tears away with his caresses and kisses and velvet hands in the night.

\* \* \*

Two Hawks' eyes jerked open, jarring him out of a deep sleep. Sweat beaded his forehead, his heart raced; his blanket lay in a tormented twist. He looked around at the sleeping warriors to make sure he hadn't awakened them. It was the dream, again. *Her* dream. T'on Ma had been calling to him, crying for him. Even awake, he could feel the sorrow in her voice. What was wrong? Why wouldn't his heart let her go? She had chosen another. Frowning, he turned angrily on his side, folded his arms across his chest and tried to find sleep.

\* \* \*

Early the next morning, Mary answered the knock on the guest quarter's door. Liam pushed his way in.

"Are the folks up yet?" he asked curtly.

"I don't know. I don't think so." Mary looked puzzled.

Liam walked over to their bedroom door. "Time to get up!" Bang! Bang! Bang!

"*What?*" Patrick jerked the door open, still in his nightshirt, his hair frazzled. "We're not ready for company."

"I don't care!" Liam snapped. "This isn't company." Leaning around his father, he called, "Get up, Mother. Now!"

"How dare you speak to me like that!"

"I will come in there and drag you out if you're not here in one minute."

Patrick started to challenge Liam's attitude, but something in his son's eyes stopped him. There was a hardness, a steel he'd never seen before.

"You'd better come out, Maeve," Patrick advised.

Within a few minutes, Patrick, Maeve and Mary sat on the sofa, still in their nightclothes and robes. Liam stood over them, the vein in his forehead throbbing.

"We need to get something straight right now," he began. "I'm sure you two know what Dad and I talked about last night after dinner, so don't pretend you don't."

Both women looked wide-eyed at him, shocked. He'd never spoken to either of them like this.

"Lana heard everything you said last night, Dad."

"Oh, Liam, I'm sorry. I didn't mean..."

Liam interrupted him. "She is my wife. I love her and I will *always* love her. She is not one of your high society debutants, for which I am eternally grateful. I can't stand those women! She might not have a high school education or have gone to finishing school, but she is the most intelligent woman I've ever met. And I'm including the two of you in that." He pointed to his mother and sister.

"You won't find anyone with more heart or courage or love if you looked for a thousand years. And — pardon me for upsetting your delicate sensibilities, Mother — she was a virgin when I took her to bed. I can assure you that she isn't one now. I make love to her every chance I can. There's that much passion between us. Do you remember what that's like, Dad? Passion? Making love to your woman with so much feeling and emotion that you think your chest is going to explode?

"*Liam!*" His father tried to stop him.

"No. I'm not done. That's how I feel about her. That's how much I love her. And if you — any of you — hurt her like that again, you will never see me as long as you live. You will never see our children. You could give me a million dollars, and I would spit on it. Are we clear?"

When no one spoke, he said, "Good!" He looked each one in the eye. "Now, when you see her today, you'll be civil — without all of these subtle little jabs. She picked up on every one of them yesterday. If you can't be sincerely nice to her, then stay the hell away!"

"There's no need to be vulgar," his mother fussed at him.

"No. There isn't. So don't be!" With that, he walked to the door. "I'm on duty all day, but I've told Lana to get me if she needs me. Hopefully, I'll see you all at lunch."

He closed the door behind him and walked back to his quarters. Lana was up and making coffee.

"Morning, beautiful," he said, all trace of his earlier anger gone, and then turned her around to kiss her. "Sleep good?"

"Yep," she smiled. "I always sleep good in your arms."

He kissed her contentedly once more and then sat at the table. "I talked to my folks."

"When? This morning?" she asked incredulously.

"Yep. Got 'em out of bed and everything." He chuckled.

"They must have really appreciated that," she grinned.

"Ah, probably not. However, they will be on their best behavior today. You've got nothing to worry about."

"Oh, Liam, honey." She sat next to him and took his hand. "They can treat me like I'm the Queen of England, but that won't make them like me or accept me."

"Maybe not, but it will keep them from hurting you. They're just too snobbish for their own good. In time, they'll come around."

"Let's hope so." She stood up. "What would you like for breakfast? Eggs and toast or oatmeal?"

"Are you on the menu?" he asked hopefully.

"Only if you want to be late for work."

Sighing heavily, he said, "Eggs and toast, then."

## Chapter 37 — Becca

Liam had been gone over an hour when there was a knock at the door. Lana opened it to discover Toby and Jason standing there, a large trunk between them.

"The Missus sent us over with this," Toby explained.

"Please, come in." Lana stepped back and gestured to the living room.

The two men picked up the trunk and carried it through, setting it with a thud on the floor next to the wall.

"Becca will be along in a minute to help with that," Toby told her.

"All right. What is it?"

"Don't rightly know."

"Have you had breakfast? Would you like some coffee?"

Toby and Jason exchanged uneasy glances with each other. To refuse the daughter-in-law of Mr. O'Connell was unthinkable. But to have her serve them breakfast was even more unheard of. Unwittingly, she had put them on the horns of a sticky dilemma and they weren't quite sure how to get out of it. Fortunately, Becca stepped through the open door.

"Morning, Miss Lana," she called out.

"Good morning, Becca."

"What are you still doing here?" Becca turned to the two men. "Shoo. You've got work to do in the stables."

Looking relieved, they nodded once at Lana and gratefully went to their chores.

"The Missus wants me to help you unpack this," Becca said as she walked over to the trunk, a large key in her hands. Kneeling, she unlocked it and pushed open the heavy lid. Lana peered over her shoulder, curious about the trunk's contents.

"What is all this?" Lana asked as she brought a chair over. "Here, sit down."

Once Becca was seated, she began talking as she pulled out items and unwrapped them.

"This trunk is full of things Miz O'Connell wanted Liam to have when she heard he was married. It's got china and tablecloths and such like."

Becca held up the most delicate porcelain teacup Lana had ever seen. It put her mother's Delft pattern to shame — complete and utter shame. The porcelain looked like it was made of pearls, with elegant dark pink roses hand-painted around the border. The rim and handle were trimmed in real gold. Lana was afraid to touch it.

"I don't know where we're going to put this," she fretted. "I don't have a china cabinet."

"Oh, don't worry 'bout that," Becca said. "There's one coming."

"There is?"

"Yes'm. Being freighted special. Heard tell it was coming through New Orleans by ship." The elderly woman reached in and picked up another item, carefully unwrapping it. "They's sending a big bed and some other furniture, too."

"Where are we supposed to put all of that in this tiny place?"

Becca laughed at that. "I don't rightly know. You'll figure it out."

"Do you drink coffee?" Lana asked.

"Yes'm."

"Good. So do I." She went into the kitchen and poured them each a cup. When she handed a cup to Becca, Becca looked up at her in surprise.

"Why'd you do that?"

"You were busy," Lana explained.

Becca shook her head at Lana's foolishness, but took a sip of coffee before she continued working.

"May I ask you something?" Lana broke their silence.

"Yes'm."

"How long have you worked for the O'Connells?"

"How long? Well, I was born into the house, so I reckon all my life."

"All your life," Lana repeated as she let that sink in. "So I suppose that's your home."

"Yes'm. As much as I'll ever have. They could sell me, but I'm too old now. No one would buy an old woman like me." She chuckled at that, but Lana failed to see the humor.

Becca pulled out a beautiful Irish lace tablecloth and walked over to the kitchen table with it. Spreading it carefully across the table, she nodded. "That looks better."

It dawned on Lana that Becca was used to having beautiful things surrounding her in the house where she worked. This place must look awful to her.

"I suppose we seem pretty bleak here at the fort," Lana said as she carried over a beautiful porcelain serving bowl and set it in the middle of the table.

"Well, just a little."

"There's not much call for finery out here," Lana explained. "It's all heat and dust and soldiers. Not many womenfolk around."

"Then the ones that are here need to do better. Keep things civilized."

Lana rolled her eyes at that.

The last thing Becca took out of the trunk was a beautiful bedspread. Lana had never seen anything so fine, as used to homemade quilts as she was.  The soft baby blue fabric had dozens of satin stripes down its length.  Exquisite dark blue and purple flowers with tiny green leaves had been embroidered between the satin stripes.  There must have been hundreds of them by Lana's count.

"Oh, Becca, this is gorgeous!" Lana took it from her and went into the bedroom.  Spreading it across the bed, she stood back to look.

"Now the room looks dingy next to this," she sighed.

"I'm glad you like that," Becca smiled as she stepped through.  "It took me more'n two years to do all that."

"*You* made this?"

"Yes'm.  Just finished it right before we was to leave for here."

Lana took the woman's two arthritic hands in hers and stared at them.  "You must have been in so much pain with all of that needlework."

"Oh, I didn't mind."  Becca became embarrassed.  "I'd do anything for Master Liam.  He's always been my favorite."

"Mine, too."  Lana giggled and then, in a spontaneous gesture, kissed both of Becca's hands.  "Thank you so much for this.  You are wonderful."

Becca pulled her hands back and nodded once.  "Welcome."  She turned to leave the room so that Lana wouldn't see the tears in her eyes.  No one — no one white — had ever thanked her for anything in her life.  And no one, white or black, had *ever* called her wonderful.

With the trunk unpacked and the china put wherever Lana could find a place, Becca walked to the front door.  "I'll be right back to start lunch."

"Lunch?  I was going to fix lunch."

"Oh, no'm."  Becca shook her head at that.  "The Missus has food brought in that I'm to fix.  I'll get it and be right back."

"All right."  Lana certainly didn't want to get in an argument over what to eat for lunch.

Within fifteen minutes, Becca came in, carrying a few items, with Jason right behind her, carrying a large, overflowing box.

"My goodness!" Lana exclaimed. "Are we going to feed the whole fort lunch?"

Jason burst out laughing as he set the box on the kitchen counter.

"Jason!" Becca shushed him. It didn't do to be too familiar with the owners. The young man shot a nervous look at Becca and then quickly left the room.

"What all have you brought?" Lana asked as she peeked into the box.

"Now, Miss Lana, you go on. I'll take care of this."

"Can I at least sit at the table and watch?"

"Yes'm. Cain't keep you from your own house, now can I?"

"I'm not so sure," Lana muttered. There were a whole lot of unwritten rules she seemed to keep tripping over around the O'Connells and their servants.

When Becca pulled out a pound of yellow squash, Lana stood up. "At least let me do the slicing and chopping," she volunteered. "I can do it so much faster. Plus, I'm getting bored just sitting here."

Becca studied her for a moment, considering her request. This girl was different than any she had met back home. This one knew how to work and wasn't afraid of it. More than that, she was genuinely kind. Finally nodding, Becca handed the vegetables to Lana, telling her how she needed them cut.

Between the two of them, they made short work out of preparing the meal.

"Should we use the china for lunch?" Lana asked. "I don't have enough plates for everyone, otherwise."

"I think the Missus would like to see that," Becca nodded.

"All right, then." Lana brought the dishes over while Becca set the table. Lana didn't know where everything went and watched Becca carefully.

When Liam walked through the door for lunch, he stopped abruptly when he saw the table. The Irish lace lay beneath beautiful, delicate china and crystal wine goblets. The table almost groaned under the weight of smoked ham, fried squash and onions, smoked salmon, hot rolls, sliced tomatoes, fresh cantaloupe, and boiled sweet potatoes. Two pecan pies sat on the kitchen counter, cooling.

"My, oh, my!" Liam exclaimed as he kissed Lana.

"You *need* to kiss Becca," Lana teased. "She did all of this."

"Oh, go on!" Becca ducked her head and slapped the air at Lana. When she looked up, she told them, "I'll go get your folks and tell them lunch is ready."

When Becca was gone, Liam turned to Lana. "You mean my parents haven't been by all morning? Or Mary, either?"

"No. They sent Becca to unpack this huge trunk full of things they want you to have."

"Oh. I see." Liam scowled at that, but he let it go, preferring to wait and see how things went at lunch.

# Chapter 38 — Little Spitfire

"Hello, dear," Maeve greeted her son with a kiss on his cheek. Looking beside him at Lana, she smiled. "Hello. I see you got the things we sent. I hope you like them."

"It is all so wonderful, so beautiful. Thank you very much."

Maeve nodded and then walked over to the table, inspecting Becca's work. "Hmmm. The tomatoes are sliced thicker than I like."

Lana was appalled. All of that delicious food on all of that beautiful china, and all Maeve could say was that the tomatoes were sliced too thick!

"I'm sorry," Lana said. "I sliced those. I didn't realize you liked them thinner."

"*You* sliced them? Not Becca?" Maeve frowned at Lana.

"No. I was bored just sitting there watching her, so I made her let me."

"I see. Well, no matter. They'll taste just the same anyway."

While this conversation took place, Mary and her father said hello to Liam. Soon, they all took their seats around the table, eating lunch and being very civil.

"So, Liam, how long before you get new orders?" Patrick asked.

"I'm not sure. I expect by this fall, I'll know something."

"Do you think you'll get assigned back east?"

"Probably. Once you do a stint west of the Mississippi, they let you come back." His family laughed at that.

"You know, I've had the most marvelous idea," Maeve said a little too brightly as she smiled at Lana. "When you find out when you'll be transferred, why doesn't Lana come ahead of you and stay with us for a while? You know, until you get settled at your new post? We could show her where you were brought up — take her to the theater — maybe do some shopping. Doesn't that sound like fun?"

Lana reached for Liam's knee under the table, squeezing it in her panic, while she lamely smiled at her mother-in-law.

"That sounds wonderful," Mary chimed in. "We could even have a ball to introduce her to all of Liam's friends."

"Of course! What a great idea," Maeve turned to Liam. "So, what do you think?"

"I think we need to wait and see where I'm assigned before we make those kind of plans. If I'm not going back east, there's no point in sending her there. But those are good ideas. All of them." He smiled back at his mother and then deliberately changed the subject. "By the way, this food is delicious. Where did you get the fresh vegetables?"

The conversation turned again to safer waters. When Liam asked what they had done that morning, Patrick told him that he and Maeve had gone for a ride with the colonel several miles away from the fort. Mary shyly told them of her walk along the river with the young officer she had flirted with the night before.

"I'm glad you're enjoying yourselves," Liam nodded. "There's not a whole lot to keep you entertained out here."

Lunch passed without incident, and Liam excused himself to go back to work. Maeve announced that she needed a nap after such a large meal, so she and her husband went back to their quarters. When they had gone, Lana began clearing the table.

"What are you doing?" Mary asked. "Becca will do that."

Lana sat the two plates back down and faced Mary. "This is my house, Mary. I'll do whatever I want in it. And that includes clearing the table."

"I'm sorry," Mary stood up, offended. "I didn't mean that you couldn't if you wanted to. Just that you didn't *have* to."

"Actually, Mary, I do 'have' to. Becca is an old woman whose every step is painful, every move of her hands hurts. To watch her work while I'm just sitting there being waited on is more than I can live with. It's too shameful!" Picking up the plates again, she carried them to the counter.

"Are you saying that I should be ashamed?" Mary sounded defensive.

"No. I'm not saying anything about you. This is about me, about how I was raised. I do for myself and for those that can't do for themselves. It's just that simple. I'd go crazy being waited on hand and foot. I'm not used to it. I doubt I ever will be. If we're ever going to get along, you're going to have to let me jump up and do things, and I'm going to have to let you sit there and watch."

"Well, aren't you the little spitfire," Mary laughed to hide her discomfort.

"More than you know, Mary." Lana carried more dishes over to the counter, wondering how Mary would take the news that Lana had killed Apaches. When she got to the food, Lana asked, "Will you want to take some of this back with you?"

"What? Oh, no. Just throw it out if you don't want it."

"Throw it out? Wouldn't Becca and Toby and Jason like this?"

Mary looked surprised, like that thought had never crossed her mind.

"Am I not allowed to give it to them?" Lana asked. Again, Mary looked surprised. She had no idea. It just was never done.

Sighing in frustration, Lana kept back enough food for Liam's supper and then put the rest aside. "If Becca doesn't want this, I know the Army cook will.  But I'm *not* throwing out perfectly good food."

"I suppose things *are* different out here in no-man's land," Mary suggested.

"Very different," Lana agreed.  "We can't afford to waste anything, not food, not water, nothing."

\* \* \*

The O'Connell's visit lasted a week.   After than, Liam's observation that there was little to keep them entertained turned out to be too true.  Bored, restless, and already tired of her new officer, Mary pouted and whimpered and made life miserable because she wanted to go home *now.*

While things seemed fine on the surface, Lana was ready to help them pack.  The uneasy truce between her and her in-laws had been held together only by Liam's firm hand on the situation.

"I hoped to be here when your furniture arrived," Maeve complained.  "But I'll just have to be disappointed."

"It will be lovely, Mother.  You were very thoughtful to send it. I'll write to let you know when we get it."  Liam kissed her cheek and then helped her onto the wagon.

"Goodbye, Lana," Patrick smiled.  "I am so glad we got to meet you.  You make my son very happy."

"Thank you," Lana said.  "That is very kind of you to say so." He smiled once before he turned to shake Liam's hand.

"Be careful out there.  Come back home as soon as you can. Your family will be waiting."

"Yes, sir.  We will."

Lana walked around the wagon to Mary.  Looking up, she said, "I hope you have a safe trip back.  Goodbye."

"Yes.  Goodbye."  Mary nodded briefly and then turned to face straight ahead.

Lana shrugged her shoulders and walked to the back of the wagon. "I think I'm going to miss you most of all," she whispered to Becca.

"Me, too." Becca patted Lana's hand. "You're a good child. Take care of my boy for me."

"I will." Just as Lana said that, the wagon jerked forward and the O'Connells' trip home began.

Lana stood next to Liam and they waved goodbye until the wagon rolled out of sight. Then Liam put his arm around Lana's shoulders. They walked back to their quarters, shut the door, sat down at the table, and gave a collective sign of relief.

"Peace at last," Liam said as he surveyed their place. "I don't know what Mother was thinking of, bringing us that china. It will break the first time we move."

"She was just trying to help," Lana smiled. "She really loves you, you know."

"Yes, I know. It's just that, sometimes, I wish she didn't love me so much." Liam took her hand and turned to face her.

"Now that they're gone, I need to tell you something."

"Oh, really? What?"

"I'll be on scouting detail starting day after tomorrow."

"How long will you be gone?"

"Two weeks at least. Probably longer. You know how far I have to travel."

"Will you be going by my parents' place?"

"I don't know. Maybe. It just depends on what we find out there."

"Find? What are you looking for?"

"Trouble. The Kiowa are raiding all up and down the Brazos again. Horses, mainly. But that can change quickly."

"I know you'll be careful, but I'll still worry."

"I know."

"I'll write a letter to my folks just in case you do see them. I'll write it tonight."

"No. Not tonight. Tonight, I have plans for you."

"Oh, you do?" she asked coyly. "Whatever could they be?"

"I have to thank you for putting up with my family. And I want to apologize for my family."

"Honey, you don't have to thank me *or* apologize."

"Are you sure?" he said with a wicked gleam in his eye. "Because I had planned on thanking you at least twice."

"Twice?" She grinned. "Then you'd better get busy, soldier boy."

"Yes, m'am." He stood up and took her hand. "But before I get to that, there's something I need your opinion about."

"My opinion? About what?"

"Come here." He led her to the living room and sat her down on the sofa. Going into the bedroom, he returned a moment later, holding something in his hand. He sat beside her and picked up her left hand.

"I need to know which you like better." He kissed her hand and then held it up for her inspection. "Do you like your hand this way?" Opening his hand, he put a diamond wedding ring on her finger. "Or this way?"

"Oh, Liam! It's beautiful! Where did you get it?"

"I had it sent in from St. Louis. It came in the day after my folks arrived, but I wanted to wait until it was just us before I gave it to you." He looked at the ring for a moment and then looked up at her. "The diamond is circled by sapphires and rubies. Sapphires for my birth month and rubies for yours. Do you like it? If not, I can get something else."

"I love it! Don't you dare get me anything else." Leaning over, she kissed him provocatively. "Now, who needs to thank who?" she whispered.

# Chapter 39 — Utmost Contempt

Liam had been gone for several days, Lana's letter to her parents tucked in his saddlebag. The setting sun found Lana in a weird, unsettled frame of mind. She had been all day. Not hungry for supper, instead, she sat outside on the porch by her front door and watched the fort settle down for the night. Sentries changed; horses were brought into the stable and corral. Cooking smells from the officer's quarters and the mess hall wafted across the compound.

This was the first time that Lana had ever been alone — really alone. She had always lived at home or with Liam. Loneliness was new to her, and she didn't like it. Perhaps that's why she felt so unsettled.

Her thoughts went back to her first day there at the fort with her family. Nathan's and Christina's wedding had been a happy time for the Cooper family. But, even through all the festivities, Lana had felt a sadness from telling Two Hawks goodbye.

Then, before she even turned around twice, she got married herself. It all happened so fast! Now, here she sat on her own porch, swatting at mosquitoes, and wondering how she had gotten to this point. Liam loved her and her pa pushed her into Liam's arms. For what she thought were all the right reasons, she agreed to marry him, even though they both knew she didn't love him like he loved her.

Even in bed, as passionate and fulfilling as that was, she still felt that shade of sadness wrapped around her, almost like a second skin. It completely covered her. Lana felt that, somehow, she was cheating Liam out of what he truly deserved.

Sighing, she leaned back against the wall and looked up at the first stars twinkling in the eastern sky. Now that she had time to really think, there wasn't that much difference between the ways the Kiowa and the O'Connells lived.

Slavery, captives. No difference there. One sold slaves in Mexico City, the other on the eastern seaboard. Both did it for commerce.

Her parents had argued that she would have difficulty being accepted by another culture.

But, after what she had just been through with her in-laws, Lana doubted that Two Hawks' family could have been any harder or more distant, or their culture more foreign.

Education? She might not know how to skin a buffalo, but she also didn't know which fork went where on a formal dining table.

More than one wife? The Kiowa's reasons for doing that made sense to her. In the white world, a widow had to fend for herself any way she could. Remarrying anyone, cruel or otherwise, was one option. Prostitution another. Starvation a third. There weren't many good choices. At least the Kiowa solution was compassionate.

Women didn't have a say in the government of either society, but the Kiowa had a balance of power. The Kiowa women owned the property and homes. White women rarely owned anything.

As her thoughts whirled around and around, back and forth, one unsettling realization kept bobbing to the surface. What if she had rejected Two Hawks for reasons that didn't really matter? Lana had to face those reasons with Liam anyway. If that was the case, and she was afraid it was, then she had married the wrong man.

How many times had she been in Liam's bed, making love with him, when the thought of Two Hawks haunted her?  It happened more and more lately, and they hadn't been married three months yet.  This couldn't be good.

Feeling more unsettled than ever, Lana stood and went inside to escape the ravenous mosquitoes.

\* \* \*

Two Hawks, with his band of warriors, had been stealing horses and burning homesteads all along the Brazos.  The unusual ferocity of this band created its own storm and, the more they razed the countryside, the more the outcry came pouring into the military.  Liam had been sent to deal with the Kiowa band, but he had no idea Two Hawks was with it.

The cavalry trailed the raiding party for days, finding charred remains of homesteads and fields along the way, but never getting close enough to give chase.  That all changed the second week out.

"Lieutenant," one of the scouts reported back to camp that night.  "We've spotted a small band of Kiowa warriors with several horses. There are no women or children with them."

"That's probably who we're after, then."  Liam stood and signaled for his sergeant and the scout to follow him. They stepped to the fringe of camp for a private strategy meeting.

"Should we wait until morning to move in?" the sergeant asked.

"No.  We'll take them tonight, while it's dark.  If we're this close to their camp, they don't know we're here," Liam reasoned.

"Surprise 'em," the scout nodded in agreement.

"Exactly.  Now, what's the land like around their camp?" the lieutenant asked.

The scout gave as detailed a report as he could, squatting down and drawing in the dirt. Within the hour, Liam had an attack mapped out and the sergeant organized the men.

Under cover of darkness, Liam sent four of his men toward the Kiowas guarding the horses. The rest quietly encircled the sleeping camp, being careful not to arouse anyone until the last minute.

When the soldiers were in position, Liam gave his silent signal by raising and then quickly lowering his saber. The Kiowa guards were killed while the rest of the soldiers galloped into the camp, quickly capturing the warriors.

Two Hawks leapt to his feet at the first sound of trouble, but, before he could reach his rifle, there was another pointed directly at his chest by a mounted soldier. Two Hawks backed up one step, his hands raised in defeat. Looking over his shoulder, he saw that his entire band was either staring down the barrel of a gun or lying dead.

Liam slowly rode in a wide circle around the captured Kiowa. When he saw Two Hawks, he stopped, looking down at the defiant young warrior. The two men stared at each other for a long moment and then, with the utmost contempt on his face, Two Hawks spit on the ground in front of Liam.

Without saying anything to Two Hawks, Liam turned to his sergeant. "Secure them for the night. We'll leave at first light."

"Yes, sir."

"Set double watch as well."

"Yes, sir."

* * *

It took five days of hard travel for the patrol to reach the fort with their captives. During that time, Liam and Two Hawks rarely came into direct contact with each other, though they were each acutely aware of the other's presence. Liam worried about bringing Two Hawks so close to Lana, about what the warrior would do if he saw her. Liam didn't know if the Kiowa still wanted Lana, or if he had moved on with someone else. Liam fervently hoped for the latter.

* * *

Two Hawks watched Liam, also wondering about the soldier's wife. Had Nathan told him the truth? Were T'on Ma and this soldier really married? Two Hawks couldn't keep his thoughts away from the last time he'd seen her. That early spring morning had been one of the worst days of his life. One minute, she was lying in his arms, covering him with her kisses and soft words, their whole future bright before them, and the next, she was telling him they couldn't be together — ever.

Two Hawks' spirit still reverberated from his cry of denial and pain that day. Her words had shaken him, left him faithless. Then, to hear of her marriage so soon after filled him with a rage that he made felt all along the Brazos. Anyone doubting that could ask the survivors of his raids. They could point to charred, gutted homes and sad graves as evidence of his wrath.

As the days passed and Ft. Worth grew closer, Two Hawks' anger became more focused. Instead of being angry at the world, he was now angry with the bluecoat, O'Connell. If he could have gotten free, Two Hawks would have ripped out Liam's beating heart! But he couldn't get free. The restraints were iron, not rope. They held his wrists during the day, and his wrists *and* ankles at night. During the day, the Kiowas' horses were tied together in one long line while a guard rode beside each prisoner.

In his angry rebellion, Two Hawks refused the soldiers' food. Every morning, they offered him hardtack. Every evening, a soldier held out jerky and hot coffee. And every morning, every evening, Two Hawks refused the meal by an arrogant turn of his head.

"Still no food?" Liam asked his sergeant on their last night out.

253

"No, sir." The sergeant scratched his head. "Do you think he's trying to starve himself?"

"I don't know. I wouldn't put it past him, though." Liam stood up and stretched. "Let me go talk to him."

"You speak Kiowa, sir?"

"No. He speaks English." Not waiting to explain to the surprised sergeant, Liam approached Two Hawks, who sat on the ground with his warriors.

"Are you not eating because you're ill?" Liam began.

Two Hawks glared up at Liam with feral, hate-filled eyes, and then looked straight ahead.

"Because, if you're ill," Liam continued, "we'll get you a doctor."

"I am not ill," Two Hawks stated flatly.

"All right. I guess you just don't like Army food," Liam chuckled. "You wouldn't be the first."

Two Hawks remained motionless.

Liam stood over him for a few silent moments. "You and I have come a long way since I pulled that arrow out of your back. I was glad you lived. I was surprised, though, when I saw you with the Apaches stealing those women, especially after you had just rescued Lana from those same men." He waited, looking for a reaction, needing to know how Two Hawks felt about her. Seeing none, he continued. "Maybe I shouldn't say Lana. Maybe I should call her by the name you gave her. T'on Ma."

"Don't say her name!" Two Hawks growled. "It is bad to speak of the dead."

"She isn't dead."

"She is to me!"

* * *

When they arrived in the middle of the afternoon, the Kiowa were pulled off their horses and led to the stockade. It hadn't been designed for comfort or privacy. The stockade was one large rectangle, the bottom half consisting of rough-hewn logs lying horizontally on each other, the top half, closely spaced vertical steel bars. The jail only had one door, and it faced the compound. Prisoners were on view at all times. All eight of the Kiowa prisoners were in irons. Once safely at the fort, their wrists were unchained as they were placed, one at a time, into the stockade.

Their arrival caused quite a commotion throughout the fort, and even Lana, on the outskirts, heard the news. Stepping to her porch to watch, she shielded her eyes from the sun and stared at the knot of cavalry and Kiowa and horses and dust. At first, it looked like organized confusion to her. But, as the irons were removed, a soldier jerked one of the Kiowa forward and turned him around so that he faced her. Lana stopped breathing. Two Hawks! If he saw her, he didn't show it.

Flushed and excited, Lana hurried back inside. Knowing Liam would come in at any second, she tried to calm down. Liam couldn't know what an effect Two Hawks had on her. Having something to do might help. With that idea, she made a fresh pot of coffee. Just as she set it on the stove, the door opened and Liam came in, hot, dirty, and wanting her.

"Hello, beautiful," he smiled, holding his arms out to her.

"You're home!" She jumped into his embrace and laughed as he covered her in kisses.

"I'm home for just a minute. I still have to file my report with the commander. Then I'll be home for good."

"All right." Lana smiled up into his eyes. "I'll fix us a really nice dinner. What would you like?"

"Let's see," Liam smacked his lips, trying to decide. "What would I like? Hmmm. Truthfully, all I want is you. Tell you what. Instead of fixing dinner, why don't you fix me a hot bath and then help me take it?" He nuzzled her hair suggestively. "Does that sound good to you?"

"You're not back for *five* minutes," she played like she was fussing at him.

"Five? I'm moving too slow, then." He laughed and then leaned down to kiss her, long and slow, moving his hands across her, enjoying the feel of her. Sighing, he stepped back. "I'd better go now, or I won't leave."

Once he was gone, Lana dutifully heated up water for her husband's bath. But her thoughts wandered to the stockade. Was Two Hawks hurt? Or hungry? Did he know she was here?

Liam came back within the hour. Stripping out of his trail-dirty clothes, he sat in the large washtub in front of the stove while Lana poured a pitcher of warm water over his head.

"Ah," he sighed. "This feels so good. I hope I can scrub off the worst of it." Reaching for a bar of soap, he began washing his hair and face.

"Did you get to see Pa?" she asked anxiously.

"Oh, honey, I'm sorry, but no. There simply wasn't enough time." Seeing the disappointment on her face, he reassured her. "As soon as another patrol goes out that direction, I'll send your letter with them. All right?"

"All right. I guess that's all we can do. I miss them so much, though."

"I know you do, sweetheart. I know."

"I saw you brought back some prisoners," Lana broached the touchy subject. "Kiowa?"

"Yep. The very ones we were looking for."

"Were any of them hurt?"

"No. We had to kill a few when we took their camp, but none of the others are hurt."

"Well, that's good." She reached for a sponge and began scrubbing his back. "What's going to happen to them?"

"I don't know. Hanging, probably. They've burned out a lot of homesteads and killed a few people."

"Hanging! Without a trial?"

"A trial?" Liam laughed at that. "No. I don't think there's going to be a trial."

Liam looked over his shoulder at her. "Lana, I guess I ought to tell you that Yi Ceŋtas is one of them." When she didn't say anything, he continued. "As a matter of fact, he's the leader of this raiding party. He's the one that's been causing so much trouble all spring."

"Oh." Lana moved around and began methodically scrubbing his chest, her mind not on the task at hand, but rather on a question — was her rejection of Two Hawks the cause of the raids, the cause of those deaths? Breaking her worried reverie, she asked, "Have they had anything to eat?"

"I don't know. I'm sure the cook will give them something."

"But will it be edible?" Lana asked. "He'll give them rancid leftovers and bad water."

"Lana," Liam sounded concerned, "Just leave it be. The Army will take care of them."

"Please, let me at least take them a decent meal. I owe him that much."

"Him? Yi Ceŋtas?" Liam scowled. "No, Lana. Leave him alone. If he sees you, there is no telling what he'll do."

"But maybe, if I talked to him, it would do some good."

Liam shook his head. His wife simply didn't understand how a rejected man would take a visit from her, especially under these circumstances."

"I wish you wouldn't," was all he said, knowing that he couldn't stop her if she was determined.

"Just a meal, Liam. Please?"

"Only if I go with you." Liam hoped that Two Hawks would refuse her food as well, making his feelings very clear to Lana.

"Of *course* you'll go with me. I'd be too nervous otherwise."

"All right. You fix them something to eat while I get dressed."

"Thank you, sweetheart. I'll repay you for this when we get home."

Liam only scowled as he reached for a towel and stood up, sending water splashing across the floor.

## Chapter 40 — Shadow of Doubt

The O'Connells walked across the compound, Liam carrying a basket of food and coffee cups and Lana carrying her coffee pot. As they approached the stockade, the guard saluted Liam and stepped back. Liam set the basket on the ground and turned to Lana.

"You sure about this?"

"Yes. It's just a meal."

Lana took the venison and cornbread she had made and walked up to the bars.

*"Food,"* she said in Kiowa. *"I've brought food."*

One of the warriors stood up, curious about the white woman who spoke Kiowa.

*"Oh, it's you, Water Woman,"* he announced, surprised. Taking some food from her, he turned back. *"Isn't she your woman?"* he asked Two Hawks.

Two Hawks had been sleeping, propped up in the corner, but at the warrior's words, he jerked awake and looked out. There, in the darkness, stood a familiar silhouette. He stood and walked slowly to the bars, where he waited until everyone else had food. Then he approached her.

*"What are* you *doing here?"* he growled as his eyes flickered toward Liam and then back to her.

"Hello, Yi Ceŋtas." She spoke in English so that Liam would understand. "Food."

When he shook his head in refusal, she offered it again. *"Please,"* she said in Kiowa. *"I brought this for you. I know you're hungry."*

The angry man almost refused a second time, but something in her eyes stopped him. He'd seen that look of love hundreds of times before, but this time it couldn't be true. She loved someone else, not him — didn't she? Even so, her expression softened his resolve. T'on Ma had made this food by her own hand, and brought it because he was here. He sensed that she wouldn't have done this for any of the others. Reluctantly, he took the offered food from her. Liam scowled as he watched, an alarm going off in his mind.

Next, Lana poured them all coffee, adding sugar to each tin cup. The cups just fit through the bars and were taken by eager hands. Sweet coffee was a treat at any time. But in these circumstances, it only proved once again how strange the white man was. Who gave treats to prisoners?

*"Is it true you married him?"* Two Hawks nodded toward Liam.

*"Yes."*

*"Do you love him then so quickly after me?"* He sounded contemptuous.

*"No."*

*"What?"* He stepped back in his surprise.

*"Only you,"* she said softly in Kiowa. *"Always you."*

"What are you saying?" Liam asked as he stepped over to them.

"He's asking me if you and I are married. And I told him yes."

"Oh, well, let the guard get their cups. You've fed them. Now, let's go home and feed me."

"All right, sweetheart."

Liam picked up the empty basket and the coffeepot in one hand and put his other around Lana's shoulders. Two Hawks watched them walk away, more confused than ever. Had he just heard right? She loved him? Only? And always? He didn't know if his heart could take this kind of puzzle.

\* \* \*

Back home, Liam finally had Lana where he wanted her, in his arms, lying beside him, holding him.

"I missed you so much," he whispered. "I used to like going on scouting details, because somewhere in that time, I knew I'd be seeing you. But now, I don't like them at all."

"I missed you, too," she smiled up at him. "I've never been alone before like this. I don't like it, either."

"My poor baby," he murmured. "I'm here now." He slipped her nightgown over her head and then began moving his hands over her in a way that he knew excited them both. While he was rocking her, kissing her, he looked down at her face. Her eyes were closed and a solitary tear shimmered, hung on her dark eyelashes." Liam stopped and brushed the tear away.

"What's wrong? Why are you crying?"

"I don't know," she told him. "I guess I missed you more than I realized."

"Oh, woman. Here. Let me take care of that." He continued making love to her, but as aroused as he was, he moved slower, with more deliberation, more tenderness, wanting that tear to disappear for good. It took all that he knew to do, but finally, she arched her back and held him tightly, moving with him, her head thrown back as she moaned.

"There you go, baby," he murmured as he watched her face. "There you go. That's what I want to see." With that, he moved faster, harder until he also moaned and let go.

A few minutes later, he lay on his side, his chest against her back, his arm across her hip, almost asleep. But a muffled noise made him alert. Listening closely, he realized it was Lana trying to hide her tears. He pulled her back to face him.

"What is it? Something's wrong."

"No. I'm fine."

"You are not. You were crying earlier, too. Talk to me, please." They lay together quietly for a moment. "Maybe you're pregnant," he suggested. "I've heard that women get moody then."

"I wish that was it," she smiled. "But my monthly visitor was here while you were gone."

"Oh." Liam frowned. "I don't like seeing you sad. Are you sure you don't know what's wrong."

"I'm sorry, sweetheart, but I don't." She reached up and kissed him. "Now, quit worrying about my silliness and go to sleep. I know you're tired."

"Goodnight, then. Sweet dreams." Liam adjusted his pillow and was soon asleep, but Lana closed her eyes and prayed to be forgiven for telling her first lie to Liam. She knew exactly why she was in tears. She had just made love to the wrong man. Her man was only a few yards away, locked in the stockade, waiting to be hanged!

* * *

The next morning, Lana presented Liam with a false cheeriness and a delicious breakfast. Unaware of her true state of mind, he kissed her goodbye and walked out the door to work. As she cleaned up the kitchen, the turmoil in her conscience came to a boil. What was she doing to Liam? What was she going to do about Two Hawks? Her mother's voice filled her mind. *"Don't take vows you can't keep."*

A plate slipped out of her soapy hands and went crashing to the floor. After staring at the mess for a moment, she threw herself into a kitchen chair and, head on folded arms on the table, burst into guilty, angry, confused tears. If Two Hawks hadn't been captured — if she hadn't seen him again — maybe she could have continued her well-meant façade with Liam. But Two Hawks' nearness jolted her back into reality, almost drowning her in her need for him. Knowing that she could never stop loving him, she wondered if she had the strength to ignore that love. It would shatter Liam into a million pieces if he ever found out. He deserved so much better.

Two Hawks watched all day long for her. She never came. But Liam did. Walking up with an interpreter, he began telling the Kiowa what was in store for them. Stealing horses from other tribes was of no concern to the soldiers. However, burning out homesteads and killing the settlers was, and they were to be hanged in two days' time for their crimes.

The Kiowa braves shouted in their anger, shaking the bars, demanding to be set free, or at least to be allowed to die fighting, not swinging at the end of a shameful rope.

During the furor, Liam approached Two Hawks, wondering why the warrior stood quietly, seemingly unaffected by the announcement of his eminent death.

Knowing that the soldiers intended to kill him, to kill them all, Two Hawks wanted Liam to know, even in death, Two Hawks was still victorious. "Lana," Two Hawks said in English as he stepped up to the bars. "Lana is mine."

Liam laughed at that.

Two Hawks shook his head, "Even if I am dead, she is mine. Her heart is mine. Forever!"

Liam turned and walked away, not believing a word of it. But the smallest shadow of doubt entered his mind and took residence there. Just a few days before, Lana had been dead to Two Hawks. What had changed? And why?

* * *

At dinner that night, Lana seemed tense. After the meal, she picked up their plates and took a step toward the kitchen counter before she turned to face Liam.

"Is it true the Kiowa are going to hang day after tomorrow?"

Liam sighed. There was no keeping a secret in a fort this small. "Yes, it's true."

Lana turned back and walked to the washbasin, angrily throwing the plates in it, not caring if they broke.

When she came back for the rest of the dishes, Liam stopped her. "That bothers you, doesn't it?" he growled.

"You know it does! They haven't had a trial or anything. It's not right!"

"Would it bother you this much if Yi Ceŋtas wasn't one of them?" Liam's anger was clear in his tone.

His question stopped her. "Honestly?" She looked down at him, worry and frustration in her eyes. "Probably not. Is that what you wanted to hear?"

"I wanted to hear the truth!" he snapped, standing up. "And now I have. He told me today that he has your heart. I laughed at the time, but now I wonder."

"Liam, we talked about this before we got married. Remember?"

"Yes. I know. But now you're my wife, my lover. I thought your feelings had changed for me, that you were in love with me. It certainly feels that way when we're in bed together."

"Liam, I don't know what you want me to say."

"I want you to say that you love me. Only me! That Yi Ceŋtas is in your past. I am your future." He looked down at her, his eyes filled with so much pain that she couldn't stand to see it. Standing in front of him, tears in her eyes, she said nothing, not wanting to lie to him, and yet, not wanting to hurt him with the truth. Her silence turned his pain to fury.

"You know, I was disappointed at first when I found out you weren't pregnant. Maybe it's a blessing in disguise." Liam stomped across the room and slammed the front door on his way out.

## Chapter 41 — Gallows

Lana stared at the door as it quivered in place. Numbly, she finished cleaning the kitchen, then she grabbed her shawl and went to look for Liam. On a hunch, she went to the Bachelor Officers' Quarters and knocked on the door of one of Liam's friends. When the door opened, cigar smoke poured out in a thick, blue-gray cloud.

"Is Liam here?" she asked, waving her hand in front of her face, trying to breathe.

Speaking over his shoulder, the officer said, "Hey, O'Connell. It's your wife."

Liam stepped to the door, a cigar in his mouth, a shot of whiskey in his hand.

"Can we talk? Please?" she asked.

"Why? Have you *finally* got something to say?" His sarcasm felt like a slap across her face. He'd never spoken to her like this before.

"Please?" She stretched her hand out toward him.

A debate raged in his mind as he stared at her. Part of him wanted to slam the door in her face, but another part wanted to grab her up and hold her so tightly that she'd never leave. Finally, giving her a sharp look, he stepped outside and closed the door behind him.

"They're just starting a game, so make it quick." Liam's words cut deeply, as he had intended.

"You're so angry right now that maybe this should wait." She briefly touched his shoulder, then turned to walk away, unwilling to be bullied, but not wanting to continue the fight, either.

He watched her take a few steps and then sighed in resignation. "No, Lana. Come back. Let's talk." Throwing the cigar down onto the dirt, he walked up to her, drained the whiskey from the shot glass, then nodded. "All right. I'm ready. What do you want to say?"

She looked around the compound, wondering if this was a conversation for such a public place. But, from the expression on his face, she realized he wasn't going anywhere with her in his present mood.

"Liam, I've been so upset at seeing Yi Centas again that I haven't done right by you. I should have answered you after dinner. I am very sorry. Please forgive me for that. I'll answer you now, if you want." When he didn't say anything, she went on. "*You* are my future. He is my past. I am your wife and that's the end of it." She put a hand on his arm. "Just understand that I am upset that he is being hanged. I can't pretend that I'm not."

Watching Liam for a moment in the dark, she smiled sadly. "Come home when you're ready." She left him standing there, filled with questions he was afraid to ask and even more afraid to hear the answers to. In spite of her words of reassurance, she hadn't said the one thing he desperately needed to hear — that she loved him, *only* him.

Lana went home and got ready for bed. She lay there for quite some time, listening to the silent house.

Liam opened his friend's door, put the shot glass on the floor beside it, and left. He walked for a long time behind the stables and the Officers' Quarters. What was he going to do? Lana would stay with him, would be his wife. But he knew, he *knew*, that Two

Hawks was right. Lana's heart belonged to another man, and that was *killing* him.

Not sure how long he had been outside, he finally went home. Liam sat on the bed, and removed his boots and shirt. Still sitting there, he held his head in his hands, feeling lost and sad. Why couldn't she love him with her whole heart? Why? It would be so easy!

Lana's soft touch on his back let him know she was awake. He twisted around to look at her, his sorrow evident.

"Come here, sweetheart," she whispered. Reaching for him, she pulled him to her and simply held him.

"I love you so much, Lana. I don't know what I'll do if I lose you."

"I'm not going anywhere. It's going to be all right."

\* \* \*

The sound of hammering woke them both the next day. Lana sat up in bed, trying to figure out the noise. She rose quickly and walked to the window, but when she looked out, she jumped back as if she had been hit.

"Gallows! They're building gallows."

"They'll have to hurry if they're going to be ready by tomorrow morning," Liam said matter-of-factly.

Lana didn't want to reopen the previous night's discussion, so she went into the kitchen to start breakfast. Her hands shook as she tried to measure out the coffee beans. They spilled across the counter and bounced along the floor. Frowning, she reached for the broom to sweep them up, but Liam came over and took it from her hands.

"I'll get this. You go ahead with the coffee."

"All right." Her second attempt was successful, and coffee soon boiled on the stove. Breakfast was a quiet time at the table, but noisy in the compound. Lana felt that the sawing and hammering would drive her crazy.

After breakfast, Liam rose to go to work. He kissed Lana's cheek rather than her lips. "I'll be home for lunch," he told her as he left.

Ignoring the dirty dishes, Lana walked to the window and looked out. Soldiers scrambled around, many without shirts, carrying lumber and saws and ropes and planes. A distraction. She needed a distraction to get her through the day. But what?

Perhaps she could go foraging like she did at home. She picked up a basket and a knife and went to tell Liam where she was going. After that, she walked away from the fort and out into the wilderness, looking for rosehip bushes or wild onions or anything she could find. It didn't matter what she gathered, as long as she was away from that noise!

To some extent, her plan worked, but she had to be back to fix Liam's lunch. That meal was as strained has breakfast had been, with neither of them saying anything of importance. After Liam returned to work, she tried sewing and then reading and then making pies from some berries she had gathered. Keeping busy helped, and she could almost tune out the workmen's noise. But, late that afternoon, a new noise took the place of hammering — a noise that sent a deadly chill down her spine — the noise of the gallows' trap floor being tested.

That did it! She had to do *something* to save Two Hawks! She *had* to! Biting her lip, she wondered what one woman could do among so many watchful soldiers. Lana wandered from the kitchen to the living room and the bedroom, looking for an idea, any idea. She walked to the front window and then to the back, searching. Then a light came to her eyes. Maybe. Just maybe she had a plan, but it relied on luck as much as anything else.

Stepping outside, she strolled across the compound toward the gallows. As she walked, she inspected the ground. In a few minutes, she found what she was looking for — a bent nail.

Smiling secretively, she put it in her apron pocket and hurried home.

After dinner and after sundown, Lana told Liam that she had a headache from all the noise throughout the day and that she wanted to turn in early.

"I understand," Liam sympathized. "I'll try and be quiet so you can rest."

"Is that game still going?"

"Game?"

"Yeah. The one from last night."

"It's still going. Why?"

"You could go there for a while until you're ready to turn in. It would certainly be less boring than sitting here being quiet."

"You wouldn't mind?" he asked, surprised.

"Not tonight. Really."

"All right. I'll only lose ten dollars. Tops. I promise." He smiled when she smiled at that. Perhaps, after tomorrow, after Two Hawks was 'gone,' things would ease up between them. Kissing her once quickly, he grabbed his money and headed to the game. Lana blew out the lamps, plunging the house in darkness, and walked to the front window, watching Liam cross the compound. When he was inside his friend's quarters, she put her plan into action.

After changing quickly into her nightgown, she twisted her hair up into a high bun. Next, she pulled on Liam's uniform shirt and trousers over her gown, and then she put on his cap. Making sure the bed covers were turned down, she took the key to the stockade off his key ring. She raised the back window and carefully looked around. To her relief, no one was in sight. She climbed through the window and pulled it almost closed before she checked again for the sentry. One had just reached a far building and was turning the corner. Scurrying behind Officers' Quarters, Lana ran from shadow to shadow until she made her way to the back of the stockade, where she knelt, watching again for the sentries.

Still kneeling in the shadows, she spoke in Kiowa in a low voice. "Two Hawks?"

Nothing.

"Two Hawks? It's me."

"Water Woman?" he whispered back.

"I'm here to get you out."

"All right. How?"

"I have a key to unlock the door. You unlock it and give me back the key. Wait for a little while before you escape so that I have time to get back home."

"I unlock the door. Give you the key and wait."

"Yes."

Hearing a soft noise, he looked at the bars and saw her hand waving a large key. He took it from her. "Do you have horses?" he asked.

"No. You'll have to steal some."

"All right."

"Also," she continued, "leave this nail on the floor by the door when you go."

"A nail? Why?"

"There's no time to explain. Just do it."

"All right." Two Hawks reached out a second time and took the bent nail. With the key and nail in his possession, he motioned to his band to be still. Going to the stockade door, he checked for guards. One stood at the other end of the stockade with his back to them. Two Hawks slipped his hand through the bars, quietly unlocked the door and then placed the nail just inside. When he came back to Lana, he simply dropped the key to the ground beside her.

She had planned to leave quickly, but couldn't go without seeing him. Checking over her shoulder for the sentry and seeing none, she stood up. Two Hawks stood just inches away, his strong face in shadow.

"I love you, Water Woman." His hand reached through the bars to caress her face.

"Still? After all that I've done?" She held his hand against her cheek.

"Yes. Always."

"I love you so much — but I have to stay with my husband."

"For now."

She couldn't risk staying any longer. "Goodbye."

"Goodbye, my heart."

He watched her slip away, wishing he could take her with him. It wouldn't be just his escape. It would be theirs. Even though she hadn't said, he knew she was in her own prison — a prison without bars. All those dreams of her crying in the night had told him so.

Lana hurried home, slipped in through the back window and closed it like it had been before she left. Taking off Liam's uniform, she carefully put it away, and put the key back on the ring. Her heart raced, her throat felt dry. She needed to look like she had been asleep. Unpinning her hair, she slipped into bed, willing herself to calm down as she mentally went over all of her steps. No, she hadn't forgotten anything.

Several minutes later, an alarm sounded. Lana heard the sound of shots and of men yelling. "The prisoners are escaping! Stop them!"

Lana closed her eyes tightly, hoping Two Hawks wasn't hurt. The sound of hooves thundering crossing the compound filled the night. Lana's heart jumped to her throat. *What had she done?* Had she sent Two Hawks to his death tonight instead of in the morning?

Somehow, the Kiowa got away, though one guard was severely wounded in the process. The melee that ensued was noisy and confusing.

* * *

When Liam heard the cry go out that Two Hawks had escaped, the tiniest suspicion leapt to his mind. Liam rushed into the house, looking for Lana, and was relieved to find her home, in bed.

"I suppose you've heard," he said excitedly.

She rolled over to look at him. "I heard a lot of shooting. What happened?"

"Yi Ceŋtas — all of them — have escaped." He hurriedly changed into his uniform and grabbed his keys.

*"What?"* She sat up, hoping she looked sufficiently surprised to be believable.

"I've got to go. I don't know when I'll be back." He stopped long enough to give her one quick kiss.

"Be careful," she called after him.

And that was it. Liam once again chased Two Hawks across the high plains of Texas. Lana fell back against her pillow, worried sick over both of them.

* * *

While giving Lana enough time to return home, Two Hawks thought about his next step. Then, drawing his warriors into a tight circle, he quietly explained his plan. It was good that Ft. Worth had no walls around it. There would be no gate to open.

The eight braves were ready. As soon as the sentry faced away and began rolling a cigarette, one of them snuck out the door and picked up a manacle hanging from the stockade wall. With a huge effort, he struck the guard on the head with the leg iron, knocking him unconscious. They quickly dragged the soldier into the stockade, where he was stripped of his uniform. Within two minutes, a Kiowa donned the uniform and resumed the guard's position outside the prison.

From his vantage, the new 'guard' checked for all the other sentries. At his nod, the first warrior stepped through the door and sprinted, bent low, toward the corral, hiding among the horses. A few minutes passed before a second warrior safely made his way to the corral and knelt by his horse. Soon, all the prisoners were free, had picked out their horses, and waited. They didn't need bridles or even halters. Their horses were trained by knee commands, which made the escape easier.

The new guard casually strolled toward the corral and unfastened the gate. Throwing off the hated uniform, he jumped on his horse and, at that signal, all eight made their getaway, sending their horses flying across the compound, stampeding the others with them.

They hadn't gotten far when a shout went up and gunfire filled the night.

"Ride!" Two Hawks yelled.

After twenty minutes of hot pursuit, Two Hawks gave the hand signal and all eight warriors split up, running in eight different directions. In the dark of night, let the bluecoats find eight trails of men who left no trail!

\* \* \*

As Liam and his men gave chase, the fort commander began asking a lot of hard questions of the Officer of the Day. The Kiowas' escape had been too easy. It didn't take long, though, for them to find the bent nail by the stockade door.

"I imagine they used this to pick the lock," the officer reasoned.

"But where'd they even get a nail?" the commander asked.

"That wouldn't have been difficult," the officer shook his head. "There are nails everywhere from building the gallows."

Satisfied with that explanation, the commander decided against any further investigation. Two Hawks wasn't the only one who had just had a narrow escape.

## Chapter 42 — You Win

Liam returned late the next afternoon, tired, hungry and mad. "Well, we didn't get them," he announced as he slumped onto a dining chair. "I suppose you're happy about that."

"Oh, honey, don't. Please." Lana handed him a glass of beer. "I'm happy that you're safe and here with me."

"Really?" He sounded skeptical. "Even though you love someone else?"

"Liam, I love *you*." She touched his face. "I always worry about you when you're away, but this time, I almost made myself sick. It was too dangerous."

To prove her point, she sat on his lap and kissed him. Pulling back to look at him, she saw hope in his eyes — hope that she was telling the truth. She leaned in again and kissed him slowly, provocatively, sliding her hands around his neck. At first, he let himself be kissed, but after a moment, he began to respond, his hands moving around her waist, his lips sensuously kissing hers.

"I've told you this once before," he said. "Don't kiss me like this if you don't mean it."

"Oh, I mean it. I *love* the way you love me, Liam. I *need* the way you love me."

She had done all she could for Two Hawks. Now she needed to do all she could for her husband. What she needed to do for herself didn't matter. Not any more.

Taking Liam's hand, she led him to their bed. She sat him down and began unbuttoning his shirt. Wordlessly, he watched her, needing her to love him, to heal his heart from its doubt and worry and fear. Lana straightened up to stand in front of him, and took down her hair, shaking it loose around her shoulders and down her back.

Kneeling, she took off his boots, then unfastened his belt and pulled off his pants as she reassured him. "Liam, don't ever doubt that I'm here for you." Standing back up, she seductively removed her clothes, letting him watch as she revealed more of her body, from her shoulders peeking from under her camisole, to her breasts, her navel, her hips, her long legs.

Pushing him back on the bed, she straddled his lap and leaned forward, her hair falling against his chest. "You are the only man who has ever touched me. I need you to touch me now." She placed his hands on her breasts while she sat straight up, closing her eyes, offering herself to him.

Liam watched her, knowing she was loving him the best way she knew how. He wondered if it would be enough. If he had any pride at all, he should walk out, refusing to be anyone's second best. But when it came to her, he was shameless. Second, third, or fourth best. It simply didn't matter.

As if suddenly making up his mind, he moved his hands to her waist and jerked her against him, rolling her underneath him. Not waiting for her, he took her — hard — desperately — needing her so much that it frightened him. Lana lay beneath him, holding him, letting this be just for him. Finally, spent, he laid his face against hers and whispered in her ear, "You win. Whatever you want. Just don't leave me."

When she looked into his eyes, his joy was gone. "Oh, Liam, no!" she cried. "Look what I've done to you. I am so sorry." She held his face, covering it in kisses while she cried. "I need you to be happy. *Please* be happy." Her tears broke his heart, but there was nothing he could do.

* * *

Two Hawks thundered across the plains, leading his raiding party back to their summer camp. It wouldn't be safe to stay there very long, but he needed to let his family know that he was all right. With every mile that passed, even with soldiers in pursuit, he felt his spirit grow lighter. Talking with T'on Ma, hearing that she still loved him, brought joy back into his eyes. Nothing else mattered to him now. They would be together. He didn't know how or when, but he *knew* it would be so.

When they returned to their camp, Two Hawks' band was smaller than when they left. The soldiers had killed four. There were no horses, either. With nothing to celebrate, the band entered camp quietly. Two Hawks stopped in front of his mother's tipi and dismounted.

"You're back!" Gray Dove exclaimed, smiling up at him. "Come in. Your father will want to talk with you."

Two Hawks went in and sat beside his father.

"You missed a buffalo hunt," Many Deer told him. "We could have used your arrows."

"I'm sorry. I'll be there for the next one."

"I don't see any new horses."

"No. We had some, but they were taken."

"By who? Osage? Kickapoo?"

"Soldiers."

"Soldiers? What do they want with your horses?"

"They didn't want our horses. They wanted us."

Two Hawks related his capture and imprisonment. "They were going to hang all of us. They even built the stand."

"What happened?" Gray Dove couldn't help but interrupt.

"Water Woman helped us escape by giving us a key to the jail."

"What? *Water Woman?*" Gray Dove scowled. Just when she thought she'd heard the last of her, T'on Ma showed up again.

"Yes. She was very brave. It was her husband that caught us."

Many Deer shook his head. "Her husband catches you and takes your horses. He plans to hang you, but she helps you escape?"

"Yes."

"Why? If he is her husband?" Many Deer truly did not understand. He would be well within his rights to beat a wife for such a thing.

"Because she loves me. She has always loved me."

"No. If she loves you, she wouldn't have married another."

"I don't care what you say. She loves me. I know it."

"White people are crazy!" Many Deer exclaimed. "I already knew they were crazy, but this...?"

"It doesn't matter if she loves you or not," Gray Dove reasoned. "She is married to someone else, so you need to find a nice Kiowa girl and get married, too."

Two Hawks smiled at his mother, knowing full well who that 'nice Kiowa girl' was.

"Four of us didn't return," he said to change the subject. "I need to speak with their families."

"Of course. I'll go with you." Many Deer stepped outside with his son and headed to the first family, bearing the sad news.

* * *

It was late, the moon already high in the sky. Two Hawks walked away from the camp, knowing he would have to leave early in the morning to protect his village from the soldiers who would inevitably come looking for him. But tonight, he had a few hours of rest, time to himself. As he stood there, he heard someone approach from the camp. Turning, he recognized Corn Flower, even in the night.

"I need to ask you something," she said. "Before you leave again."

"All right." He looked down at her, waiting.

She took his hand, holding it in both of hers, before she spoke. "Iron Crow has asked me to marry him. Before I answer him, I need to be sure of one thing."

"Me?"

"Yes."

"Corn Flower, I have told you before not to wait for me."

"I know. But are you sure? Absolutely sure? Things change."

"I am very sure. I already have a woman. She's not here with me yet. But she will be. So marry Iron Crow. Be happy."

Releasing his hand, Corn Flower stepped closer to him, held his face in both hands and kissed him.

"That is as close to happy as I will ever be, but I won't trouble you about this any more." Taking a few steps back toward the camp, she stopped and turned for a moment. "Be safe." With that, she was gone.

Two Hawks stood beside the river, looking across it to the western horizon. He let his mind return to T'on Ma. Seeing her the first time at the fort exhilarated him, although he wouldn't admit it to her or to anyone. Just the sight of her made his heart jump. And then, to hear that she was still his caused all the anger in him to drain away. All he wanted to do was hold her.

But to have her risk everything to save his life brought a fierceness that he thought he'd lost for good. This fierceness was an unshakable faith, a pre-knowing, that he would find a way to be with her. He must pray and listen to the spirit guides to find the path. But he knew it was there.

# Chapter 43 — Shreveport

"I've got my orders," Liam announced at the supper table one late August night. Since Two Hawks' escape a few months earlier, neither had spoken of him. Lana tried her best to love her husband with all of her heart and Liam tried his best to be content with that.

"Oh, really? Where to?" Lana set his plate down in front of him and put her hand on his shoulder, waiting for the news.

"Boston."

"Boston! That's so far away." Getting her own plate, she sat beside him. "When do you have to be there?"

"In six weeks."

"All right. We'll be ready by then."

"*I'll* be ready by then," he corrected her.

"What do you mean?" she asked, her fork paused halfway to her mouth.

"I want you to leave for Atlanta in a few days and go ahead of me. I think Mother had a good idea about you seeing where I lived and meeting my friends. It will help whenever you meet the officers I'll be working with and reporting to in Boston."

"Oh." Lana put her fork down, suddenly not hungry. "It will help *what* exactly?"

"You'll be more familiar with how things are done back east. It's much different than here in Texas."

281

"I see." Lana looked down at the table, frowning.

"What?"

"I don't want to leave you," she admitted. "I don't know anyone back east."

"You know my family. Well, most of them, anyway."

"But Liam, you *know* how they feel about me."

"This will give them a chance to get to know you better. Plus, they can introduce you to so many important people."

"Oh," she said again, not quite sure who the important people were.

"Lana, you have to realize that when I get out of the Army, I will go into politics. My family has groomed me for this all of my life. You need to know what to do, how to speak and dress, what the current topics are, how to entertain. My mother will be more than happy to teach you all of that."

"When do I have to leave?"

"There's a supply wagon going east to Shreveport day after tomorrow. From there, you can catch a stage to the nearest train, and that will take you to Georgia."

"Day after tomorrow?" Her eyes flashed. "But I need to see my family before I go!"

"Lana, honey, I don't have enough leave coming to take you there for a visit and back."

"Then I'll go by myself!"

"No! Absolutely not!" Liam's voice raised. "There are too many hostiles between here and your family."

"Liam!" She jumped to her feet. "I'm not going *anywhere* without saying goodbye to my family! I may never see them again!"

"There isn't enough time!" Liam stood up as well.

"There would be if I didn't have to go to *Georgia!*" she retorted.

"I *need* you to go to Georgia!"

282

"And *I* need to see my family!!" Lana had never been angrier with anyone in her life.

Trying to calm down, Liam lowered his voice. "I'm sorry, sweetheart. But if you're going to have enough time in Georgia to learn all that you need to, you have to leave for Shreveport day after tomorrow."

*"I WON'T GO!"* Lana stamped her foot, stomped across the living room, and slammed the bedroom door so hard that the windows rattled. Neighbors on either side of the triplex listened in fascination from the comfort of their own kitchens.

Liam stared at the bedroom door in disbelief. Remembering his father-in-law's words on the eve of his wedding, Liam went out in search of a barn. He needed to cuss something awful.

When he returned a few hours later, their uneaten meal had been put away and the kitchen cleaned. The house was dark except for a line of yellow coming from underneath the closed bedroom door.

Liam tapped once and then slowly opened the door. Lana sat propped up in bed, her arms defiantly folded across her chest, her face tear-streaked. She looked at him with sad, resentful eyes.

"Please, Lana. It will mean the world to me if you'll do this. It's for us, for our future." He sat down beside her on the bed.

"But, Liam, my family...!" She burst into fresh tears. Liam pulled her to him, grateful that she let him hold her.

"I know, honey. I know. But that's the way the military works. Everything is on its time, not ours." After a few minutes, she sat up and dried her eyes.

"I tell you what," he smiled and laid his hand on his heart. "I *promise* that I will get your letter to your parents before I leave for Boston, even if I have to pay someone to take it. Will that be all right? Will you go to Shreveport?"

Lana studied his face while she considered his offer. "I suppose," she reluctantly agreed, knowing neither one of them had any choice in the matter.

"All right, then.  That's what I'll do."  Liam walked to his side of the bed and began to undress.  Later, when he reached for her, she turned her back.  "Please, no, Liam.  I don't feel like it."

Scowling, he slowly withdrew his hand and then, reluctantly, blew out the lamp.  There had been more and more of this lately, and he hoped the move would lessen this distance between them.

* * *

Lana sat in the back of the wagon, under the canvas, her two suitcases by her feet.  Two soldiers sat on the drivers' seat, one holding the reins and the other with his rifle at the ready.

Liam stood behind the wagon, saying goodbye to his wife.  "I'll miss you so much, honey," he said, reaching for her.  "I already do."

"I don't have to go," she reminded him.

"Yes, you do.  But it will pass quicker than you know."  He was trying to encourage himself as much as her.  "Let me kiss you before you have to leave."

She offered her lips and returned his kiss with real tenderness.  "Take care of yourself," she whispered.  "I love you."

"I love you!"  The wagon jolted into motion, and carried her away from the fort and toward Shreveport.  Liam stood there and watched until she was out of sight.  It took all he had to keep from running after the wagon and pulling her off.  It was going to be a long, lonely, distracted six weeks.

* * *

As Lana sat in the back of the wagon, watching the fort grow smaller and smaller in the distance, she couldn't help it.  She burst into tears.  Why did she have to leave?  And, especially, why did she have to go to a place where no one liked her?

284

It was bad enough when her family left after the weddings to go back to the homestead. But this? There had been no time for her to tell them goodbye, to explain what was happening to her. As she sat in that bumpy, uncomfortable wagon between boxes, crates and her suitcases, her tears turned to anger.

What was she *doing?* Moving clear across the country to a place she'd never been for a husband she shouldn't have married! Would she ever see Texas again? Or her family? And politics? What did she know of politics? How on earth was she supposed to help Liam further *that* career?

With every step the horses took, with every mile that rolled beneath the wagon wheels, she became more and more convinced she was making the mistake of her life. But what could she do? Nothing — at least nothing that she knew of.

* * *

The wagon had been on the trail for three days, passing a small, new settlement and a few homesteads along the way. Many places offered them meals in exchange for the rare commodity of cash money. They had just left the settlement when they passed a young woman walking in the same direction along the trail.

As Lana saw her, Lana spoke to her from the back of the wagon. "Where are you going?"

"Anywhere. Just away from here," the woman told her.

Lana looked up at the sky where storm clouds were brewing. "And you're walking?"

"Have to. Don't have a horse."

"Well, we're going to Shreveport. Do you want to ride with us?"

"You and two soldiers?"

"Yes. My husband is an officer for the Army."

"Oh, I see." The woman continued walking alongside the wagon as she considered this offer. "Shreveport, huh? That's a far piece."

"Yes. It is," Lana agreed.

"Think I could find work in Shreveport?"

"I'd imagine if you could find work anywhere, it would be Shreveport."

"All right, then. Thanks!" Without waiting for the wagon to stop, the woman climbed up the back and settled in beside Lana.

"My name is Nan." No sooner had she made this announcement than raindrops began to pound the side of the canvas and raise little bursts of dust on the road.

"Nan. I'm Lana." Lana looked at her new friend. Her dress had been mended several times and was now nothing more than rags held together by patches. The women looked to be about her age. "Hungry?"

"I could eat," Nan admitted.

Once Lana had given Nan food, she broached another subject.

"I have some extra dresses in here," she patted one of her suitcases. "You're more than welcome to change into one. That one looks — well..."

"Looks like it was rode hard and put up sweaty," Nan laughed. "But thanks. I'm all right." A violent jag of lightening lit up the western sky.

Lana pulled out a sweet, light blue dress and shook out the wrinkles. "Are you sure? I bet this would fit you perfectly."

Nan reached out and touched the dress admiringly. "It sure is pretty."

"Well, try it on."

Looking over her shoulder at the soldiers in the front and then back at Lana, she asked, "Do you think they'll peek?"

"No. I'll sit between you and them. How about that?"

Nan nodded and, within a few minutes, sat across from Lana, feeling like a princess in her borrowed dress. "Goodness," Nan smiled, studying Lana, "We could be sisters."

"We do look a lot alike," Lana agreed. "I've got one sister-in-law and three brothers, but no sisters." Thunder clashed and boomed, making them both jump.

"Shouldn't we stop or something?" Nan asked fretfully.

"I don't know. I'm sure the soldiers know what to do. They might just be looking for a good place to get out of the storm."

Nan nodded. "Yeah, probably." Storms made her nervous and she felt edgy. Lana noticed and tried to think of some way to distract her.

"Are you from the settlement we just passed?" Lana asked.

"*That* place. No! That place is *awful!* My folks' place got burned out and they got killed. I've been looking for work or something ever since. Been slowly making my way east, toward civilization."

"Oh. Well, perhaps Shreveport will have what you're looking for."

"I hope so."

They sat there silently, struggling to keep their balance as the wagon jolted down the rough trail. The two women tried to ignore the storm.

"I saw you looking at my ring," Lana said. "Want to see?"

"Oh, I'd love to." Nan moved to sit next to Lana. Holding up Lana's hand, she gently touched the ring.

"I've never seen anything so beautiful in all my born days," Nan exclaimed. "What are the red ones?"

"The red ones are rubies. The blue ones are sapphires."

"And the white one?"

"That's a diamond. This is my wedding ring. My husband had it made special."

"Goodness. You must be rich."

Lana laughed at that. "No. Not rich." Her distraction was working, the storm nearly forgotten. "Do you want to try it on?"

"You mean, you'd *let* me?" Nan looked at her in astonishment.

"Of course. Just give it back, all right?" They both laughed while Lana pulled the ring off and gave it to Nan. Slipping it on, Nan held it up to inspect her newfound, though temporary, wealth.

"I feel like the Queen of England," she gushed.

A clash of thunder boomed immediately overhead, instantly followed by wicked lightning searing the ground near them. The terrorized horses bolted and careened down the muddy trail. The trail turned but the horses didn't. The soldiers tried desperately to stop the runaway animals, but to no avail. They plunged off an embankment that led to a river. Horses, wagon and people flew through the air, dashing on the rocks below.

## Chapter 44 — Make Her Wake Up

Liam stood facing his commander, receiving orders in the colonel's office.

"We've received a report of an accident involving an Army wagon and possibly Army personnel. It's about three days east of here. Take a detail with a wagon and investigate."

"Yes, sir." Liam saluted and, as he walked out of the office, tried to shake the uneasy feeling in the pit of his stomach. Lana left almost a week before. Surely, this had nothing to do with her. Within the hour, he led his detachment out of the fort.

The trip east proved non-eventful. When Liam reached the settlement, he found the person who had reported the accident. The young man led the cavalry to the site where deep ruts ran off the road and eventually over the embankment.

Thanking him, Liam sent him back home, telling him, "We'll take it from here."

Liam sent scouts up and down the embankment. It took over two hours to find a safe route to the river, and the sun had almost set when Liam arrived at the scene. The first alarm went off in his heart when he saw a dress that looked like one of the new ones he had bought Lana. Walking over to it, he picked up the pink fabric from the rocky river bank and stared at it. No matter how hard he wished otherwise, he knew the dress was hers.

"Lieutenant!" his sergeant called out.

Carrying Lana's dress with him, Liam walked over to the sergeant. Wordlessly, the man pointed to the ground. There, behind busted boxes and sprung suitcases lay a young woman's torn body, her face beaten beyond recognition. As Liam forced himself to walk closer, he saw her wedding ring — the ring he had specially made just for her — the diamond and rubies and sapphires sparkling cruelly in the light.

"Oh, God! Lana!" Liam didn't remember going to his knees — or screaming. He wanted to hold her, to *make* her wake up, but the sergeant wouldn't let him, as he held Liam by his shoulders. Her body was too badly decomposed from the heat and humidity.

"Sir? — Sir!"

Liam looked up, as if he didn't know where he was. "What?"

"We need to make camp for the night. Don't you think?" The sergeant hoped to give the lieutenant something else to focus on.

"Yes, I suppose." Liam slowly stood up, all life gone from his eyes. "In the morning, make three caskets as best you can out of the busted wagon. That will do to transport the bodies back to the fort. Bury the horses."

"What about her things?"

"Gather up what you can find. I'll take them back to her parents."

"Yes, sir."

"And, Sergeant, unless it's an emergency, don't come looking for me tonight. I'll be down the river." Liam handed the pink dress to him.

"Yes, sir. Want me to bring you supper?"

"No." The distraught young officer answered too quietly. When the sergeant turned away to give the orders, Liam knelt beside her body and, jaws clenched, removed her ring. Kissing it once, he put it in his top pocket and then, after covering her with a blanket, stood up to walk away, leaving his soldiers to their gruesome tasks.

Somehow, his numb legs carried him a half-mile down the riverside. He stared at the water for a long time as the sunlight faded and the stars came out. Liam refused to let his mind think or his heart feel for as long as he could. But, in spite of himself, the pain rolled in like thunderclouds, black and billowing, full of wind and fury and inescapable destruction.

"Why?" he whispered to the moon. "*Why?*" he asked the stars. "WHY!" he shouted at God. None of them answered. His mind went red, the anger and rage bursting from him like an erupting volcano, spewing from his mouth in curses and cries.

Hurrying over to a large tree, he rammed his fists into it, first one and then the other. "Damn it! Damn it to hell!" His fists, not feeling the pain, pounded the rough bark, one punch after another. With his feet splayed apart, his torso twisting, each jab was accompanied by another curse. For several minutes, the uneven bout continued — man against tree. Suddenly spent, he flung his arms around the tree and sobbed uncontrollably.

"Lana, no! Baby, no! I need you."

Placing his back against the trunk, he slid down to the ground, hopelessly lost, eternally empty, the sorrow so heavy he couldn't get enough air in his lungs to breathe. Time passed by unnoticed. The moon rose and set; the constellations moved across the heavens. Somewhere in that time, Liam fell asleep, sheer exhaustion taking over.

"Lieutenant?"

Liam jerked awake, startled. For a split second — one merciful split second — he didn't know where he was or why he was there. But then it came rushing at him — the fanged sorrow, the black, airless grief — and wrapped its life-sucking tentacles around his soul. Liam looked around him, at the ground, at the river, and then up at his sergeant as he tried to get his bearings.

"Yes?"

"Sir, I just wanted to make sure you were all right. There's coffee on back at camp."

"Thank you." When Liam put his hands on the ground to stand up, a sharp pain made him wince. Looking down, he saw both hands were a bloody, blackened, swollen pulp.

The sergeant noticed them at the same time. "Sir, why don't you come with me and I'll tend to those."

"I suppose you'd better." Liam slowly stood up, the muscles in his back, neck and shoulders sore and stiff, making his first few steps awkward.

"The men wanted me to tell you how sorry we all are about your wife."

"Thank you." Liam sounded expressionless.

"We've already seen to her casket and her things are collected."

"All right."

"And if there's..."

"Thank you, Sergeant, but I'll be fine." Liam stopped any further discussion. "As soon as everything is ready, we'll ride."

"Yes, sir."

Somehow, Liam made the trip back to the fort with his composure intact. Somehow, he gave rational orders and spoke in coherent sentences. At the fort, he requested and was given permission to take Lana's body to her family's homestead. Since he would be transferred soon, he didn't want her buried at the fort where she wouldn't know anyone. She needed to be home.

* * *

"Pa, we've got a visitor," Jake announced as he walked into the barn.

"Who?"

"Can't tell. He's in a wagon, though."

Joshua and Jake stepped out into the yard to look. As the wagon got nearer, Joshua broke into a wide grin. "Why, it's Liam! Go tell your ma."

When the wagon pulled into the yard, Joshua's grin slowly faded as he watched Liam get down. Something in Liam's demeanor worried him.

"Mr. Cooper," Liam walked over, hand extended.

"Now, it's Pa, remember?"

Liam said nothing to the lighthearted admonishment. The two men silently faced each other, one wondering what was wrong and the other unable to tell him. As Joshua tried to read Liam's eyes, the light in his own died.

"I — I'm so sorry." Liam finally spoke, wishing that the tear he felt in the corner of his eye would disappear.

"Liam, what is it?" Joshua looked alarmed.

Turning to point to the wagon, Liam said quietly, "I've brought her home to stay."

Joshua felt his heart stop, but he made himself look into the back of the wagon. At the sight of the casket, he slowly turned back to Liam.

"No! Tell me no!" he demanded.

May stepped into the yard, excited at the company, but one look at the two men, and she ran to the wagon. She screamed and dropped to her knees, her hands over her heart, as if she were trying to keep it from exploding in her chest.

Rocking back and forth on the dirt, inconsolable, her wailing brought the others out. It took a long time before they understood — before they allowed themselves to understand — that Lana was gone.

Liam reached for May, pulling her to her feet. Taking one look into his sad eyes, she flung herself into his arms, holding him tightly, as if that would bring Lana back.

"What happened to my baby? What happened to my little girl?"

Joshua took May by her shoulders and pulled her against his chest. "Come here, sweetheart." Looking over his shoulder at Nathan, he said, "Get the whiskey out. All of it."

"Yes, sir."

"Paul, Jake, take the wagon into the barn and take care of the horses. Then come to the house." Laying his hand on Liam's shoulder, Joshua said, "You'd better come in, son."

They all gathered around the long table, waiting for Liam to tell them why they were in this nightmare. What happened? He told them all that he knew, which wasn't enough. After explaining about his new orders sending him to Boston, and Lana leaving to visit with his parents in Georgia until his arrival, he told of the accident.

"Apparently, there was a bad storm. The wagon left pretty deep ruts when it went off the road. They went over a steep embankment. None of them survived; not the people, not the horses." Liam looked around the table at the grief-stricken faces, knowing his looked that way, too. Reaching for his top pocket, he pulled out the ring, and set it in the middle of the table.

"I took her wedding ring off her hand when I found her. I want you to have it." He pushed it toward May. "She would want that."

May burst into fresh tears as she stared at the ring. As lovely as it was, she knew she would never wear it.

"There's something else," Liam said softly.

# Chapter 45 — A Psalm Was Read

Liam pulled a worn letter from his back pocket and handed it to Joshua. "Lana wrote this letter over two months ago. I promised her I'd get it to you before I left for Boston." His voice cracked at the end, making it difficult to finish the sentence.

Joshua stared at the letter in his hand, not knowing what to do. When he looked at his wife, she was staring holes into the letter. It had been written before Two Hawks had been captured, before Lana and Liam argued about her living in Georgia with his parents. It had been written when circumstances had been happier between them.

Joshua slowly sat down beside May and pulled the lantern closer for its light. With thick, trembling fingers, he broke the seal and unfolded the paper.

*Dear Ma and Pa,*

*Can you believe it? Two of your children are married! And one of them is me! I must tell you that Army life isn't too bad. The other wives here have made me feel welcome. Please tell Christina that I finally went to my first quilting bee. Goodness! What a bunch of gossips we were. And, with the wives' help, Liam* and I have a house full of things we need. I've even gotten used to cooking on a wood stove instead of the fireplace.

Liam is such a wonderful husband! You were right, Pa. He's smart and generous and kind and loves me as much as any man has ever loved his wife. I'd even say that he loves me as much as you love Ma. And that's saying a lot because I've seen how you two still look at each other when you think us kids aren't watching.

Ma, remember you told me that I'd have my own wedding ring one day? You should see the ring Liam gave me. It puts the sun to shame, it is so beautiful. Maybe one day, you'll get to see it. I'll let you try it on if you promise to give it back.

I met Liam's parents and one of his sisters when they came for a visit last week. I don't understand their ways, but it's important to Liam that we become a family, so I am going to do my best to fit in with them.

Liam is going on patrol tomorrow, and I hope he can make it to you to give you this letter. I worry about him when he's gone. So much can go wrong. The one small comfort I have is that he isn't alone out there. But if anything happened to him, I would die. I just know I would.

I'm running out of paper, so I'd better close. I love you all more than life itself and I miss you so much! Sometimes I sit on the porch and cry when Liam's not home. Please take care of yourselves and hug each other for me. Write when you can. I love you!! Your daughter,

*Lana O'Connell.*

Joshua folded the letter and pushed it to the middle of the table. Christina buried her head in Nathan's chest, sobbing. Jake ran to his mother and clung to her, unashamed to cry at his age. The family sat around the table in tatters, unable to speak, unable to move.

\* \* \*

"It's close to sundown," Christina said when she finally let go of Nathan, needing to find something to do. "I'll start supper." Walking behind May, she kissed her mother-in-law on her head and then went to the kitchen counter. Joshua scooted his chair closer to his wife and put his arm around her shoulders.

Nathan stood up and walked to the front door. "I'm going out. I've got something to do."

"Don't be long. Supper will be ready soon," Christina told him.

"I'm not hungry." Stepping outside, he walked to the barn to get a shovel.

As he left the barn, Liam approached him. "What are you going to do?" he asked as he looked at the shovel in Nathan's hand.

"I'm going to take care of my sister."

"If you've got another shovel, I want to help."

Nathan nodded and returned in a few seconds with one, handing it to Liam. The two young men walked away from the house and down the riverbank.

"Here. Right here," Nathan said after they'd walked a short distance. "She used to come to this spot and sit under these trees to think and to read."

"All right." Taking off his shirt, Liam walked to a high spot and began digging. Nathan began digging about six feet away. It was well past dark when they returned to the house, hot, sweaty, dirty, tired. When they sat at the table, Paul handed them each a glass of whiskey.

"We've dug the grave," Nathan announced just before he gulped his down.

"Good," Joshua nodded. "We'll bury her in the morning." May sat in her rocking chair, staring unfocused into the fire. The gentle wish-swish, wish-swish of the rocker was the only sound she made.

"Oh, I've brought her things, too," Liam broke the silence. "Maybe Ma and Christina can make use of some of them."

"All right." Christina stood up. "Where are they? I'll go get them."

"No. I will." Liam finished his whiskey and went back outside. When he walked into the dark barn, he went to the wagon seat, reaching under it for her things. When he straightened, his eyes locked on the casket. He stayed there for a long time, thinking.

"Honey," he whispered. "You're home now. Your brother and I have got you all fixed up by your favorite place next to the river. I finally got your letter to them, just like I promised. And Ma has your wedding ring. I thought maybe that's what you'd want. And now, I'm taking in your things hoping they can use them. I can't keep them around me. I'll lose my mind if I do." Reaching out, he touched the edge of the casket. "I miss you so much, Lana. I wish it had been me instead of you. How am I supposed to go on now? How?" Liam looked around in the darkness. For what — he didn't know. "Bringing you here was hard," he continued. "But at least you were with me. I don't know how I'm going to make myself leave. You'll be here. My heart will be here. My life will be here."

When he didn't come back, Joshua went looking for Liam and heard the last part of Liam's words. When Joshua touched him on the shoulder, Liam whirled around and then held on to Joshua, crying, not like a baby, but as only a grown man can cry in the face of unbearable grief. Joshua understood and let him.

The next morning brought a hint of the coming fall. The Texas sky was deep blue and wide open. Joshua stood at the head of the grave, the family Bible in his hand. A Psalm was read, a prayer said, a hymn sung, tears shed. When the grave was filled, Joshua set up a crudely-made cross. May laid what flowers she could find beneath it. There was nothing left to do but go back to the house.

Liam refused to stay. "I've got to get back. I leave for Boston very soon, and I have a lot to do before I go."

"Yeah, Boston." Joshua looked somberly at Liam. "I suppose you won't be back this way, then."

"Probably not. Not with my family in Georgia."

"Well, then, this is goodbye for real." Joshua extended his hand. Liam shook it and then hugged Joshua.

"I loved her with everything I had," he said quietly, so that only Joshua heard him.

"I know you did, son. I know." Patting his back once, Joshua stepped away to let the others say their goodbyes. In a short time, Liam was back on the wagon headed east to a life he no longer cared to live.

* * *

Whether by chance or by fate, three days later, Nathan ran across Two Hawks while he was out hunting.

"Nathan! How is it with you?" Two Hawks asked as he prodded his horse nearer.

"Yi Ceɳtas." Nathan hadn't thought of the Kiowa for a long time.

"How is your wife?" the warrior asked.

"She's fine." Nathan studied him for a moment and then decided he had a right to know. "I have some bad news, though."

"Bad? What?"

"Lana is dead."

"*What?* What happened?" Two Hawks didn't believe him.

Nathan told him the story and ended with, "We buried her by the river just a few days ago. Come with me and see."

Two Hawks followed Nathan for several minutes before they came to her grave. She was buried underneath the very trees where they had spent many delightful Sunday afternoons, where they had almost made love that last spring morning. Sliding off his horse, Two Hawks walked slowly to the grave, his disbelief turning to pain. Looking up at Nathan, he could see the sorrow there. This was true, then. A heavy monster suddenly sat on his chest, not allowing him to speak. Nodding once, he jumped back on his horse and rode away without a word.

Somewhere between her grave and his village, Two Hawks' world shattered. Instead of going home, he turned his horse west and rode for several hours before he stopped. Hobbling his horse, he sat on the ground — motionless — waiting.

Even though T'on Ma was married, she loved him. Only him. His love for her was so fierce that it consumed him. He counted on that to bring them together one day. Now that there was no possibility of having her in his life, he was devastated.

As he sat in the prairie grass, he felt the numbness wear away, replaced by pain that grew in its intensity. With his arms wrapped tightly across his chest, Two Hawks rocked back and forth, keening. The pain stayed, bringing with it anger.

Two Hawks fought with the anger throughout the night, tearing at the earth with his knife, shouting at the sky with his threats. As the morning sun rose, he finally fell exhausted to the ground and slept. When he awoke late that afternoon, the anger was gone, but in its place was a sorrow so deep that he couldn't stop the gulping sobs that wrenched his body. T'on Ma was his! They had a future together. Who had stolen it? *Why?*

Three days later, he rode into his camp. Putting his horse with the remuda, he went to his mother's tipi. "I'm back," he announced lifelessly.

"Good." Gray Dove looked up from her work. "Where have you been?"

"With the dead." He offered no further explanation.

Studying his face, she knew better than to ask what that meant. Something had broken his spirit. Perhaps, in time, he would tell her what that was.

## Chapter 46 — Two Horses And One Rifle

Something hurt her eyes. And someone wouldn't quit moaning. Why wouldn't they be quiet? Didn't they know she didn't feel well? Lana slowly squinted against the sun. There was that moan again! Wait. That was *her.* What was going on? She tried to sit up, but fell back unconscious.

Much later — hours? — days? — something tickled her ear. Moving her hand to swat it away, she rolled over onto her side, gasping from sharp pain as she did. Lana opened her eyes to darkness. Confused, she tried to get her bearings. Something moved beside her. Carefully turning her head, she saw a coyote pacing close by.

"Shoo! Shoo!" she whispered weakly and then grimaced. Even that hurt. Rolling onto her stomach, she lifted her head to look around. Lana remembered riding in a wagon. It set to one side, busted into six large pieces. The team of horses lay at odd angles in their traces. That couldn't be good.

Looking to her left, she saw a bare foot. Crawling the short distance to it, she pushed back the busted suitcases and scattered clothes to find Nan lying underneath the rubble, dead. The flying debris had bashed in her face and crushed her chest. Lana turned away, retching. Peering into the darkness, she saw the two soldiers, also lying too still to be alive.

Lana crawled away from the macabre scene and slowly, painfully, sat up. Checking herself, she wondered if she didn't have broken ribs. She knew she was badly bruised and her face bloody. How long had she lain there? She didn't know. Exhausted, she fell into a deep sleep beside the river as it ran along, oblivious to the human tragedy on its shore.

The wounded woman awoke several hours later to find the sun up and not a storm cloud in sight. Thirsty, she made a wide path around the wagon and got a drink. As she stood, gasping against the fierce pain in her side, her first thought was to get help. But help from where? She didn't even know where she was.

Then she thought of the small settlement they had passed just before they picked up Nan. Making up her mind to go there, Lana tried to climb the embankment, but it was too steep. It seemed to take hours before she finally reached a place where she could climb out. After emerging at the top, she couldn't see any road. Getting her bearings from the sun, she set out west, each halting step agony.

* * *

Lana passed out — again — from pain and hunger and exhaustion. When she came to, she was bouncing roughly on a travois as it made its way across the uneven ground. Squinting her eyes against the sun, she looked to her right. An old woman walked beside her. Behind Lana rode a mounted warrior; to her left lay open prairie and rolling hills.

Studying the woman, Lana realized that she wasn't with Kiowa, but she didn't know who they were. She was too far west for them to be Caddo and too far east for them to Apache. Kickapoo? Comanche?

"Water," she said in English. The woman glanced at her once but kept walking. "T'on," she said in Kiowa. Again, the old woman did nothing. Using sign language, Lana told of her thirst. This time, the woman frowned at her and shook her head.

The warrior behind her watched and, when the old woman walked ahead, he tossed Lana his flask. It hit her in the chest, sending sharp spasms of pain across her. But, grateful, she drank enough water to ease her parched throat. When she finished, he rode up beside her and reached down for his flask.

"Thank you," she smiled. Making no response, he simply fell into line behind her travois.

The band of ten Kickapoo warriors, fifteen women and seventeen children traveled for six days in a northwesterly direction. The children would often walk beside the travois to stare silently at the strange woman with blue eyes. Lana tried to befriend them, but before she could make any progress, a nervous mother would grab their hands and hurry them away, or a warrior on horseback would chase the child to its mother.

By the middle of the seventh day, the band reached their destination. Runners had come through their village many weeks before, announcing a powwow of many tribes — Apache, Kiowa, Kickapoo, Comanche. They had learned that the new forts built the year before were going to be joined by another long line of forts cutting through their lands yet again. This would bring more soldiers, more settlers. Something had to be done.

The Kickapoo band had gotten there early, hoping to get a choice spot to set up their camp. This would also give them plenty of time to catch up with news from distant relatives and old friends. As the week went on, more and more bands of various tribes arrived until the encampment looked like someone had scattered pebbles all around, with no rhyme or reason to how things were set up. That wasn't entirely true, though. Camp organizers stayed busy directing new arrivals to their appropriate locations. Each band set up camp next to others of their tribe, lodge openings facing east. Barking dogs and laughing, yelling children played between the tipis, around the horses and through groups of adults, adding their own touch to the already chaotic scene.

Lana's captors carried her into a tipi. The painful travois no longer had to be endured. From what she could figure out, the tipi belonged to the daughter of the old woman. The daughter's husband, Leaf That Falls, had pulled Lana's travois.

\* \* \*

Leaf That Falls wasn't quite sure what to do with the white woman, but when he found her lying in the middle of nowhere, unconscious, hurt, and alone, he decided to bring her along. Perhaps he could trade her for horses or, better yet, a rifle, at this large gathering.

They had been there several days when Leaf That Falls noticed a new band arriving. As he watched them ride by in a long line, he recognized some of the warriors. Once they got their camp set up, he decided he would visit them.

Before the supper fires were started, Leaf That Falls went to the newest camp and walked over to one of the men. "Dark Fist, it's good to see you again."

Dark Fist looked up from the person he was talking with. "And you, too. How are you?"

"Doing well. Looking forward to this meeting. Almost everyone is here now, so it should start in the next day or two."

"Good. There is much we need to talk about."

"Yes, there is."

"Too many whites are moving in. Too many soldiers." Dark Fist frowned.

"Speaking of whites," Leaf That Falls crossed his arms, "I found one all by herself a few days ago, badly hurt."

"Oh, really? How did you kill her?" Dark Fist laughed. Leaf That Falls was notoriously squeamish, even among other tribes, about such things.

"I didn't kill her. I brought her here. I'm hoping to trade her."

"Is she skinny? If she's skinny *and* hurt, you won't get much for her," Dark Fist teased.

"Maybe. Maybe not," Leaf That Falls defended himself. "She's got blue eyes."

Dark Fist's head snapped around at that. "Blue eyes?"

"Yes."

"And she's here with you now?"

"Yes. In my tipi."

"Show me."

Dark Fist followed his host across the large site and into his tipi. When Dark Fist entered, even in the poor lighting, he knew it was Lana.

"You!" he pointed at her. "You won't get away so easily this time."

Lana looked up into eyes she'd prayed she would never see again.

"You know her?" Leaf That Falls asked, astonished.

"Yes. I captured her once, but she escaped." Dark Fist walked over to her, grabbed her arms, and pulled her to her feet, ignoring her cries.

"She escaped?" That surprised the Kickapoo. He'd never heard of anyone getting away from Dark Fist.

"With help. How many horses do you want for her?"

Leaf That Falls knew he was in a good bargaining position. "Six."

"Six!"

"Yes. Six and one rifle."

"Two and one rifle."

"Five and…

"Two and one rifle or I'll slit your throat and take her anyway."

"All right. Two horses and one rifle."

"Follow me," Dark Fist ordered Leaf That Falls and then, grabbing Lana's hand, he dragged her back to his camp. She didn't resist. She didn't have the strength to. A little while later, Leaf That Falls returned home with his new horses and a used rifle.

Once inside the tipi, Dark Fist threw Lana to the floor. He said something to a woman, who then turned to Lana and tied her hands behind her. That evening, they fed Lana supper and then ignored her.

The next morning, the woman led Lana to the river, where four other Apache women met them. She was stripped and told to bathe. One of the women handed her extract from agave plants and instructed her to wash her hair. While she did that, another women took her clothes and washed them. The women began discussing her, knowing she didn't understand them.

"She's too skinny," one said.

"And too pale."

"Her bruises are almost gone, though."

"I don't know what he wants with her. He already has three wives."

"And why does he want her cleaned up if she's just a slave?"

"With Dark Fist, it's hard to know. Maybe he's got a wealthy buyer in mind and wants her looking better before he shows her to him."

"Maybe."

"Maybe it's those blue eyes. Have you ever seen blue eyes before?"

And so went the conversation and gossip. Within the hour, Lana was back in the tipi, wearing a borrowed buckskin dress, while her clothes dried on the bushes in the sun.

\* \* \*

The Kiowa band of Many Deer and Crying Fox were the last to arrive at the powwow. After they set up camp, Red Flint and Many Deer went to find the other tribe leaders and let them know of their arrival. Returning, they told their band that the big meeting would be the next night.

When Gray Dove learned of this over supper that night, she told her worries to her husband. "I hope Two Hawks makes it in time."

"He will. He knows to hurry."

"He *used* to know to hurry," she corrected him. "But he hasn't been the same for a while. I don't know why he had to go hunting now. We don't need fresh meat right away."

"It will be all right, woman," Many Deer tried to reassure her. "He'll be here."

But, as if justifying his mother's concerns, Two Hawks didn't show up that night — or the next morning — or the next afternoon. His mother's mood progressed past frustration and irritation to anger. If he didn't show up by that night, she would go from there to worry.

* * *

That evening, all the people were in high anticipation. Runners went through each camp, announcing for all to come to the meeting. They had no lodge big enough to hold all the men, so they selected a large clearing.

Each tribe chose three leaders to sit in the center circle. Beyond that circle was a larger circle, consisting of the rest of the men, from teenagers to old grandfathers, each eager to listen to, and perhaps even contribute to, the discussion. Behind that ring sat the women and children, not allowed to participate, but keen to watch. Even the youngest children sensed the gravity of the occasion and sat still.

The men in the center circle began by washing themselves in sacred smoke that had been sweetened with sage, cedar, and sweetgrass. The ceremonial pipe passed from right to left around the inner circle, with each man inhaling deeply from it.

One of the Apache leaders rose and looked around the gathering before he began.  He spoke of the recent history of bluecoats and settlers dividing up the land between them, scaring off game, and tearing the earth to build towns and forts and to plant crops.  A sense of anger swelled throughout his audience when he sat down.

One of the Comanche leaders spoke next and told of the current troubles they were having with the soldiers.  Skirmishes constantly broke out between the Comanche and the settlers.  Inevitably, the bluecoats showed up with their guns and horses, leaving many Comanche dead.  Several in the audience nodded, their jaws clenched, remembering the loss of loved ones.

A Kickapoo leader added his part, telling of the next string of forts planned to be built after winter was over.  It would again divide their lands, making it difficult to follow the buffalo.  And, without buffalo, all the people would starve.  Indignant muttering rumbled through his audience when he finished.

The last speaker was a Kiowa leader.  He spoke of a plan — a plan using lightning fast guerrilla attacks on new fort sites and homesteads, along with the burning of what construction had already been done.

When he sat down, the debate began.  Men from different tribes spoke of being at a disadvantage because they didn't have enough rifles for these attacks.  Even if they had rifles, there was no ammunition, no powder, no bullets.  And, if they were busy tearing down the new forts, who would hunt the buffalo?

Dark Fist stood up and waited for the voices to grow quiet.  When he had everyone's attention, he pulled Lana to her feet and held her roughly by her elbow.  Whispers filled the night air as all eyes inspected her.  They had heard there was a blue-eyed captive in camp, but most of them just thought it was a rumor.

"You see this woman?" Dark Fist asked when it finally grew quiet again.  "She is beautiful, isn't she?"  Looking around, he saw several heads nod in agreement.  But not Many Deer, not Red

Flint. The two men froze when they saw T'on Ma. Maybe it was a good thing Two Hawks hadn't arrived. That would only bring trouble.

Dark Fist went on. "She's been here with Leaf That Falls for over a week. She traveled with him for a week before that. Do you see any soldiers looking for her? Have any of you been asked about a missing white woman with blue eyes?"

No one said anything.

"No. You haven't." He pushed her forcefully around in a circle so all could see. "Wouldn't you come looking for this one if she was yours?" Turning Lana to face him, he stroked the side of her face in a lover's gesture. He looked thoughtfully into her eyes for a moment and then back at the crowd. "Yes, you would. I certainly would." A chuckle rippled through his listeners at that.

Looking haughty, he said, "I'll tell you why no one looks for her. Because there aren't enough of them. They can't protect the forts they have now, let alone look for this one. So it will be easy for us to attack soldiers at the new forts before they are built, especially when they realize they are fighting not just the Apache — not just the Kiowa — not just the Kickapoo — not just the Comanche. They will be fighting all of us!"

A roar of approval went up through the crowd. The women began trilling their enthusiasm. Their courage was high.

"Is that your woman?" one of the Comanche braves teased Dark Fist, "Or is she for sale?"

Dark Fist looked around at the speaker, no smile on his face. "This one is mine!" With that, he led Lana back to his place and, pushing her to the ground, sat beside her, his point made.

## Chapter 47 — I Choose You

Two Hawks walked into the crowded meeting. He stood tall, fierce, strong, proud, and many eyes followed him. His reputation preceded him. Many knew of his raiding parties throughout the spring and summer. The escape from hanging at the soldier fort only added to his notoriety. Many whispered behind hands into ears whose owners shook their heads in wondering admiration. Young women craned their necks to see the handsome warrior and, hopefully, to catch his eye.

As he studied the people, he did a double take. There, sitting with the men, a pair of unmistakable blue eyes looked right at him, stopping him in his tracks.

Unable to breathe or think or even focus on what he was doing, he took a first tentative step toward T'on Ma, and then a second. Unable — no — afraid to believe his sight, he kept staring, waiting for her ghost to disappear, her image to turn into a wisp of smoke and whirl away. But when she didn't disappear, when she kept looking at him, his chest exploded with a fierce light, a piercing joy, as rushing wings carried his love back to his soul and light back into his spirit.

T'on Ma's eyes went wide with their pleading. Looking to her right, he saw Dark Fist sitting beside her, glaring at him. The challenge was clear, the hatred between the two warriors palpable.

Two Hawks stepped through the people and walked up to T'on Ma, wordlessly holding out his hand. She eagerly took it and stood up. Dark Fist jumped to his feet and slapped her hand out of Two Hawks'.

"Sit down!" he ordered T'on Ma.

Two Hawks grabbed her arm and quickly pulled her to stand behind him.

"You've taken her from me for the last time," Dark Fist hissed. "I'm going to enjoy killing you in front of her."

"Laughing Turtle," Two Hawks called, not taking his eyes off his adversary. "Take her out of here!"

The young brave hurried over to T'on Ma and, as he escorted her away, Dark Fist ordered, "Don't take her too far. When I'm done killing this fool, I'll want her."

They kept walking, but when they got to the edge of the crowd, T'on Ma stopped Laughing Turtle. "Let's stay here," she said. "He may need me." Laughing Turtle didn't want to miss the fight and was more than happy to stay.

The Kiowa and the Apache still glared at each other.

"I gave you two women for her," Two Hawks reminded him. "She isn't yours to take."

"You didn't keep her very well," Dark Fist laughed derisively. "Someone found her all alone, hurt. I paid for her. Paid well. So, yes, she *is* mine to take."

"You'll have to kill me first!"

"I plan to." Dark Fist went to a crouching position as he pulled his finely honed knife from its sheath. The men around them moved back, giving the two foes more room. The Kiowa pulled his knife as well, and they began slowly circling each other.

The tribal leaders looked on with great consternation. This was supposed to be a time of unity against the soldiers. A fight between one Kiowa and one Apache could cause a rift between those two tribes. Then what would all of these plans be worth?

Dark Fist lunged first, slashing his knife upward at Two Hawks' chest. Two Hawks leapt back and spun around, missing the Apache by a fraction of an inch. But in that movement, Dark Fist brought his blade across the Kiowa's shoulder, cutting him.

Taking advantage of the wound, Dark Fist pushed Two Hawks hard on both shoulders. At the same time, he kicked Two Hawks' legs out from under him. When Two Hawks fell backward, Dark Fist threw himself on top, his knife-hand raised. Two Hawks held the Apache's wrist, preventing him from stabbing downward. The two men locked in an even test of strength and will, neither moving, as their arms trembled with their great effort.

Finally, Two Hawks bucked once, throwing Dark Fist off. When Two Hawks leapt to his feet and kicked him in the chest, Dark Fist grabbed at Two Hawks' foot and twisted, sending Two Hawks slamming to the ground.

Dark Fist lunged again, but this time, Two Hawks was ready. Two Hawks thrust his knife upward, piercing Dark Fist in his stomach. With one vicious movement, Two Hawks jerked the knife up, slicing Dark Fist open to his chest. Then, with a death-dealing blow, he twisted the knife into the Apache's heart, his blood spurting down onto Two Hawks.

He pushed the dead man off and stood up, swaying on his feet, trying to catch his breath. Ignoring his wound, he looked around for T'on Ma. She hurried through the people and, when she broke clear, stopped a few feet away from him.

He stretched one hand out toward her. T'on Ma jumped into his arms, holding him as tightly as he held her. When she raised her head, with tears in her eyes, he leaned down and kissed her long and sweet, momentarily forgetting that onlookers surrounded them. He had fought the devil himself for the right to do this. Let anyone say anything against her, and they would have him to deal with. She was his. There would be no more separation, no more waiting. Putting his arm around her shoulder, they walked past his father, past his mother, out of the camp, and to his place by the river.

* * *

As T'on Ma built a fire, Two Hawks sat on the ground, watching her, his back resting against a tree. Then she brought water from the river and began washing his wounded shoulder and cleaning Dark Fist's blood from his chest.

"I thought you were dead," he told her.

"What?"

"Your brother told me you were dead. He showed me your grave."

"My grave?" At first, she was confused. As she continued washing his chest and shoulder, she began to understand what had happened. "They must have buried Nan." After a pause, she said quietly, "So, my family thinks I'm dead."

"Yes."

"Then so does Liam."

"Probably."

T'on Ma set down the bowl of water and the cloth, tied a bandage around Two Hawks' arm, and then sat facing him. "Oh, poor Liam! My poor family! They must be grieving something awful."

"I know I did. When I saw you tonight, I thought you were a ghost." He touched her face. "I lost my mind when I heard you had died."

"Oh, love, I am so sorry. I didn't know." Moving to sit beside him, she rested her head on his chest, needing to be held by him, needing to feel him in her arms.

"What happened to you?" he asked quietly.

T'on Ma related her part of the wreck and her capture as best as she could remember. When she told him about being hurt, Two Hawks pushed her away, holding her shoulders to study her.

"You're hurt *now?*" He frowned at that, worried.

"I'm better," she explained. "My ribs still hurt some, especially if you squeeze me too hard, but only a little."

"Then I will be more gentle." He pulled her to his chest again, not willing to have her out of his touch.

They held each other for a few moments before she broke the silence. "What am I going to do?"

"About what?"

"If I tell my family that I'm alive, I will have to go back to Liam."

Two Hawks looked stricken at that. "No, Water Woman! You belong here with me. I'm not losing you again."

"I don't want to lose you, either," she sighed. "I love you too much. I've tried not to, but I can't help myself. You're in my blood."

"Then, stay with me."

"If I do, I'll be dead to my family."

"You already are, my heart," he gently reminded her.

"Yes. I am, aren't I? And, if I went home, I'd have to move back East. I'd never see my family again, anyway. Plus, I'd be living a life that I hated. Absolutely hated!" She looked up at Two Hawks, tears shimmering in her eyes. "I have to choose, don't I?"

He only nodded, knowing that any decision she made would be painful.

Laying her head on his chest again, she closed her eyes, her mind going back.

"*Don't take vows you can't keep,*" her mother said.

"*... you let a white woman choose to be a squaw,*" Liam had told her. "*Lana, in many ways, she'd be better off dead.*"

314

*"No matter that it kills Ma or breaks Pa's heart?    No matter that you turning Kiowa means you never get to see us again?"* Nathan had warned her. *"And, do you want to shame your family like that?"*

Liam's warning was harsh. *"You will be an outcast among your own people as well as theirs. Your children will be half-breeds, and will live a life even worse than your own."*

And the conversation she'd overheard between Liam and his father still stung. *"She's not the type we'd hoped you'd marry.... Someone with more than an eighth grade education. Someone raised around culture and society who could help you further a political career once you left the Army.... So, you love her. Good for you. But you didn't have to marry her. Have your fling here in Texas and then, when you get home, marry the right woman."*

Then, the last conversation she'd had with her husband, the one that made her future look so bleak, filled her mind. *"Lana, you have to realize that when I get out of the Army, I will go into politics. My family has groomed me for this all of my life. You need to know what to do, how to speak and dress, what the current topics are, how to entertain. My mother will be more than happy to teach you all of that."*

Her mind whirled around and around as these sentences and phrases tumbled over each other, pulling her back and forth. How could she be so selfish to desert her husband and family, to break her vows? She *couldn't* do that. But looking up at Two Hawks, wrapped in his arms, she knew she couldn't hurt him any more, either.

And then there was her own life, her own needs. What could *she* live with?

Two Hawks watched the debate in her eyes, knowing there was nothing he could say that would make it any easier for her.

"I love you, woman," he murmured in her ear.

"I know. I feel it."

"Please — don't leave me again." The young warrior kissed her forehead and silently held her while she decided his future.

## Chapter 48 — Thirsty For You

Finally, after many moments of silence, T'on Ma knew what she needed to do. Her heart simply wouldn't be denied any more. If she was already dead to the white man's world, then let her be happy in this one.

"I choose you, love. I choose you."

At her words, Two Hawks lifted her chin to look into her eyes. He knew the sacrifice she had just made and vowed to honor her for it. "And I will *always* choose you."

"I guess I'm Water Woman from now on. Lana O'Connell is dead." Her voice quivered as that meaning became real. Her eyes filled with sadness at the thought of never seeing her family again. Liam and Nathan had made it clear that it would be kinder if she let them all think she was dead.

Needing time to compose herself, she turned and pointing to her buttons. "Help me, please."

Two Hawks unbuttoned her dress for her, kissing her shoulders while his hands moved down her back. T'on Ma stood up and let the dress fall to the ground. She knelt beside him again and unbraided her hair while Two Hawks leaned back against the tree trunk to watch her. The firelight reflected in her beautiful face and cast her hair in gleaming highlights. When she slipped out of the rest of her clothes, she said quietly, "I'll be right back."

He watched her, contented to be with her, soaking in the intimacy between them. Nude, she walked into the river, sending the shimmering white-yellow moontrail rippling across the dark water.

She leaned forward and swam a short distance away, her heart still at war with her conscience. Even though she had made her choice, Liam's face haunted her. Tears filled her eyes when she thought of how much he loved her, of how much she knew he grieved over her. Their last words to each other had been of their love. She didn't want to hurt Liam — not *ever*.

In the water, with her face in dark shadows from Two Hawks, she let herself grieve over Liam, over her parents, over her old life. She could do nothing else, could send them no comfort. Her only solace was that they would never know of her betrayal.

Her next thoughts were of Two Hawks and the future. The Kiowa were her people now. She had much to learn, but she was willing — more than willing — because it meant she would be with him. That thought brought a smile to her face. The man she loved waited for her, needing her as much as she needed him.

Feeling more at peace with herself, she swam back to the riverbank, cool, clean, reborn. In a way, T'on Ma felt like she had just been baptized into her new life, her old one left to be swept away in the river's slow current.

T'on Ma walked out of the water, her silhouette in dark blues. She resolved that there would be no more sadness that night. There had already been too much. The rest of the night was just for them.

When she neared Two Hawks, he reached for her, wanting her body and her love. Needing his reassurance about her decision, she took his hand, straddled his lap, and leaned forward to whisper, "Kiss?"

With one strong hand behind her neck, he gently pulled her to him while his other hand rested on her thigh. That kiss, that hungry, rich, long-dreamt-of kiss was sweet and passionate.

They took their time with that kiss. They had both waited too long and gone through too much to hurry it. It marked the beginning of their life together.

When she sat back up, Two Hawks smiled at her, his hands slowly moving up her arms to push her hair behind her shoulders. There were so many ways he wanted to make love to her, to touch her, but for a moment, he was lost in her amazing blue eyes — those bewitching blue eyes.

"Do you know the first time I wanted to kiss you?" he asked softly.

"No. When?"

"When you fed me blackberries. It was all I could do to keep from taking that berry you put in my lips and feeding it to you in a kiss. And then another berry and then another."

"I didn't know," she smiled and then asked coyly, "Since you're telling me secrets, when did you first want to make love to me?"

With that, he chuckled. "The night you kissed me after the prairie fire. If you hadn't had three brothers and a father, all with rifles, I would have, too."

"Oh, I see." She looked down at him, her eyes twinkling. "So, when *are* you going to make love to me?"

"You're sitting like this?" he gestured to her naked body, "And ask me that?"

"Yes. I'd really like to know. Because, if you're not interested, I'm getting dressed."

"Not...?" Two Hawks shook his head in mock disbelief at what she had just said. But then his expression softened.

He looked at her body in the soft firelight and pulled her closer. "Come here, my heart." His sultry whisper felt delicious in her ear. "Let me show you how a Kiowa warrior loves his woman."

His kisses started with her lips, his hands holding her face. "I am so thirsty for you," he sighed.

Moving his arms around her waist, he laid her down on the blanket. Quickly undressing, he laid on her. Pushing her hair back, smiling into her eyes, he kissed her sweet lips once, twice more. Next, her throat and shoulders received his attention. As he moved down her body, caressing and kissing her breasts, he heard her sigh in contentment. Moving slowly lower, his lips found her navel, his hands running up and down her sides and hips.

In that beautiful Texas night, under the moonlight, beside the river, his hands memorized the contours of T'on Ma's body, his lips, the taste of her skin. He filled her with a passion and anticipation she could no longer contain. After a few moments, she touched his shoulder.

"Please. I need you now." Her voice both demanded and pleaded, her body almost writhing in its urgency.

Moving back up, he did as she asked, looking deeply into her eyes as he took her, reveling in her touch, and in the way she moved against him — and with him. She held him in her arms, kissing his shoulders and chest while he rocked her, sometimes in a slow, sensual rhythm, and sometimes with the heat and force of a strong, hungry man. When he heard her breathing change and felt her body's excitement, he watched her face, deeply satisfied to bring her that intimate pleasure. Then, closing his eyes, he thrust once, twice, a third time, and threw his head back, as he held himself against her. Still lying on her, he wrapped her in his arms as his breathing slowly returned to normal.

The young warrior had waited all of his life for this kind of love, for this woman. He held nothing back from her, not his heart, not his emotion, not his soul. T'on Ma understood what she was being given. There was no going back. He was totally committed to her, completely in love with her. That strength resounded in her, connecting her to him, giving her a home on this earth where she was not only welcomed, but needed, by the man she couldn't live without.

Her tears sparkled in the starlight.

"What is it?" he whispered as he held her.

"I am so happy. So incredibly happy."

Her lover smiled. "Good. That's the way I want you always to be." He kissed her once more before he said, "Tomorrow, I will tell everyone that we are married. I only wish I could give your father horses to make things right."

* * *

Several days later, lying next to T'on Ma under the warm buffalo robe, Two Hawks awoke with a smile. Having her with him like this brought him joy and filled him with contentment. He kissed her awake even though it was very early. The sun wouldn't be up for three hours.

"I have to do something this morning," he told her. "But I'll be back by this afternoon."

"All right," she smiled up at him. "I'll be here. Besides, I think your mother is coming over to show me how to tan hides."

"Good." He leaned down and kissed her one more time as he ran his hand across her soft body. Forcing himself to leave the comfort of their bed, he stood up and dressed. Walking outside, he went to the remuda and got two horses — his black stallion and the palomino.

In a few minutes, he rode the black stallion out of camp, the palomino led behind on a rope. Two hours later, just as sunrise began to streak through the eastern sky, the palomino stood in the middle of Joshua's corral. The Coopers were stirring awake inside the house. Two Hawks rode away, unseen, and turned to look back only once. He honored T'on Ma by giving for her the best thing that he owned — the horse that had almost cost him his life. Now, he felt at peace. His debt was paid. T'on Ma was his woman — forever.

## The End

ISBN 141209729-0

9 781412 097291